Essays on the Punjab History

ESSAYS ON THE PUNJAB HISTORY

Kulwinder Singh Bajwa

Commonwealth

Essays on the Punjab History

Edition : 2009
ISBN 978-81-311-0251-0

Published by :
COMMONWEALTH PUBLISHERS PVT. LTD.
4831/24, Prahlad Street,
Ansari Road, Darya Ganj,
New Delhi - 110002
Ph. : 23272541, 23257835
Fax : 91- 011- 23257835
e-mail : campusbooks@hotmail.com
commonwealthbooks@gmail.com

Laser Typesetting by :
Dimple Typesetter
Delhi

Printed at :
Roshan Offset Printers
Delhi

Dedicated

to

my

revered

parents

Foreword

History must, from time to time be re-written, and reinterpreted. However, here would like to add a word of caution. Casual attempt to re-discover new aspects of the past events in the light new standards of thought, behaviour and beliefs of society in later times, can may easily lead to an imaginary analysis of the past. Therefore such effort should always be based on unimpeachable contemporary evidences. Objective analysis of significant land marks of human endeavor in the past is possible merely when the quest continues for new information on past happenings.

There is, naturally no dearth such source material of the history of the Punjab, especially of the later medieval times or of more recent past. This is quite evident from the large number of documents selected by the author of this book which contains sixteen Essays related to different important issues pertaining to the history of Punjab and also of the Sikhs apart from the reference political aspects, these essays give detailed but analytically information on various subjects such as Guru Arjun Dev In Western Historical Writings; Revelation of the Khalsa in Mehma Parkash Vartak; Eighteenth Century Sikh Traditions; Western Writings on Banda Singh Bahadur; Sikh-Muslim Relations during the Late Eighteenth Century; Jassa Singh Ahluwalia's Relations with Bharatpur State; Western Perception of Sri Harimandir Sahib During the Nineteenth Century; Western Perspective of the Sikh Scripture; The Kingdom of Lahore in the 1830s; Maharaja Ranjit Singh's

Rule : Western Perception; Charles Masson's Account of the Sikhs; John Malcolm's Perception of the Sikh Scripture; Early Nineteenth Century Punjabi Society in European Travel Literature; Liberation of Sri Darbar Sahib Tarn Taran; The First Martyr of Gurdwara Reform Movement Gurdwara Shahid Ganj Lahore (1764-1936), of course on such divorce subjects which are not only important but require special intention of the scholar of the history of Punjab in particular and India in general because there we find re-interpretation not only of the events but also of the social religious conditions of the people of the region.

Dr. K.S. Bajwa has done wonderful job to take up the publications of selected issues, based on the primary source material of the region of Punjab which also constitutes an important subjects of the history of the country. Undoubtly this volume by the author is in it self valuable research. Of particularly interests are the reports and correspondence of British envos. Their views about this country are as useful today as they were in the nineteenth Century.

This publication will have usefulness not only by itself as a forerunner of other studies in the same field by the author–K.S. Bajwa the author is well noon for his scholarship and for his outstanding work in his area of special expertise. In Punjab historiography, he enjoys patriarchal status. The contribution Dr. Bajwa has made to the study and understanding of the history of the Punjab and the Sikhs is of abiding value. For new entrants in this field, he remain guide, friend and philosopher. I deeply admire the opportunity I have had of offering tribute to the author who has dedicated this volume to his revered parents who were is source of inspiration to him.

S.D. Gajrani
Professor of history
(Retd.)
Punjabi University, Patiala

Acknowledgement

I am grateful to Dr. J.S. Paul, Professor *Namdhari* Chair, Guru Nanak Dev University, Amritsar who was kind enough to write forward for this book. In fact, he has gone through the draft of the book with his habitual thoroughness before writing the forward. He admired the present work and feels convinced that it will positively leave impact on the young generation to take interest in the History of the Sikhs and Punjab.

I started writing this book with the patience revived time to time by the encouraging and loveable attitude of my parents. The occasional complications in the present work, sometimes made me feel dejected; at such moments I could not forget my parents words that used to say me, "it is better to struggle in life then to compromise with the circumstances." I shall always remain indebted and beholden to my parents who too acted as spring board for my ideas.

I feel a sense of pleasure and pride while acknowledging the love and encouragement shown by Dr. H.S. Dilgeer for his guidance and cooperation which he extended ungrudgingly throughout the period of my research and writing the present work.

We are fully aware, librarians provide the crucial link between a researcher and his source material, so I acknowledge with gratefulness the help of all those who have helped me at their respective places. In particular my special thanks are due to the Director, National Archives of India, Janpath, New Delhi; Librarians of various libraries like Central Public Library, Patiala; Bhai Mohan Singh Vaid and Dr. Ganda Singh Sections, Bhai Kahan Singh, Library, Punjabi University, Patiala; Nehru

Memorial Museum Library, New Delhi; National Library, Alipur, Calcutta; Desh Bhagat Yadgar Library, Jallandhar; Dwarkadass Library, Madhya Marg, Chandigarh; Punjab State Archives, Patiala, Khalsa College Librarty Amritsar, etc.

I thankfully acknowledge the encouragement that was given by Dr. Navtej Singh, Professor and Head Department of Punjab Historical Studies Punjabi University, Patiala to edit this work and get it published. I am equally thankful to Sardar Manmohan Singh of USA, S/o Kartar Singh Jhabbar who gave me the original manuscript that enabled me to complete this work. It was due to his advice I finally completed three books and sent for publication. He gave me freedom to pursue my own ideas. That in spite of the constant and valuable criticism and suggestions given by him many errors still have crept in is entirely due to my own imperfection and intellectual limitations.

I shall always remember with deep gratitude the benign interest which Professor Dr. S.D. Gajrani, Formerly Professor of History and Head Department of Correspondence Courses, Punjabi University, Patiala, took in my present work. He not only inspired me to complete the present work, rather he has edited the final draft. It was due to his efforts, I could complete the present work. I shall never forget his help which he gave in form of going through the final draft of the present work and finally getting the present work published from renounced Publishers.

I will be failing in my duty if I don't express gratitude to Jasbir Singh Mann of California, USA for his usual courtesy and ungrudging help that he has extended to me from time to time. My thanks are also due to my better half (Wife) who always encouraged and inspired me as well as financially assisted whenever I was a need of some money without which the present work would not have been completed. I shall remain always indebted to her for help, love, encouragement and assistance that she gave me at every step during the last four years of my research period. I feel a sense of gratitude to my two daughters and a son for their patience and love that they showed to me. They were really very cooperative and helpful. 1 acknowledge their this gesture with love.

Contents

1

Guru Arjan Dev in Western Historical Writings

For any meaningful interpretation and appreciation of the life and achievements of Guru Arjan Dev as perceived by the Europeans, it is pertinent to know their writings in totality rather than their isolated observations, as has been done by many historians of the Punjab in general and of the Sikhs in particular, for a number of reasons. However, Father Jerome Xavier, a Jesuit,[1] writing from Lahore nearly four months after the martyrdom of Guru Arjan Dev observed, 'when the Prince (Khusrau) came flying from Agra, he passed where a gentile called (Goru) Guru, who amongst the gentiles is like a Pope amongst us. He was held a saint and was as such venerated; because of this reputation of his and because of his high dignity, the Prince went to see him, desiring, as it seems, some good prophecy. He gave him the good news of his new reign, and gave him a *tikka* (otria) on his forehead; although this man (the Guru) was a gentile and the Prince, a Moor; to the pontiff it seemed that it would be good to give this symbol peculiar to gentiles, as a sign of success in his undertaking; as the Prince was the son of a gentile woman and because of the Prince's opinion of his saintliness."

'The King (Jahangir) came to know of this and after having imprisoned the Prince, he ordered for the said Goru

(Guru) to be brought. Having him imprisoned, some gentiles interceded for their saint; finally they managed to get him sentenced to a hundred thousand cruzados, a petition of a rich gentile who remained his guarantor. This individual took care that either the king (El-Rei) annul this sentence or the saint have or at least negotiate that money; but in all he got frustrated; and he seized from his poor Pope everything he could find not sparing his clothes nor the clothes of his wife and sons; and seeing that all of this was not enough, as the gentiles do not have loyalty towards neither Pope or father regarding money, each and everyday he gave new affronts to the poor saint. He ordered him to be beaten many times with shoes on his face and forbade him to eat, so that he (the Guru) would give him more money, as he was not willing to believe that he did not have it, but he did not have it nor did he find anyone, who would give it to him; and thus amongst many trials, pains and torments given by the ones who ordered him, the poor Guru (Goru) died. The guarantor tried to save himself, but he was imprisoned and killed after they have taken everything they could find.[2]

Inspite of being brief, this letter is very significant as it denotes many things relating to Guru's position among the contemporary Sikhs as well as non-Sikh world. Besides, it indicate the alleged cause and mode of Guru's martyrdom. For instance, it asserts Guru's association with the rebel Prince, Khusro. It signifies that the Guru was not tortured to death by the Mughals, as is emphasized in Sikh tradition but was murdered by a "gentile" who stood credit for the Guru's fine of 100,000 cruzados. This is, however, contradictory to Jahangir's own assertion in his Tuzuk-i-Jahangiri, that refer to a clear order to be 'put to death with tortures.'[3] Xavier's claim that this 'gentile' murdered the Guru after the surety could not be returned to him, is in part corroborated by the other contemporary account, namely, Dabistan-i-Mazahib, which quiet clearly mentions the method of torture as being inflicted by the collectors' and hastening the eventful demise of the Guru[4]. However, Father Xavier's comments that Guru Arjan Dev was the equivalent of the Pope deserve an exceptional attention. The use of such a strong and unusual comparison from a European shows how important the influence of the Guru was. During the life time of Guru Arjan Sikhism's influence was not just restricted to the Punjab but extended to all parts of Northern India.[5] Many Udasi and Nirmala establishments throughout Northern India are clear proof of that influence. In fact, it seems that Sikhism, at this point of Sikh history had much more influence than most official historiographies, Indian or Western, would let us believe.[6]

A.L.H., Polier writing about the Sikhs in 1780 did not even mention the name of Guru Arjan[7] . Charles Wilkin, who visited Takhat Patna Sahib in 1781, does refer to the Sikh scripture, the compilation of which he attributes to Guru Nanak Dev. But he too have not mentioned even the name of Guru Arjan.[8] James Brown writing in 1788 observed that 'Gooroo Arjan who wrote the Gurhnt (Granth), now generally followed as the rule of discipline'.[9]

Writing in 1790, George Forster observed that Guru Arjan succeeded his father Guru Ram Das in 1581. "He incurred the displeasure of a Hindoo (named Chaundoo) favoured by Jahangir, was committed by that Prince to the persecution of his enemy; and his death which happened in the year 1606 at Lahore, was caused, it is said, by the rigour of confinement."[10] Thus, Forster attributes the martyrdom of Sri Guru Arjan Dev to the enemity of Chandu Shah, who was favoured by Jahangir. But he does not mention the cause of the enemity and the reason of his being favourite to the Emperor. However, the Guru died due to 'the rigours of confinement'.

John Malcolm holds that the most significant achievement of Guru Arjan Dev during his life time was the compilation of 'the Adi Granth or the first sacred volume of the Sikhs'. No doubt, beginning in this direction had been made by Guru Nanak, for 'it was partly composed by Nanak and his immediate successors, but received its present form and arrangement from Arjunmal, who blended his own additions with what he deemed most valuable in the compositions of his predecessors'. Furthermore, 'it is Arjan, then, who ought, from this act, to be deemed the first who gave consistent form and order to the religion of the Sikhs.' This act of his went a long way in uniting the Sikh 'nation more closely' and increasing their numbers'. However, it 'proved fatal' to him. For, says Malcolm, the 'jealousy of the Mohammedan government was excited, and he was made its sacrifice'. The mode of his death, which happened in the year of Christ 1606 and of Samvat 1663, is related very differently by different authors, but several of the most respectable agree in stating, that his martyrdom, for such they term it, was caused by the active hatred of a rival Hindu zealot, Dunichand Kshatriya, whose writings he refused to admit into the Adi-Granth, on the ground that the tenets inculcated in them were irreconcilable to the pure doctrine of the unity and omnipotence of God, thought in that sacred volume.' This man, according to Malcolm, 'had a sufficient influence with the Mohammedan governor of the province to procure the imprisonment of Arjan : who is affirmed, by some writers, to have died from the severity of his confinement, and by others to have been put to death in the most cruel manner. In whatever way his life was terminated, there can be no doubt from its consequences, that it was, considered by his followers, as an atrocious murder, committed by the Mohammedan government; and the Sikhs who had been, till then, an inoffensive, peaceable sect took arms under Hargovind, the son of Arjunmal, and wrecked their vengeance upon all who they thought concerned in the death of their revered priest.'[11]

However, for Malcolm, the most significant achievement of Guru Arjan was the compilation of the Adi Granth. Also, it became the root cause of his martyrdomi for it (Adi Granth) 'provided consistent form and order' to Sikhism which helped in increasing the number of Guru's followers and uniting the Sikh 'nation more closely' than ever before. But the instigator to the Mughal authorities as well as the reason for instigation is quiet novel and does not find support in Sikh history and tradition.[12] Nevertheless, 'an atrocious murder' of the Guru with the order of the Mughal Emperor went a long way in changing the character of the Sikh movement as the Sikhs took up arms under Guru Hargobind Sahib to defend their faith. This in turn caused estrangement in Mughal-Sikh relations, W.L.M. Gregor asserts that Guru Arjan was the favourite son of his father. He became famous for the compilation of Adi Granth which he placed in the temple named "Harmunder or God's House' erected by him in a large tank. Large number of devotees started visiting Ramdaspur (Amritsar) frequently 'for the purpose of bathing and hearing the Grunth read'. Amongst his followers, many were '*Zamindars*'. Not only the Sikh devotees but also the 'Hindu merchants flocked to the Punjab in the time of Arjun, bringing all kinds of curiosities for sale'. With the increased commercial activities and the number of devotees, the town of Ramdaspur expanded. Resultantly. Guru's wealth began to increase which considerably effected his life style and caused envy to his brother Pirthi Chand, as the Guru "kept great state and lived in splendour unknown to his predecessors. He kept fine horses, and was clothed in costly raiments.'[13]

Quite contrary to the Sikh tradition, M'Gregor holds that on the advice of his followers, Guru Arjan himself went to Baba Buddha Ji to be blessed with a son.[14] However, he consider the enmity of Chandu the sole cause of the martyrdom of the Guru. According to him Chandu Shah was Prime Minister at Lahore and there was enmity between him and the Guru for the latter had refused Chandu's proposal to have his daughter wed to his only son Hargobind.[15] He argues that, 'Chandooshah had a beautiful daughter, whom his father wished to bestow in marriage on his succession in office; this resolution he communicated to his friends, but they advised him to give her in marriage to Urjun's son. as he was a very comely youth. Chandooshah spurned the advice and added 'Though Urjun is a wealthy man and a Hindoo Gooroo, still he is a fukeer. I am like the upper story of a house, he is like the drain for receiving the water'.[16] Being pressed, however, Chandu consented to the match and marriage presents were sent to the house of the Guru. M'Gregor continues that 'one of the bystanders related the speech of Chandooshah to the Gooroo, and the comparison he had drawn between them. On hearing this Urjun was very angry and said, "That Hindoo is a fool compared to me, and I will not allow my son to marry his daughter." When the presents were brought, the Gooroo refused his consent to the purposed union, adding, "He is a noble man, I am a fukeer; he must be mad in wishing his daughter to wed my son." Chandoo Shah entreated Urjun's forgiveness for the words he had used and went himself to visit the Gooroo, taking with him nearly a lakh of rupees. On coming before Urjun, Chandooshah joined his hands and asked permission to address him, but the latter said it was useless, adding "Oh! Chandooshah my words are engraved on stone and cannot be washed out; I will never gainsay them, and were you to give the whole world as a dowry with your daughter, she shall never wed my son; this is fixed and irrevocable." On hearing these words, Chandooshah remained silent, but from that time meditated revenge against Urjun."[17]

However, M'Gregor has erroneously placed this event in the reign of Emperor Shah Jahan instead Jahangir. He asserts that when Shah Jahan enroute to Kashmir visited Lahore, Chandu having obtained audience related to the Emperor that "a Hindoo fukeer had sprung up in the, Punjab who assumed a state of royalty and had crowds of people as his followers, who raised tumult and disturbances." Upon this a horseman was sent to fetch him. On seeing the Guru the Emperor exclaimed." He has fukeer's face; I will befriend him" and dismissed him. But Chandu was determined to get the Guru murdered. Addressing the Guru, he said, "I will again bring you before the Emperor tomorrow, when you must either defend your own cause, or be punished." On hearing these words, 'Urjun knew well that he would not escape with his life' and the next morning he requested leave to go to the ravee for the purpose of bathing, promising, that he would afterwards return and do whatever was required of him. His request was granted. On reaching the river, the Gooroo plunged into it, sank and disappeared." However, his corpse was recovered and cremated by the Sikhs. A temple, elegantly built, with a dome covered with gold, stands within the city of Lahore in memory of this event, which took place in 1607.[18]

Clearly M'Gregor attributes the martyrdom of Guru Sahib to the enmity of Chandu Shah and does not mention about the role of the Mughal Emperor in this event of great significance in Sikh history. Curiously enough, he does not mention about the torture inflicted on the Guru, but gives a new story about the mode of Guru's death which suggests that the Guru sought his own demise not to defend his claims but to escape from any kind of punishment given to him. This sort of explanation is quite contrary to both; the Sikh tradition, as well as the personality of the Guru. Therefore, it is inappropriate and misleading.

Enumerating the achievements of Guru Arjan Dev, H.H. Wilson describes: the compilation of the Adi Granth, increased wealth and influence which drew upon him the jealousy and persecution of the Mohammedans. He 'was seized and thrown into prison, where he either died or put to death.' However, the act was widely resented by the Sikhs who took up arms under (Guru) Hargobind and 'exacted vengeance from all whom they regarded hostile to their religion'.[19]

Referring to the achievements of Guru Arjan, J.D. Cunningham asserts that during 'the ministry of Arjun, the principles of Nanak took a firm hold on the minds of his followers'. For, he was the first successor of Guru Nanak to clearly understand 'the wide import of his teachings and perceive how applicable they were to every state of life and to every condition of society'. He made Amritsar, 'the proper seat of his followers, the centre which should attract their worldly longing for a material bond of union'. Resultantly, Amritsar became 'a populous city and a great place of pilgrimage of the Sikhs'. To provide fixed rules of religious and moral conduct', to his followers, he compiled the Adi Granth. Amongst other, accomplishment of Guru Arjan, Cunningham refers to; the reduction of the customary offerings to a systematic tax, which among other things made the Sikhs accustomed to a regular government of their own, encouragement to extensive trade, particularly in horses.[20]

Celebrated among pious devotees, Guru Arjan attracted the attention of those in high position. Among them was Chandu Shah, the finance administrator of the Lahore province, who approached the Guru, to betroth his daughter to his son. Prince Khusrau, the son of Jahangir, who was in rebellion and in temporary possession of the Punjab, sought Guru's political partisan. Enraged emperor summoned the Guru, fined and imprisoned at the instigation chiefly of Chandu Shah. He died in 1606, a death hastened by the rigours of his confinement.[21]

Ernest Trumpp looks upon Guru Arjan as 'an enterprising and active man' who had 'a great talent for organization'. His main object was to provide to his followers an authenticated sacred text 'in order to unite them more closely by one common religious tie and to separate them from the mass of the Hindus'. This was, according to Trumpp, the objective behind the compilation of Adi Granth, to which he describes as the 'Bible of the Sikhs' and which gradually supplanted 'the authority of the Vedas and Puranas, which the unlettered people had never been able to read, whereas the Granth was composed in their mother-tongue and intelligible to the vulgar.' To equip the Sikh Community with an organization and to ensure regular financing for his aspiring schemes, the Guru reduced 'the voluntary offerings of his disciples to a kind of tax, which he levied by deputies, whom he nominated in the several districts and who forwarded, whatever they had collected annually to the Guru'. Another measure which he adopted to have more funds was to deal extensively in horse trade. Regular flow of considerable sums enabled the Guru to keep 'an establishment like a grandee; to hold a court and to keep always a strong band of adherents around his body and extend his authority' in the far flung areas. Gradually, the Sikhs became 'accustomed to a kind of government of their own, and began to feel themselves as a firmly organised and strong party within the state'. Due to his organizational measures, the Sikh 'community increased very considerably and spread fast over the Punjab; but in proportion as the Sikhs began to draw public attention on themselves, the suspicion of the Mohammedan Government was roused, and Guru Arjan was the first who fell a victim to it.[22]

About the reason and mode of death of Guru Arjan Trumpp repeats the same story as found in M'Gregor's account, but does not consider the enmity of Chandu as the only cause of the martyrdom of the Guru. However, relying on the account of Dabisian-i-Mazahib, he asserts that Guru Arjan Dev was 'arraigned on the charge that he had joined (with his adherents) in the rebellion of Khusrau. Whichever way he died, his death was ascribed to the bigotry and cruelty of the Mohammedan Government, and his disciples were burning to revenge it. The death of Guru Arjan is therefore the great turning-point in the development of the Sikh Community, as from that time the struggle commenced, which changed the whole character of this reformatory movement.[23]

In retrospect, an analysis of these writings reveals to the reader that none of these scholars have used the word 'martyrdom'; they have used the word 'death' either by 'torture' or 'murder'. But this does not mean that they did not look upon it as an event of great historical significance in Sikh history. Also, Cunningham and Trumpp's assertion that Guru Arjan reduced the voluntary offerings of his disciples to a systematic tax, is wrong. For, the Sikhs paid a part of their income. (usually known as Daswand, 1/10 part of one's income), out of reverence for the Guru and not under any kind of compulsion. However, Guru Arjan was a favourite son of his father, Guru Ram Das. He was an energetic and enterprising leader having great organizational skill. His measures to spread the Sikh faith; instituting and consolidating new institutions; completion of Amrit sarovar, construction of Harmandar, compilation of Adi Granth, to organise masand system, establishment of new townships, instituting daily worship at Harmandar Sahib etc; resulted in the proliferation and consolidation of the Sikh Panth. Increased following followed by considerable wealth and influence, rendered his position not only amongst the Sikhs, but also amongst the non-Sikhs, analogous to the 'Pope'. He came to be looked upon as *Sacha Padshah* (true king); in other words, he was being regarded more than a spiritual guide. This position of the Guru in the Sikh as well non-Sikh world was not cherished by the Emperor Jahangir himself as well as by the orthodox Muslims. For this the Guru had to pay the price with his head. His martyrdom for the Sikh faith, inflamed the religious passions of the peaceful Sikh Panth, converting it into a warlike nation, ready to defend their faith with the sword. Thus his martyrdom proved to be a turning point in Sikh history which changed the whole character of the Sikh movement.

REFERENCES

1. Father Jerone Xavier wrote a letter in Portugese on September 25,1606 from Lahore to his provincial superior at Goa. The substance of it was reproduced by Father Fernao Guerreiro, S.J., in his *Relacao Annual das Cosisas que Fiseram os Padres da Compenhia de Jesus nas. Partes da India Oriental,* Printed at Lisbon in Portugal in 1609 (New edition, 3 vols., Coimbra-Lisbon, 1930-42); An English translation of the relevant portion of this letter is given by Mr. John A. D'Silva in his article : "The Rebellion of Prince Khusrau, according to Jesuit sources", Published in the *Journal of Indian History*, Vol. V. 1927, p. 278; also in C.H. Payne's *Jahangir and the Jesuits* (The Broadway Travellers Series) pp. 11-12; Ganda Singh, (ed), *Early European Accounts of the Sikhs,* Indian Studies Past and Present, Calcutta, 1962, pp. 45, 48-49; See also; Amandeep Singh Madra and Paramjit Singh (eds.) *Sicques. Tigers or Thieves.* Palgrave Macmillan, New York, 2004, p. 3.
2. Amandeep Singh and Paramjit Singh, *Ibid*., p. 7; Ganda Singh, *ibid*., pp. 48-48.

3. Ganda Singh, *ibid.*, p. 46.
4. When after the capture of (Princ) Khusrau, His Majesty King Jannat Makani Nuruddin Muhammed Jahangir punished and mulcted Guru Arjan Mal, on accout of his having prayed for the welfare of Prince Khusrau, the son of His Majesty Jannat Makani, who had rebelled against his father and a large amount was demanded from him (Guru Arjan), he found himself powerless to pay it. He was tied up and kept (in the open) in the desert around Lahore. He gave up his life there, owing to the strong sun, summer heat and injuries inflicted by the collectors' Irfan Habib (trns) Sikhism) and the Sikh 1645-46: From 'Mobad', *Dabistan-i-Mazahib*", in Sikh History from Persian Sources (eds. J.S. Grewal and Irfan Habib), Tulika, New Delhi, 2001, p. 67.
5. Author of the *Dabistan-i-Mazakib* states that in every *mahal* (each Gura's reign) the Sikhs increased in numbers, till the reign of Guru Arjan Mal, they became very numerous, not many cities remained in the inhabited region where the Sikhs had not settled in some number. Irfan Habib, *ibid.*, p. 66.
6. Amandeep Singh and Paramjit Singh, *ibid.*, p. 6.
7. A.L.H Polier, "The Siques", Ganda Singh, *ibid.*, pp. 55-64.
8. Charles Wilkins, "The Seeks and their College at Patna." Ganda Singh, *ibid.*, pp. 71–74.
9. Major James Browne, "History of the Origin and Progress of the Sicks," Ganda Singh, *ibid.*, p. 22.
10. George Forster. "*Journey form Bengal to England, Through the Northern parts of India, Kashmir, Afghanistan and Perisia and into Russia by the Caspian Sea*, Language Department Punjab, Patiala 1970 (first Published in 1789, London), 2 Vols., Vol. 1, pp. 297-98.
11. John Malcolm, *Sketch of the Sikhs*, London 1812, pp. 30–33.
12. Sikh tradition holds Chandu Shah responsible for the martyrdom of Guru Arjun Sahib as he wanted to settle his old scores with the Guru Who had refuessed the hand of Chandu's daughter for his only son (Guru) Hargobind.
13. W.L. M. 'Gregor, *The History of the Sikhs*, Language Department Punjab, Patiala 1970, (first edition 1846, 2Vols.), Vol. I., pp. 23–54.
14. *Ibid.*, pp. 54-55.

15. *Ibid.*, pp. 55-56.
16. *Op. cit.*
17. *Ibid.*, p. 56.
18. *Ibid.*, p. 57.
19. H.H. Wilson, 'Civil and Religious Institutions of the Sikhs'. *The Sikh Religion: A Symposium*, Shushil Gupta, Calcutta 1958 (first published in *Journal of Royal Asiatic Society*. Vol. ix, 1848) p. 57.
20. J.D. Cunnigham, *A History of the Sikhs*, Low Price Publications, Delhi 1990 (First 1849 London), pp. 46-47 & 48.
21. *Ibid.*, p. 48.
22. Emest Trumpp, *The Adi Granth*, Mushiram Monoharlal, New Delhi, 1997, pp. Ixxx-ii.
23. *Ibid.*, p. Ixxxii.

2

Revelation of the Khalsa in Mehma Parkash Vartak

Mehma Parkash Vartak occupies a significant place amongst 18th century Gurmukhi literature.[1] It is an earliest source which gives an integrated account of the lives and mission of ten Sikh Gurus. It is in prose, written in *Sakhi* (anecdot) style. In the scriptural hierarchy of Gurmukhi literature, Prof. W.R Mcleod had placed it in the later *Janamsakhi* traditions.[2] It contains 170 instructive *Sakhis*.[3] Nearly 40 *Sakhis* are related to Guru Gobind Singh's life and mission. However, in the present paper we propose to understand the Khalsa of Guru Gobind Singh in the light of the evidence presented in *Mehma Parkash Vartak*.

To understand and appreciate the nature of evidence presented in *Mehma Parkash Vartak,* it is essential to know about its author, though briefly. The available text does not contain any reference to the author of the manuscript. Bhai Kahn Singh was, perhaps the first scholar to attribute its authorship to Kirpal Singh Bhalia.[4] Bhai Vir Singh accepted the views of Bhai Kahn Singh, Lal Singh attributes its authorship to Bawa Kirpal Dass.[5] Prof. Kirpal Singh states 'according to Bhai Vir Singh its author is Bawa Kirpal Singh.[6] W.H. Mcleod is also of the same view.[7] Yet another scholar attributes its authorship to Kirpa Diyal Singh.[8] However, Kirpa Diyal Singh was the son of Sarup Dass

Bhalla. He wrote *Fatehnama Sri Guru ji Ke Panth Ka* in Sambat 1853 (1796 A.D.).[9] Interestingly, none of the above mentioned historians have cited any evidence, either internal or external, in support of Bawa Kirpal Singh or Bawa Kirpal Dass, as its author. Since the name of this alleged author is absent in the manuscript, therefore, some scholars have hurriedly concluded that its author is anonymous.[10] However on folio 126 of the manuscript a reference is made to Gurdas Singh of Bhagnagar as its scribe.[11] On folio 127, there is also a reference to Nihal Singh of Bhagnagar who prepared a copy of the manuscript in extant, in 1824 A.D.[12] Since we do not have access to the original copy of the manuscript, therefore, in the absence of Eternal evidence about its author in the copy in extant, the issue of its authorship remains open.

Like its authorship, the date of its compilation is too a controversial issue. For instance Ganda Singh on the basis of a reference in the manuscript itself on folio 127,[13] draws his inference that this manuscript was written in 1798 B.K. (1741 A.D.).[14] Where as Kirpal Singh states that, it was compiled in 1830 B.K. *viz.* 1773 A.D. and the present copy which was prepared by Nihal Singh dated 1824 A.D.[15] W.H. Mcleod argues that of these two dates, 'the former bears the greater weight of authority, but like the later date it lack satisfactory evidence. The most we can say is that indications given in the text itself strongly support an indeterminate date within the middle or later years of the eighteenth century.'[16] A recent study has placed its authorship between 1776 A.D. to 1824 A.D. But, its arguments are not convincing.[17] G.B. Singh in his book, *Sri Guru Granth Sahib Dian Prachin Biran Bare,* has running to a manuscript in possession of *Purani Sangat Mel Wadda Burhanpur* (M.P.). which includes *Parchi Patshahi Dasvin Ki.* It is a transcribed copy dated 1753 A.D. and its scribe *is* Behal Singh of Nihchal Nagar. Perusal of the contents *of* this manuscript clearly points that while writing the account of Guru Gobind Singh, the author *of Mehma Parkash Vartak* had heavily borrowed from this manuscript, further more, a *Sakhi* about the tenure of *Guruship of each Guru with* date of its compilation *e.g.* Samat *1798* (1741 A.D.) appears to be a ditto copy of the above mentioned manuscript.'[18] On the basis of these facts and the arguments put forward by W.H. Mcleod, it can safely be suggested that *Mehma Parkash Vartak* was written around mid 18th century.[19] But it was certainly written before Sarup Dass Bhalla's *Mehma Parkash,* for, there are evidence to suggest that Sarup Dass used this manuscript while writing his *Mehma Parkash.*[20]

Though author of this manuscript does not straight way delve into a situation in which the Khalsa was revealed on the Baisakhi Day of 1699 A.D. Yet, purport of several anecdotes gives us some important clues to that situation in which it was revealed. They also unfold its characteristics. To delineate its revelation, we may turn to the contents of some anecdotes. Guru Gobind Singh's account opens with an anecdot which depict his message to the wailing, Sikhs at the time of the execution of Guru Teg Bahadur, the father of Guru Gobind Singh. His message is very important to understand the contemporary condition of the *Sikh Panth* as well as Guru's mission. Shocked and grief-stricken Sikhs were told in plain terms by Guru Gobind Singh that there was no use to mourn the execution of Guru Teg Bahadur. For, life and death was alike to him. He was God's own image while living. After leaving his body he merged with the Almighty. By doing this, he had exposed the falsehood of the Mughals. He was a saint, who had sacrificed his life in defence of his 'dharama.'[21] He was not a political offender in either sense : for, he had neither usurped any territory of the Mughals nor killed any of their men. By executing a saint like him, the Mughal rulers have done great injustice. Their falsehood would extirpate their rule. Now it is my (Guru Gobind Singh) turn to fight and finish their unjust rule.'[22] To prove the falseness of the Mughal rule, in the same anecdot, the author has given contents of the *Zafarnama.*[23] Thus it is clear from this anecdot that one of the purposes for the revelation of the Khalsa was to fight against oppressive and injust Mughal rule, to defend *'dharma'* (righteousness).

One day Guru Gobind Singh was sitting on a *damdama* (raised platform), when an informer told him that a Sikh *sangat* coming for his *darshan* has been robbed of by a Mughal official. The Guru did not respond immediately. Next day, similar incident occurred and the same was reported to the Guru. The Guru asked to the informer that why do not he say that it was the Sikh *sangat* who robbed of the Mughal Official. Then after a pause, the Guru said, '*sangat* is right' for earlier Gurus had blessed it with 'rosaries.' Now I would bless the Sikh *sangat* with 'arms.' He, then and there, enjoined upon the Sikh *sangat* to bring arms as an offering instead of money. Henceforth, the, Guru started imparting regular training to the Sikh *sangat* in the art of warfair.[24]

Guru Gobind Singh rightly perceived the danger which the malapert *masands* could pose to the institution of Guruship. They had become too powerful and corrupt. They had openly started challenging the authority of the Guru. To know and understand their attitude towards the institution of Guruship and the Sikh masses, we may turn to the contents of another anecdot. The anecdot goes like this : Once Mata Gujri (Mother of Guru Gobind Singh) asked the *masands* that they collected more from the Sikhs than what they deposited in the Guru's treasury. Instead of disgorging the appropriated offerings, they, bluntly told the holy mother that, your son is not capable to scrutinize to account.'[25] Afterward, the Guru himself heard; them saying among themselves that, 'Guru is of our own making. Did we not, contribute the money necessary for his maintenance, no one would call him Guru. But we hesitate. If he does not possess attribute of a Guru, yet he retains a name.[26] Reacting to such audacity of the *masands,'* Guru decided, to, punish them. Meanwhile another incident took place which further heightened his wrath. He decided to deal with them in an exemplary, manner. The story runs as follow; once the Guru was sitting, a company, of mimes came to, him. They begged to show their performance and asked the Guru to express his likeness. The Guru ordered them to imitate the *masands* without any reservation.

Accordingly, one of them dressed as *masand*, another as a *masand's* courtesan riding behind him on horseback as he went to collect offerings for the Guru. One of them as a servant offering a bowl of liquor to the *masand*. They entered into a poor Sikh's house. The owner of the house served them with a coarse food comprising *Dal* (crushed pulse) and *Parsadi* (unleavened bread). The *masand took* the bread, threw it into his host's face and dashed the crushed pulse on the ground, beside abusing him saying, 'curse upon you, a Guru has visited your house and you are not even providing him with good foods. Such kind of food is not even relished by our dogs.' On questioning the *masand* about the kind of food he used to have, he replied that the dishes must include *Karah* (sweet pudding) and *Mahan Parsad* (meat). The poor Sikh sold his wife's ornaments and prepared the kind of meal demanded by the *masand*. The *masand* and the prostitutes took food. Next day the *masand* asked for offerings. Now penurious Sikh mortgaged his quilt and offered one rupee. As the offering was much less than his expectation, the *masand* again became angry. In his rage threw the coin towards his courtesan and showered blows on the poor Sikh. The Guru enquired from the mimes, if the *masand* perpetrated such a oppression on the Sikhs. They replied that they have narrated only one; tenth of the whole truth. Eventually the Guru resolved to free his Sikhs from the tyranny of the *masands*.[27]

These anecdotes don't leave any doubt about the situation in which the *Sikh Panth* was put in at the time of the execution of Guru Teg Bahadur. The execution demoralized the Sikhs to such an extent that they did not gather courage to claim the dead body of their Guru. At that time the Sikh *Panth* was not a cohesive body. It was divided into two major categories : *(a)* Sikh *sangat* directly controlled by the Guru called *Khalsa* and *(b)* Sikh, *sangat* controlled through the mediacy of the *masands* called *Sehlang*. Considering the ramifications of the Sikh Panth, the role of the *masand* was very vital. But the attitude of these indiscreet *masands* towards the institution of *Guruship* and the Sikh *sangats,* as noticed in these anecdotes, was quite dangerous. Besides, attitude of the Mughals and the hill chiefs towards the Sikh movements was not favourable. Thus, all these issues; the depressed morale of the Sikhs, the impudent *masands,* the unjust Mughal rulers and the hill chiefs, were of great concern to Guru Gobind Singh. Therefore, before measuring sword with the unjust rulers, it was incumbent to bring the Sikh *sangats* under one banner and infuse into them instinct of sacrifice for the cause of righteousness.

Khalsa was enjoined upon to sever all kinds of social interaction with the *masands* and their followers.[28] He was prohibited to cohabit with a woman except his own wife.[29] He was asked not to adore tombs, cemeteries and man-worship etc.[30] He was to shun all formalities and rituals and to be a true devotee of the Almighty.[31] He was not to engross himself into the corrupt and pillaged atmosphere. Instead he should remain pure amidst the impurities of the world.[32] He should live as a householder but at the same time fix his mind at the Almighty like a hermit.[33] He was to shun vanity, for egoism is detrimental to secure the grace of God. Without God's grace one can't repeat the 'true name' which in turn ends one's transmigratory cycle.[34] Above all, he was asked Disked to be true to his words; lead selfless life and be fair in his dealings; serve the humanity, remember name of the true lord and follow the *rehat* (code of Conduct) prescribed by the Guru. Whosoever would observe the *rehat* would secure blessing of *Akalpurkh* (Almighty) in both the worlds exhorted the Guru.[35] Surely, in his own life item, Guru Gobind Singh made the Khalsa competent enough to observe and safeguard the *rehat.*[36]

Khalsa was commanded to wear arms and keep his hair intact.[37] For the 'Guru was under vow to make the Khalsa a perfect human being. And, 'without *Kesas* (hair) and *shastras* (arms) the man is imperfect.'[38] Offering of arms was hailed and encouraged. Arms were worshipped like God.[39] To be skilled in the use of various weapons had made an important duty of the Khalsa. To make him a supreme warrior, necessary training was imparted. Since the Khalsa was to fight against 'oppression' therefore the use of arms was justified to check the tyranny of any kind or shade. But the use of force by the Khalsa was limited to repel the oppression. For, the use of force for oppression by the Khalsa made no difference between him and a tyrant. However, to die in defence of one's *'dhanna'* (righteousness) was far better than to die with any other calamity.[40] Plundering in war was not a rule, but compulsions of the situation. To attack the defenceless and pursue the defeated enemy was described unethical.[41] Fighting spirit of the Khalsa was due to the grace of the Guru who had been ordained by the God himself to fight against evil doer and the unjust rulers. Thus every success in war was the grace of God, therefore, the Khalsa was restrained to be proud of his achievements. Instead, he should be thankful to the Almighty for his success.[42]

However, the perusal of the contents of Mehma Parkash Vartak reveals that the revelation of the Khalsa was a result of Guru Gobind Singh's mission *i.e.* to fight against tyranny and defend *'dharma'* (righteousness). It was not a sudden and dramatic step as most of the historians of the Sikhs assert. In fact Guru Gobind Singh was prescribing Khalsa *rehat* to his followers much earlier the formation of the order of the Khalsa on the *Baisakhi* of 1699 A.D Equation of the Khalsa with the Guru further enhanced its radiance. Thus, Khalsa *sangat* became supreme but while establishing its supremacy, doctrine of infallibility of the Guru was maintained.[43] The Khalsa sangat was a true representative of the Guru. Furthermore, the Mehma Parkash Vartak author of does not make any difference between the Khalsa and the Guru, and the Guru and *Akalpurkh* (Almighty). By implication, the Khalsa is both, the very image of the Guru and the embodiment of God.[44] However writing in the 18th century, when the Khalsa was fighting for survival against the Mughal forces, the author depicts an ideal picture of the Khalsa of Guru Gobind Singh in consonance with Sikh doctrines.

REFERENCES

1. The manuscript under study is a transcribed copy of a manuscript copied by Bhai Vir Singh in 1928 A.D. from the manuscript in possession of Akali Kaur Singh. Later on Prof. Ganda Singh made a copy from the copy of Bhai Vir Singh in 1932 and placed it in the Sikh History Research Deptt., Khalsa College, Amritsar, M.S. No. 2308. It has been edited by K.S. Bajwa entitled, *Mehma Parkash Vartak*, Singh Brothers, Amritsar, 2004.

2. Entire Sikh literature from Guru Nanak to the times of the Singh Sabha Movement has been divided by Prof. Mcleod into eight categories : *(i) Adi-Granth; (ii) Dasam Granth*; *(iii)* Compositions of Bhai Gurdas and Bhai Nand Lai; *(iv)* The *Janamsakhi* traditions; *(v) RehatNamas; (vi) The Gurbilas* traditions and later historical works; *(vii) Nirankari's* and *Namdhari's* literature; *(viii)* The literature produced under the influence of Singh Sabha Movement : W. H. Mcleod, *Textual Sources for the Study of Sikhism,* Manchester University Press, U.K., 1984, pp. 1-18.

3.

(1)	Guru Nanak Sahib	20
(2)	Guru Nanak Dev ji	11
(3)	Guru Angad Dev ji	28
(4)	Guru Ram Dass ji	07
(5)	Guru Arjan Dev ji	15
(6)	Guru Hargobind Sahib	20
(7)	Guru Har Rai Sahib	18
(8)	Guru Harkrishan Sahib	01
(9)	Guru Teg Bahadur ji	05
(10)	Guru Gobind Singh ji	38
(11)	Miscellaneous	07
		170

4. Bhai Kahn Singh, *Encyclopaedia of Sikh Literature,* Language Department Punjab, Patiala, 1990 (5th ed.), p. 936.

5. Ganda Singh, *A Bibliography of the Panjab,* Punjabi University, Patiala, 1996, pp. 202–208.

6. Kirpal Singh, *A Catalogue of Punjabi and Urdu Manuscripts*

in the Sikh History Research Department, S.H.R.D., Khalsa College, Amritsar, 1963, pp. 17-18.

7. W.H.Mcleod, *op. cit.*, pp. 18 and 149.
8. Madanjit Kaur, 'Devi Worship Story—A Critique', *Fundamental Issues in Sikh Studies* (eds.), Kharak Singh, G. S. Manuskhani and Jasbir Singh Man, Institute of Sikh Studies, Chandigarh, 1992, p. 173.
9. Uttam Singh Bhatia (ed.), *Mehma Parkash Sarup Dass Bhalla,* Language Department of Punjab, Patiala, 1999, pp. 45 and 68.
10. Rai Jasbir Singh (ed.), *Guru Amar Dass Sarot Pustak,* Guru Nanak Dev University, Amritsar, 1986, pp. 48, 38.
11. It is written on folio 126: Bhul Chuk Bakshni Sadka Guru Ki Sangat Tehllia Gurdas Singh Bhagnari, Mehma Parkash Vartak, MS. No. 2308, SHRD, Khalsa, Amritsar.
12. On folio 127 is written, Samat 1881, Asarvadi Panchvi Pothi Sakhian Sanpuranhoe. Guru Akal Purkh Di Kirpa Se Nihal Singh Tehel Kari. Guru Dayal Hoth Bhagnagar meh Pothi Sahib Sampuran Hoea., *ibid.*
13. On folio 127 is written as 'Samar', 1798, Miti Mah Sudi Panchvi, *op. cit.,* 2308
14. Ganda Singh, *op. cit.,* p. 202.
15. Kirpal Singh, *op. cit.,* p. 18.
16. W.H. Mcleod, The Light of Glory from the Mehma Parkash Vartak', *The Panjab Past and Present,* Vol. II, Punjabi University, Palinla, 1969, p. 55.
17. Rai Jasbir Singh, *op. cit.,* pp. 438-39.
18. G.B. Singh, *Sri Guru Granth Sahib Dian Prachin Biran Bare,* Lahore, 1944, pp. 325-35.
19. W.H. Mcleod, *op. cit.*, pp. 55-58.
20. Uttam Singh Bhatia, *op. cit.,* p. 41.
21. Mehma Parkash Vartak, p. 102.
22. *Op cit.*
23. *Op cit.*
24. *Ibid.*, folio 108.
25. *Ibid.*, folios 109-10.

26. *Ibid.*, folio 110.
27. *Ibid.*, folios 110-11.
28. *Ibid.*, folios III & 122.
29. *Ibid.*, folio III.
30. *Op., cit.*
31. *Ibid.*, folio 117.
32. *Ibid.*, folios 115-116.
33. *Ibid.*, folios 117,118-119.
34. *Ibid.*, folios 117, 121.
35. *Ibid.*, folios 116, 118, 121, 125, 129.
36. *Ibid.*, folios 122.
37. *Ibid.*, folio, 108.
38. *Op., cit.*.
39. *Op cit.*
40. *Ibid.*, folio 116.
41. *Ibid.*, folios 114-15.
42. *Ibid.*, folio 117.
43. *Ibid.*, folio 122.
44. *Ibid.*, folios 125, 127, 129.

3

Eighteenth Century Sikh Traditions

Born in 1750, Charles Wilkins was the son of famous Walter Wilkins. Not much is known about his early career. However, in 1770, a young Charles Wilkins landed in Bengal and started his career as a writer in the East India Company. Like many Englishmen of his day, he was interested in the study of oriental languages, and was the first non-missionary to master Sanskrit, which earned for him special favour of Warren Hastings, the then Governor-General (1772–1785). Under his patronage Wilkins translated *Bhagvad* Gita and deciphered many Sanskrit inscriptions. He was the first to prepare Bengali and Persian types and set up printing presses at Calcutta for oriental languages. He also assisted the famous orientalist. Sir William Jones, to found the *Asiatic Society of Bengal* (Later the *Royal Asiatic Society of Bengal)*, now the *Asiatic Society*, at Calcutta and establishing a well-known series of the Asiatic Researches.[1]

Charles Wilkins returned to England in 1786 and published his translations of the Sanskrit book of fables, the *Hitopdesha*. and of Kali Das's drama *Shakuntla*. Four years later, in 1800, he was made custodian of the vast collection of oriental manuscripts taken away from the library of Tipu Sultan at Seringapatam. He was also credited of being the first librarian of the Indian House Library, London[2] . Besides, he was no mean scholar of Islamic literature too, as he edited Richardsons' *Persian and Arabic Dictionary* in 1806, which speaks so highly of the depth of Wilkins learning. In 1808, he produced another Sanskrit Grammar which was greatly an improved edition of his first work on the subject. In addition to these works, he wrote a large number of valuable papers on Indian subjects which created a good deal of interest in England about Indians.[3]

In recognition to his services to the cause of literature and scholarship, the University of Oxford conferred upon him the degree of the 'Doctor of Civil Law' and Royal Asiatic Society of Literature honoured him with the medal as *'Princep Literature Sanskritac'*, and was elected as an Associate of the French Institute. He was also a Doctor of Laws and Fellow of the Royal Society. King George IV was pleased to knight him with the badge of the Guelphic Order, in 1833. Above all, he occupies a significant place among the eminent Orientalists of the late eighteenth and the early nineteenth century. He died on May 13, 1836.[4]

Enroute to Benaras in 1781, Charles Wilkins visited *Takhat Patna Sahib* also known as *Harmandir,* the birth place of Guru Gobind Singh. His short visit of about two hours to this historical shrine was not without specific purpose. For instance, before leaving Calcutta, he had come to know from a native gentleman that a considerable number of Sikhs lived at Patna where they had college of their own for teaching the tenets of their philosophy.[5] Obviously, being Indologist, he might have thought of learning about the customs and culture of the people, who had not only established their sway from the riser Jamna to the river Indus but were also making inroads into the territories of the Nawab Vazir of Oudh, an ally of the British[6]. However, his preparatory letter to the secretary of the Asiatic Society is an added proof of his objective. He wrote, "As *Patna* was my way to *Benaras,* I no sooner arrived there then I enquired after the college, and I was presently conducted to it; and now I request you will please lay before the society the few observations and enquiries which a single visit of about two hours could admit of my making. If such as they are they should hereafter be found useful either as a clue to guide another in his researches in the same path, or to add to some future account to render it more complete, my end in troubling you to lay it before the society is fully answered."[7]

However, Wilkins combined his observations with oral traditions and wrote as sympathetic and appreciative of the Sikh society. He was astonished to learn that the Sikhs do not forbid the stranger or people belonging to other communities and faith to enter their place of worship. When Charles Wilkins asked them, "if I might ascend into the hall. They said it was a place of worship open to me and to all men; but at the same time, intimated that I must lake of my shoes."[8] Wilkins had given a graphic description of the Sikh *sangat* assembled in Gurdwara (Takhat Patna Sahib) and their reverence for *Sri Guru Granth Sahib,* besides other rituals. He asserts that after taking of his shoes and covering head, he was politely conducted into the hall and seated on a carpet, in the midst of the assembly, which was so numerous as almost to fill the room. The whole building form a square of about forty feet, raised from the ground about six or eight steps.[9] The hall in the centre, divided from four other apartments by wooden arches upon pillars of the same materials, all neatly carved. The room is rather longer than it is broad. The floor was covered with a neat carpet, and furnished with six or seven desks, on which stood as many as the books of their law; and the walls above the arches, were hung with European looking glasses in the gold frames..." He goes on describing. "A little room, which, as you enter, is situated at the left end of the hall is the chancel, and is furnished with an altar covered with a cloth of gold, upon which was laid a round black shield over a long broad sword, and, on other side, a *chowry* of peacock feathers mounted in silver handle. The altar was raised a little above the ground in a declining position. Before it stood a small kind of throne plated with silver; but rather too small to be useful; above it were several flower pots and rose-water bottles, and on the left hand stood three *Urns* which appeared to be of copper, furnished with notches to receive the donations of the charitable. There stood also near the altar, on a low desk, a great book of folio size, (here he is referring to *Sri Guru Granth Sahib),* from which some portions are daily read in their divine service. It was covered with a blue mantle, on which were painted, in silver letters, some select passage of their law."[10]

His description of the divine service and performing of the *Kirtan* (Singing hymns in praise of the Almighty) is also not less vivid and of significance. 'The congregation', holds Wilkins "arranged themselves upon the carpet, on each side of the hall, so as to leave a space before the altar from end to end. The great book, desk and all, was brought, with some little ceremony from the altar, and placed at the opposite extremity of the hall. An old man, with a revered silver beard, kneeled down before the desk with his face towards the altar; and on one side of him sat a man with a small drum, and two or three with cymbals. The book was now opened, and the old man began to chant to the tune of the drums and the cymbals; and at the conclusion of every verse, most of the congregation joined chorus in response, with countenance exhibiting great marks of joy.'[11] Conclusion of the *Kirtan* was followed by *ardas* (supplication). Wilkins affirms that the 'Hymns being concluded, which consisted of about twenty verses, the whole congregation got up and presented their faces with joined hands toward the alter, in the attitude of prayer. A young man stood forth, and, with a loud voice and distinct accent, solemnly pronounced a long prayer or a kind of liturgy, at certain periods of which, all the people joined in a general response, saying *Wa Gooroo* (Glory to thee, O Lord!). They prayed against temptation; for grace to the God; and for the general good of Mankind, and a particular blessing to the *Seeks;* and for the safety of those who at that time were on their travel. The prayer was followed by a short blessing from the old man, and an invitation to the assembly to partake a friendly feast (langar)."[12]

"Before dispersing for the *langar. Guru Granin Sahib* was closed and restored to its place at the alter with due reverence. The people being seated as before", asserts Wilkings, "two men entered bearing a large iron caldron called *curraiy (Karahi),* just taken from the fire, and placed it in the centre of the hall upon a low stool. These were followed by others with five or six dishes, some of which were of silver, and a large pile of leaves sewed together with fibres in the form of plates. One of these plates was given to each of the company without distinction, and the dishes being filled from the caldron, their contents were served out till every one had got his share: myself was not forgotten; and, as I was resolved not to give them the smallest occasion for the offence, I ate my portion. It was a kind of sweet meat, (he is referring to *Karah Parsad)* of the consistence of soft brown sugar, composed of flour and sugar mixed up with clarified butter, which is called *Ghee.* Had not the *Ghee* been rancid, I should have relished better. We were next served with a few sugar plums; and here ended the feast and the ceremonies of the day.[13]

However, his observations about the Sikh faith and of the Sikh scripture are not without significance. The Sikhs as people, asserts Wilkins, were to be 'distinguished from the worshippers of *Brahm* and the followers of Mahommed,'[14] By implication, the Sikhs subscribed altogether to a new faith having different beliefs and practices from the other religious communities of the world. To him, Guru Nanak was not only the founder of the Sikh faith but also of the Sikh scripture—the *Adi Granth* (now *Guru Granth Sahib).* It was written in Punjabi language in Gurmukhi script, a script introduced by Guru Nanak himself. He calls it 'a book of Sikh law', which teaches that there is but one God, omnipotent and omnipresent, filling all space and pervading all matters: and that He is to be worshipped and invoked.' He continues, 'that it not only commands universal toleration, but forbid murder, theft, and such other deeds as are, by majority of the mankind, esteemed crimes against society, and inculcates the practice of all the virtues, but particularly universal philanthropy, and a general hospitality to strangers and travellers'.[15] Wilkins had also commented upon the ceremony of initiation into the fold of Sikhism and that of *Khalsa* brotherhood. To him, 'a person having shown a sincere inclination to renounce his former opinions' must inform to any five (baptised) or more Sikhs assembled together 'in any place, as well on the high way as in a house of worship'. After knowing his/her inclination to be a Sikh, "they send to first shop where sweet meats arc sold and procure a small quantity of a particular sort which is very common, and as I recollect, they called *Batasa,* and having diluted it in pure water, they sprinkle some of it on the body, and into the eyes of the convert, whilst one of the best instructed repeats to him in any language with which he is conversant the chief cannons of their faith, exacting from him a solemn promise !o abide by them the rest of his life. This is the whole ceremony'.[16]

In retrospect, the Sikh faith originated with Guru Nanak and the canonization of the Sikh scripture *(Adi-Granth)* too originated with him. Gurmukhi script, the language of the Sikh scripture too was invented by Guru Nanak himself. Unlike the Hindus and the Muslims, the Sikhs admit strangers into their places of worship. Their places of worship (Gurdwaras) are open to every one without any distinction of caste, colour or creed. Also, everyone present there could participate in the Sikh rituals. However, to enter into the fold of Sikhism, more precisely into the fold of *Khalsa* commonwealth, one is required to lake *Khande-di-Pahul.* To Wilkins, for this 'sincere inclination' of a person who wishes to be a Sikh and the availability of the five baptized Sikhs are the most important requisite. Reverence of the Sikhs for *Guru Granth Sahib* amounts to adoration; its teachings have universal appeal and validity, above all, the capacity to ameliorate human beings. Notwithstanding, Wilkin's account is not without blemish. For instance, while describing the initiation ceremony, he had not mentioned the recitation of the *Banis* while preparing *Khande-di Pajul,* and five Ks. as a part of the *Khalsa rehit.* His silence over this issue later on provided clue to John Malcolm to assert that while initiating the five Beloveds *(Panj-Piyare)* into the fold of Khalsa Common Wealth, Guru Gobind Singh did not asked them to keep five Ks as a part of the *Khalsa rehit,* but they were presented with five weapons.[17] Also, his assertion, that he had seen another *Granth* in *Hindoovee* language at Patna that too without any author, was enough for Malcolm to declare it as *Dasam Padshah-Ka-Granth'* in 1812.[18] Above all, misconception and mis-representation of the Sikh traditions by John Malcolm, which later on many a modern historians of the Sikhs took as established facts, finds their origin with this account. Nevertheless, being pioneer account about the religious beliefs and practices of the Sikhs, the observations of Charles Wilkins are significant in many ways. For example, his description of the Sikh rituals in the eighteenth century conforms with the twenty first century Sikh traditions. Implicitly, one can argue that there is a continuity of the Sikh traditions from the times of the Gurus to the present, which automatically refutes the claims of those who argue that the Sikh identity was established with the establishment of the Singh Sabha in 1873 A.D.

REFERENCES

1. Ganda Sing (ed), *Early European Account of the Sikhs*, Indian Studies, Calcutta 1962, p. 69; J.S Grewal. *Guru Nanak in Western Scholarship* Indian Institute of Advanced Study, Shimla 1992, p. 2. Amandeep Singh Madra and Paramjit Singh (eds). *Siques, Tigers, or Thieves' :Eyewitness Account of the Sikh (1606–1809)*, Palgrave Macmillan, New York., 2004, p. 291.
2. Ganda Singh, *ibid.*, p. 69.
3. *Ibid.*, p. 70
4. *Op. cit.*, Grewal, *ibid.*, p. 291
5. Ganda Singh. *Ibid.*, pp. 71 and 72.
6. The indologisls or Orientalists fully subscribed to the Enlightenment view that differences among large aggregates of human beings, as for example, between European and Asians, arc not to be explained by their nature which is constant

and universal, but by their customs and culture which bears diverse fruits. *E. Shreedharan, A Taxi Book of Historiography:* Orient Longman, New Delhi, 2005, p. 388: See Also James Brown's letter to the Chairman of the Court of Director, Ganda Singh, *Ibid.*, p. 12.

7. Ganda Singh, *ibid.*, p. 71.
8. Ganda Singh, *ibid.*, pp. 71-72.
9. The description given by Wilkins is of the old building of the Gurdwara which does not exist at present. Most probably it was the same structure which was raised by the local Sangat on the behest of Guru Teg Bahadur for the accommodation of his family while he was on a tour to Assam. However, it was burnt in the beginning of the nineteenth century and it was re-erected by Maharaja Ranjit Singh and other Sikh Chiefs and Sardars during the earth quake of January 1934, the buildings of the Gurdwara were rudely shaken and some of them fell on the ground. But, strangely enough, no serious harm was done to the Gurdwara proper. The demolished portions were reconstructed by the Sikh Community with the funds raised by the Chief Khalsa Diwan. Amritsar and other institution and sangats Ganda Singh, *ibid.,* Foot Note 1, p 72. Ved Parkash, The Sikhs in Bihar, New Delhi, 1979 pp. 97-101.
10. Ganda Singh, *ibid*, p. 72.
11. Ganda Singh, *ibid*, pp. 72-73.
12. *Ibid.*, p. 73.
13. Ganda Singh, *ibid.*, p. 73.
14. *Ibid.*, p. 71.
15. Ganda Singh, *ibid.*, pp. 73-74.
16. *Ibid.*, p. 74.
17. John Malcolm, *Sketch of the Sikhs*, John Murray, London, 1812, pp. 181-182.
18. Malcolm, *ibid.*, p. 54.

4

Western Writings on Banda Singh Bahadur

Political ascendancy of the Sikhs in the North-Western parts of Hindustan in the third quarter of the eighteenth century and their Persistent incursions into the Gangetic-Doab which brought them face to face with British forces stationed at Avadh, alarmed the authorities at Fort William. Activities of the Sikhs were viewed as a potent threat to the British designs in India. To frame a define policy regarding them required information about the intrinsic source which caused enhancement of their political power. Consequently besides commissioning civil servants, the British residents with the Nawab of Avadh, the Marathas and the Mughal Emperor at Delhi, were asked to collect as much information as could be extracted from any source. Resultantly, due to the efforts of both : the commissioned agents of the British East Indian Company and of some individuals many accounts on the Sikhs appeared in the last two decades of the 18th century in the form of letters, papers, tracts, travelogue etc.[1]

While writing on the Sikhs, however, the Western scholars confronted with several problems like, dearth of authentic source material, absence of incessant personal contact and ignorance of Punjabi language, the language of the Sikhs and their scripture.[2] Therefore, these accounts are based on occasional observations of their authors and the information they got from the persons who pretended of possessing authentic knowledge about the Sikhs. Some of them had based their accounts on the Persian Chronicles which at times were not correct and free from prejudice. Resultantly, a number of factual error have krept into their accounts which have been repeated by the later historians of the Sikhs both, Indians and non-Indians. Also, some of them presents incoherent accounts, besides reflecting strong bias towards the Sikhs.[3] However, inspite of all these shortcomings these accounts are very important as these shed much light on Banda Singh Bahadur and the nature of Sikh Movement under him.

An earliest information about Banda Singh Bahadur and his associates has come to us through a letter. This letter was addressed to Hon'ble Robert Hedges, President and Governor of Fort William, Council of Bengal by John Serman and Edward Stephenson. Both of them were ambassador of the East India Company's Council in Bengal to the Court of Emperor Farrukhsiyar.[4] Written from Delhi this letter is dated 10th March, 1716. In this letter Banda Singh Bahadur has been described as 'The great Rebel Gooroo' who was captured along with his family and 780 associates by Abduls Samad Khan, the Governor of the Province of Lahore, However, all of them were fettered and brought to Delhi. All alives were severally mounted on camels which were sent out of the city of Delhi for that purpose. Besides, there were about 2000 heads struck upon poles, being those who died by the sword in the battle. All alive were sent into close Prison/except Banda Singh and his close confidents, all were beheaded at the rate of 100 a day. Banda Singh and 'most of his mutsuddy's were kept alive for some time 'to get account of his treasures in the several parts of his kingdom'. Later on, however, they too were put to death. Both of these British agents were astonished to find that none of them apostatized for the sake of life. They asserts that, 'it is not a little remarkable with what patience they undergo their fate and to the last it has not-been found that none apostatized from his new formed Religion.[5] Though this information is very brief, yet it is very significant to understand the true character of Sikh movement under Banda Singh Bahadur besides delineating his firm faith in Sikhism.

Writing in the 1770s, A.L.H. Polier, a Swiss engineer, confused the achievement of Banda Singh Bahadur and Guru Gobind Singh. For instance, while narrating the Sikh struggle against the Mughals, he asserts that, 'the fame of Gorou Govind, who then made his appearance and of whom many prodigies were related, contributed greatly to establish this sect. This reputed saint soon found himself at the head of a numerous force, and began to make excursions and converts, sword in hand. He exerted himself so successfully, that at last he drew the attention of Government towards him'.[6] He further asserts, though wrongly, that 'an army was formed in or about 1715 under the command of Abdus Semad Khan Subedar of Lahore' by the order of Emperor Furrukhsiyar who ordered him 'to exterminate the sect.[7] However, 'after many marches and pursuits he came up with their main body, which he totally defeated. He had even the good luck to take Gurou Govind himself prisoner. The Gorou was sent to Delhi, set up in an iron cage, and afterwards put to death, and his disciples, wherever they were caught, were on their refusal of turning Mohammedans, immediately executed'.[8] Thus the information provided by Polier besides being sketchy in factually inaccurate.

Writing nearly a decade after polier, Major James Browne provided a bit systematic account of the life and achievements of Banda Singh Bahadur. According to Browne, Banda Singh was 'the native of a village Pundory' in the Jullundhar Doab. Before commencing his carrer as a warrior, he was 'a *Biragee Fakeer*' and had been for many years the intimate friend of Guru Gobind Singh. About the mission of Banda Singh Bahadur Browne holds that after 'hearing the destruction of his (Guru Gobind Singh) defenceless family, he gave way to the deepest impression of grief and resentment, which at length settled into fixed determination to seek revenge'. To achieve his determined end, Banda

Singh contacted' to all the most powerful and zealous sicks, who had been the follower of Gooroo Gobind'. Having 'excited in them the same spirit with which he himself was actuated and enrolled himself in the fraternity of the Sicks, with surprising diligence and activity, and aided uncommon abilities', he, 'collected the sect together in arms from all quarters and inspired them with the most ardent spirit of revenge'.[9]

Political chaos which resulted due to the struggle for throne between the sons of Aurangzeb gave an opportunity to Banda Singh Bahadur to collect together a large number of irregular army of the Sikhs and attacked Nawab Wazir Khan at Sarhind. Wazir Khan came out to give battle to the Sikhs with all the troops he had under his command. The Sikhs 'inspired by enthusiasm and revenge' gave a total defeat to the Mohammaden forces. Wazir Khan himself was killed at the spot and a greater part of his army was cut into pieces. The Sikh forces occupied Sarhind : entire family of Wazir Khan was put to death alongwith every dependent and servant belonging to him.[10] Diwan Sucha Nand was 'torn to pieces, with every circumstances of cruelty which savage revenge could dictate'[11] All the mosques and tombs were destroyed. Browne further holds that such was the terror of the Sikhs that all the inhabitants of both Muslims and Hindus sought safety not only in submitting their authority but professing to be a member of the Sikh fraternity by embracing Sikhism. This, however, is an exaggeration. To Brown, Banda Singh was 'a man of great art and address'. To increase his force he encouraged with a view : treating those with the most flattering kindness who came into his sect, and those who refuse with unrelenting severity'.[12] As a result of this policy, very soon territories from Panipat to Lahore came under the authority of the Sikhs. Besides his policy, Banda Singh was benefited from absence of Emperor Bahadur Shah from the capital with the army. The forces available in the provinces of Lahore, Delhi were not sufficient to 'undertake the reduction of the insurgents'.

However, from the news of the defeat and death of Wazir Khan, Bahadur Shah surmised the intensity of the Sikh movement under Banda Singh Bahadur. He at once decided to move with his whole force from Deccan to the Punjab. Consequently, Sultan Kuli Khan was ordered to command an advance army of cavalry and artillery with instructions that, 'he should march by way of Delhi, and thereby stop the progress of the sicks on that side, protecting the inhabitants as much as possible, to prevent the insurrection from spreading, and to put every man to the sword that he should find with his hair and beard at full length–that being the characteristic external of the Sicks.'

Sultan Kuli Khan attacked the Sikhs near Panipat. In the ensuing battle, 'there was a great slaughter on both sides, but especially on that of the sicks, who being destitute of discipline, and unprovided with artillery, suffered very severly'. The defeat of the Sikhs was total. However, the survivors fled towards Sarhind to join Banda Singh.

Joined by reinforcement sent by the Emperor under the command of Munim Khan, Sultan Kuli Khan marched towards Sirhind. To meet the Mughal forces, Banda Singh drew up his army which consisted to forty to fifty thousand horse and foot. The battle was long and bloody but eventually the royal army was victorious with 'terrible slaughter of the Sicks'. Banda Singh alongwith the remainder of the army shut himseif in the fort of Lohgarh. The fort was closely invested by the Imperialists. Meanwhile, the Emperor Bahadur Shah himself joined the camp of Sultan Kuli Khan. By that time siege had lasted for a month. The 'besieged finding their provisions and ammunition fail them, and being determined to sell their lives as dear as possible, they sallied out of the fort sword in hand.' A desperate but unequal conflict ensued. The 'greater part of the Sicks were cut into pieces on the spot, many were taken prisoners, and together with other prisoners were sent to Dehli, where they were all publically executed, after having been offered their lives on condition of embracing, the Mussalman faith, which they rejected with contempt'[13] .Thus

Browne's treatment of Banda Singh is though, is in detail and systematic as compared to Polier yet it does not differ materially so far his perception of Banda's mission and achievements, is concerned. Also, it is not free from factual errors and appears to be based on the information of Gulam Muhiuddin's Siyarul Mutakhrin.

Writing in 1790s, George Forster, describes Banda Singh 'a deciple' of Guru Gobind Singh who had attended him at Deccan before coming to Punjab, after the demise of his master. Claiming a merit from his late connection with Guru Gobind Singh, he raised a 'small force" and 'in various desulatory enterprises, established the character of 'a brave but cruel soldier'. However, his successes at length drew to his standard whole body of the Sikh nation. Having confidence in the strength of his army and emboldened by the absence of the Emperor. Banda Singh after subverting the petty Mohammedan Chiefs, attacked Wazir Khan at Sarhind. Wazir Khan fell in an action which 'was faught with an obstinate valour but ended in the total defeat of the imperial troops'.[14] The Sikhs, holds Forster, 'expressed an extraordinary joy at this victory, as it enabled them to satiate their revenge for the death of the sons of Govind Singh'. Wazir Khan's family along with a multitude of the inhabitants were put to death. Not only this, mosques were 'overthrown or polluted' and the dead, turn out of their graves, were exposed to the beasts of prey.[15] However after the fall of Sarhind in 1710, the Sikh forces laid waste the territories up to the neighbourhood of Delhi.

'Alarmed at the progress' asserts Forster, and 'irritated at the cruelties they had exercised, he (Bahadar Shah) marched towards their stations with a determination to crush the sect, and revenge the injuries that had been inflicted on Mohamedan religion'.[16] Sultan Kuli Khan, however, attacked the Sikhs near Sarhind and 'put them to fight a bloody conflict'. They took refuse in the fort of Lohgarh. The fort was beiseged. Many of them were made prisoners while Banda Singh escaped. Those who survived the disaster alongwith Banda Singh could not be subdued till the death of Bahadur Shah. Like Bahadur Shah, Jahandar Shah, who succeeded him, was unable to put restraint on the progress of the Sikhs. However, during the reign of Furrukhsiyer, Abdus Samad Khan, the governor of Lahore, attacked the Sikh vigorously and in a battle gained a decisive victory. Those who escaped 'took shelter with Banda in Lohgarh, but being closely invested and reduced to extreme distress from hunger, they surrendered at discretion'. The captives were carried in triumph to Delhi where they were 'exhibited to the inhabitants of the city in an ignominious manner'. Forster asserts that they 'met a deserved fate, for their savage and often unprovoked cruelties. Yet they met it with an undaunted firmness, and died amidst the wondering praise of the populace'.

To Forster, the contribution of Banda Singh Bahadur to the Sikh movement was not less significant. He asserts that 'The Sicque Common-wealth acquired an active strength from the spirit and valour of Banda, who had inspired them with zeal which rendered meritorious every act of cruelty to the enemies of his faith, and gave their attack, until opposed by the collective force of the empire, can irresistible impulse. The success of this fierce adventure, had allured to his standard a numerous body of proselytes : some to obtain a protection against the rapacity of the Sicque Government, others to take shelter from the oppression or just demands of the empire: whilst many embraced the new doctrine, from the hope a participating in the plunder of the Punjab'.

Thus, we see that none of these scholars have delved either on the early career of Banda Singh or his meeting with Guru Gobind Singh. Besides, being sketchy, these accounts are factually inaccurate. Almost all of them have concentrated on only three points, mission of Banda Singh Bahadur; nature of the Sikh struggle under his leadership; and his character and personality with varying degree of emphasis. They have misunderstood and therefore misrepresented his mission and achievements. In other words many misconception about this leading light of the

18th Century Sikh History which generated with these scholar were latter on followed by many Indians as well as non-Indian Scholars of Sikh history. Inspite of all these shortcomings, these writings are significant in providing several clues to understand Banda Singh Bahadur and his achievements. For example, we can infer from these writings that Banda Singh was baptized and appointed leader of the Khalsa by Guru Gobind Singh before his demise at Nander. He had a firm faith in Sikhism and died as a Sikh martyer. Also, we do not find any information about the innovations about diet, dress and salutation which were attributed to him by the 19th century western as well as Indian historians. Above all, he was brave and desperate fighter who shook the very foundation of the Mughal rule. He was the first to establish a Sikh state under the banner of the Khalsa of Guru Gobind Singh.

REFERENCES

1. Ganda Singh (ed.), *Early European Accounts of the Sikhs.*, Calcutta 1962, pp. i-9; Fauja Singh, *Historians and Historiography of the Sikhs*, Oriental Publishers, Delhi, 1978, pp. 1-2.
2. Darshan Singh, *Western Perspective on the Sikh Religion*, Sehgal Publishers, New Delhi, 1991, pp. 79-81.
3. For Instance, A.L.H. Polier describes the Sikhs as '*The terror and plague' and desired the British to exterminate this 'evil'* from India : A.L.H, Polier, The Siques', Ganda Singh, *ibid.*, p. 64.
4. Ganda Singh, *ibid.* p. 49. John Serman and Edward Stephenson, 'Massacre of the Sikhs at Delhi in 1716'. Ganda Singh. *ibid.* p. 52.
5. John Serman and Edward Stephenson, 'Massacre of the Sikhs at Delhi in 1716', Ganda Singh, *ibid.*, p. 52.

6,7,8. Colones A.L.H Polier, 'The Siqes', Ganda Singh, *ibid*, p. 56 and 57.

9-12. James Brown, 'History of the Origin and progress of the Sicks, Gands Singh, *ibid.*, p. 28,29.

13-14. *Ibid.*, pp. 29-30.

15-19. George Forster, *Journey From Bengal to England*, Language Deptt., Patiala, 1970, 2 Vols. Vol. 1, p. 303, 305, 306, 311 and 312.

16-17. *Ibid.*, pp. 303-04 and 305.

18. *Ibid.*, p. 306.

19. *Ibid.*, pp. 311-12.

5

Sikh-Muslim Relations during the Late Eighteenth Century

Sikh faith originated with the utterances : "There is no Hindu and there is no Musalman" of its founder GURU NANAK SAHIB. By implication, all are men of God: Absolute, Almighty and Creator of the Universe. Since He is the only One ; therefore all his creation be regarded as equal to each other. Inequality of any kind or in any sphere of life, on the basis of caste, colour or creed is against His will. In other words Guru Nanak Sahib, exhorted fatherhood of God and brotherhood of Mankind. Guru Nanak's cosmopolitan vision advocated for the establishment of egalitarian society; a society devoid of injustice, inequality and religious bigotry. His nine successors worked hard not only to spread these ideals in for off places, but upheld even at the caste of their lives. The basic ideas like service to humanity, clemency, forgiveness, humility, liberalism, democracy, respect and regard for women etc., which were emphasized in the teachings of the Sikh Gurus and now enshrined in Sri Guru Granth Sahib, had have a direct bearing on the late 18th Century Sikh Polity. In other words, these ideas and the institutions which the 18th Century Sikh rulers evolved, served as beacon light for them in determining their attitude towards non-Sikh population of the Sikh state.

However, for any meaningful evaluation and appreciation of Sikh-Muslim relations in the historical perspective, it is imperative to understand the nature of the Sikh rule during the late 18th century which further oblige us to understand the working of the institutions like *Sarbat Khalsa, Gurmata, Dal Khalsa* and *Rakhi*. But before commenting on these institutions we must be clear what the term Theocracy means. Was the late eighteenth century Sikh polity really a Theocracy as has been conceptualized by the western as well as some of the Indian Historians. Going by a dictionary meaning we find in Chamber's Dictionary, 'Theocracy is that constitution of a state in which God or god is regarded as sole sovereign and the laws of the realms as divine commands rather than human ordinances, the priesthood necessarily becoming the officers of the invisible ruler'. But we find no instance on record when and where the Sikh priests had any kind of influence over the policies of the Sikh Chiefs. In fact observance of certain Khalsa ideals as referred earlier by the Sikh chiefs has misled the historians in thinking that Misal rule was a 'Theocracy'.[1]

Western scholars : A.L.H. Polier, James Browne, George Forster, John Malcom, H.T. Prinsep and J.D. Cunningham writing in the late 18th and early 19th centuries about the Sikhs has characterized the late 18th century Sikh polity as 'theocratic confederate feudalism.'[2] Even N.K. Sinha writing in the 20th century have adopted their views about Sikh polity in toto.[3] In their views, the peculiar features of this polity were the bi-annual meetings of the Khalsa called *Sarbat Khalsa* at Amritsar and the institutions like *Gurmata, Dal Khalsa, Misals* and *Rakhi*. However for proper understanding of Sikh Polity, we have to clarify our conception of these institutions.

About their understanding of the concept of *Sarbat Khalsa*, the historians are not unanimous. For instance, Prinsep had used the term *Sarbat Khalsa* for an assembly of the 'Sikh Chiefs' whereas J. D. Cunningham had equated *Sarbat Khalsa* with the entire body of the Khalsa. For N.K. Sinha, the *Sarbat Khalsa* was like a 'Diet' which acted as the Central Government of the Sikhs.[4] In its literal meaning the term *Sarbat Khalsa*, no doubt, refers to the entire Khalsa. It is also true that during the 1750s and 1760s the Khalsa used to come to Amritsar at the time of *Baisakhi* and *Diwali* in a very large numbers. But, available historical evidence does not suggest that all the members of the Khalsa were participating in all the deliberations at Amritsar. Nevertheless, because of the doctrine that Guruship was vested in the *Khalsa Panth*, as the collective body of the Khalsa, the gathering of the Khalsa at Amritsar and their deliberations did possess a mystic connotation for all the members. It is very much clear from the historical literature of the period that all the Sikhs were never present in Amritsar on any occasion. Generally the assemblage at *Akal Takht Sahib* used to be in proportion to the magnitude of the danger facing the Sikhs. Also, all the Sikhs present did not necessarily participate in the meetings, those who deliberated in the name of the *Sarbat Khalsa* were regarded as doing so on behalf of the entire body of the *Khalsa*.[5] Thus it is very clear that the *Sarbat Khalsa* cannot be regarded as the central government of the Sikhs; nor can it be equated merely with the assembly of the Sikh chiefs.[6]

Like the *Sarbat Khalsa*, the institution of *Gurmata* has been termed variously and sometimes confused with the institution of *Sarbat Khalsa*. For instance, Polier regarded *Gurmata* as the greatest counsel of the Sikhs. James Browne refers to *Gurmata* as 'Grand Diet'. To Forster it was a 'Grand convention' of the Sikhs. For Malcolm and Princep, it was a 'special council' of the Sikhs.[7] The word 'mata' in Punjabi language means a resolution. When it is passed in an assembly of the Sikhs in the presence of the holy Guru Granth Sahib with a hymn read on its conclusion, its is believed to have been endorsed by the word of the Guru and is called *Gurmata*.[8] However, John Malcolm has given a very elaborate procedure of performing *Gurmata* at *Akal Takht Sahib* in Amritsar which was always held by the Akalis. On this occasion the Sikhs Chiefs used to decide the line of action to be followed against the common enemy, to deliberate upon the defensive as well as offensive alliances, to pool the resources of the Sikh nation, to choose a common leader to lead the Sikh forces and to review the management of the Sikh shrines.[9] Thus, collective decision taken in the presence of Sri Guru Granth Sahib was considered as an order from the Guru himself which morally bound the Sikh chiefs to carry it out with all sincerity and diligence. However, looking at the scope of the institution of *Gurmata*, it is very clear that it was not a 'council' or 'government' of the Sikhs. No doubt, sometimes its scope was extended to territorial occupation too, but it was never extended to administrative arrangements of the acquired territory.

Lack of clarity and unanimity about the institution of *Dal Khalsa Ji* is too obvious amongst the historians. For example, James Browne holds that the *Dal Khalsa* was formed by Jassa Singh Ahluwalia, Charhat Singh Sukarchakia and Karora Singh during the governorship of Mir Mannu in 1748. He looks upon it as the army of the state. To Prinsep, *Dal Khalsa* was the joint forces of several *Misals* to collect *Rakhi*, 'for expeditions of importance or any matter of more than ordinary moment'. Cunningham equates *Dal Khalsa* with the army of the theocracy of Singhs and attributes its creation to Jassa Singh Ahluwalia, N.K. Sinha refers to it as the 'grand army' of the confederacy.[10] However, taking into consideration the arguments and conception of these historians together with the actual activities of the *Dal Khalsa*, it becomes very clear that *Dal Khalsa* was essentially a combination of forces of several Sikh Sardars for a specific purpose. Thoughout the late 18th century Sikh history, it never assumed the character of a single unit or standing army of the Sikhs, but a temporary combination of several units acting in concert.[11] Had it been so, Jassa Singh Ramgarhia had never joined Adina Beg Khan and fought against his own co-religionists. Institution of *Dal Khalsa*, along with *Sarbat Khalsa* and *Gurmata*, however, did play a significant role during the late 18th Century Sikh History' enabling the Sikhs to survive incredible state repression and acquire political power. Significantly, these institutions did not have any kind of negative influence on the administration of the territories of the Sikh chiefs. History bear witness to it. Each Sikh Misaldar or chief was a monarch in his respective domain.

An other peculiar feature of the 18th century Sikh polity was *Rakhi* system. Under this system, the offer of *Rakhi* (lit. protection) was made to the people of the towns and villages of the Punjab and was actively pursued by the Sikhs as a regular feature of their activities. However, chaotic conditions created by political turmoil caused by conflicting political claims put forward by the Mughals, the Afghans, the Marathas and the Sikhs, to extend their control over the province completely shattered the peace of the Punjab. During the 1750s to 1760s, the Punjab virtually remained under dual monarchy. During this phase the people of the Punjab did not know whether they were under the protection of the emperor of Delhi or Kabul or Kandhar. Due to internal lawlessness and external danger, the state political apparatus had literally collapsed which further made plight of the Punjabis desperate. The poor peasants were being squeezed by various authorities. There was no prospect of law and security. Thus, when the Punjabis were being ruined economically and politically and there was no hope of peace or justice, the Sikhs like true sons of the soil devised the institution of *Rakhi*.[12]

Under the *Rakhi* system, the protection was granted to the people irrespective of caste, colour or creed against foreign invasion and internal exploitation of *Zamindars,* government officials and against the depredations of the local adventures. Verily, the full safety of their persons and property was ensured in return for one fifth of their income twice a year after each harvest, that is *Hari* and *Sawni* or *rabi* and *kharif*. Soon, almost whole of Punjab came under the protection the Sikh chiefs and by 1770s this offer was even extended to the inhabitants of the Gangetic Doab.[13] For example, writing in the 1770s, A.L.H. Polier, observed that the Sikhs had come into possession of 'the whole Soubah of Lahore the greatest part that of Multan and part of that of Delhi, including all the country called Punjab'. At this point of time, the Sikh chiefs used to collect a certain yearly tribute from some areas of the Delhi and Agra provinces, and even from the Nawab of Avadh. Polier further noticed that this tribute was called *Racky (Rakhi)* and 'in general a trifle will satisfy them, from two to five percent on the revenues, particularly if at a distance; and provided this is regularly paid, it is said no further hindrance or molestation will be received from them. On the contrary, the chief, to whom the tribute or Racky is paid, takes the district under his protection and is ready to fight against any of the brethren who might think of disturbing it.'[14] Writing in the 1780s, Jame Browne asserts that, 'the Sikh chief not only himself refrains from plundering him but will protect him from all others; and this protection is by general consent held so far sacred that even if the grand army passes through a Zamindari; where the safe guards of the lowest Sikh chief are stationed, it will not violate them.'[15]

George Campbell commenting on the managing of State affairs, observed that the Sikh chief were not 'exclusive and unduly prejudiced in favour of their own people but employed capable Mohammedans and others almost as freely as Sikhs.'[16] There is no denying the fact that during the first half of the eighteenth century the Sikhs suffered a lot at the hands of the Mughal and Afghan rules, but when they became the sovereign ruler, they were not revengeful or intolerant to the Muslim subject as such.[17] However, as a rulers they ungrudgingly appointed Muslims to responsible posts in almost all the departments of state administration. For instance, Lakhana Doger, a Muslim was appointed commander-in-chief of his Army by Maharaja Ala Singh.[18] Ghoshi Khan and Mian Khushal was serving as Topchi under Mahan Singh Shukarchakia and Imam Hussain under Jodh Singh Wazirabadia. It appears that almost all the Sikh rulers had have Muslims as their artillery officers.[19] Afghans of Urmar, Yahyapur and Tanda (now in district Hoshiarpur) had joined the forces of Jassa Singh Ahluwalia due to his non-sectarian policy. Besides he had a large number of

Muslims in his service who had full liberty to perform their religious rituals as they pleased.[20]

Beside Army, a large number of Muslim *Chaudhari Muqaddams, Diwans, Kardars and Lambardars* were serving as state functionaries and were performing the same functions as they used to do under the Mughal/Afghan rule. For instance, Usman Khan under Jai Singh Kanhiya Ahmad Khan under Kapur Singh Saurianwala, Ghulam Qadar under Jodh Singh Wazirabadia, Suba Khan and Teeka Khan of Talwandi under Bhag Singh Hallowalia, Rahmat Khan Wariach of Jalalpur under Gujar Singh Bhangi, Dasundi Khan of Chimiari under Nahar Singh Chamiariwala, Khudadad Khan and Yadgar Khan of Firozke under Suddh Singh Chhina, Mian Muhammad Ashiq, Mian Mohkam Din, Mir Shadi Khan and Mir Badruddin (all from Lahore) were some of the important *Chaudharis* under the Sikh rulers. Nur Burhan under Ran Singh Nakkiye, Sahib Khan under Nahar Singh Chammiarawala, Muhammuddin of Mauza Kot Budha under Gulab Singh, Mohammuddin of Mauza Saggian under Lehna Singh, were serving as *Muqaddams.*[21] Fateh Singh Ahluwalia appointed Qadir Bakhsh as his special officer and sent him to Maharaja Ranjit Singh as his ambassador. Also, Qazi Nur Muhammad served him as Diwan and *Mukhtiar* and Sher Ali Kakezhi of Danwali as Diwan.[22]

As during the Mughal rule, the primary unit of administration was the village itself. Here the village *Panchayat (Panches)* was always chosen from men of the best reputation amongst the villagers without any consideration to religion. Significantly the office of *Qazi* and *Mufti* continued to function under the Sikh Rule as it was during the Mughal period. For instance, Qazi Kamaluddin was performing his duties at Wazirabad, Qazi Hazi at Gujrat and Qazi Abdul Rahman at Gujranwala. In the case of the city of Batala, the name of five Qazis has been mentioned in the contemporary documents. Qazi's court was quite popular amongst the non-Muslims too because of the uniform application of law. Mostly, the cases were decided according to traditions. In the case of succession the Muslims were allowed to follow their own law of succession.[23]

Dispossessed Muslim chiefs were treated with indulgence. For example, when Tara Singh Dalewalia took over Nakodar from Rai Ahmed Manj, he was granted land for subsistence. In 1767 when Charahat Singh Shukarchakia took over pind Dadan Khan, few villages were granted to Sahib Khan Khokhar, the ousted chief. Likewise, five village were also granted to the wife of Ghulam Muhammad Khan Chattha by Mahan Singh Shukarchakia. When Milkha Singh Thepuria occupied Rawalpindi in 1767, he allowed Mansur Khan and Shadman Khan the sons of Muqarrab Khan Gakkhar to retain Pharwala in subsistence *Jagir*. Significantly, the most notable tribes of Rawalpindi were allowed to retain 192 villages in *Jagir*.[24] When Maharaja Ala Singh ousted Sadar Khan Rajput of village Munak, he was provided a lucrative post. These examples are multiple.[25]

While conferring religious land grants, service *Jagirs*, *Inam Jagirs* etc. to persons and institutions no discrimination was made with the Muslims. As a rule the Sikh rulers confirmed the imperial grants and gave fresh one to *Sayyids, Shaikhs, Pirzadas, Mirasis, Khanqahs, Takiyas* and *Masjids*.[26] For instance, Maha Singh Shukarchakia granted few villages to Khudadad Khan, son of the *Chaudhari* of Jalalpur on the condition of serving with twenty horsemen. Mian Khan was receiving *Jagir* worth 15,000 rupees to perform military services under Sada Kaur. Qazi Abdul Rahman was given land grant to perform civil duties by Mahan Singh Shukarchakia. *Chaudhri* Nagalia received 22 *bighas* of land as *Inam* from Jai Singh Kanhiya. Jai Singh Kanhiya gave 160 *Ghumaos* of land worth 100 rupees to *Chaudhari* Mian Khan, in addition to five per cent commission (*Pachotra*) and two *Sers* of grain per *Maund*. Some other known grantees were Chaudhari Sultan Khan under Gurbakhsh Singh Kanhiya, *Chaudhari* Ikhlas Khan under Jodh Singh Vegila, *Chaudhari* Khudadad Khan under Suddh Singh China, *Chaudhari* Mohammad Azim and

Chaudhari Imam Bakhsh under Jassa Singh Ahluwalia. Not only the *Chaudharis*, but Muslim *lambardars* too received land grants as *Inam* from the Sikh rulers. For instance, Jai Singh Kanhiya gave 150 *Ghumaons* of land worth 90 rupees in Gurdaspur district to Sultan Ali, a *lambardar*. Gurbakhsh Singh Khanhiya granted fifty *Ghumoons* of land to Mayya and Jiwan the *Guzzar Lambardars* of the village Dagowal. Similar grants were received by Munim Khan from Milkha Singh of Amritsar and Muhammaduddin from Lehna Singh of Lahore.[27]

Village community or the life in the rural Punjab was the best example of Sikh-Muslim rapprochement, even the Hindus for that matter. In the rural population which formed the vast majority in the country, several faiths were so strongly mixed up that one could hardly be distinguished from the other. In a village, people of all castes and creeds lived amicably. The same village often contained Hindus, Muslims, Sikhs, Rajputs, Jats and people of other castes. On important occasions such as births, deaths, marriages and holy days or festivals, they fraternized with one and other. On social and religious occasions, they used to exchange greetings and presents, and enjoyed festivities in common. However, the most significant aspect of the village life was the worship of the common village deities. Of course, the women played an important part in this respect. For instance, a Muslim woman who had not offered to the smallpox goddess felt that she had deliberately risked her child's life. Even on special occasion, she fed Brahman priests. Similarly a Sikh or a Hindu woman regularly made offerings at the shrines of Muslim Saints on every Thursday and at the time of a marriage in the family.[28] T. Forrtescue has given a very graphic picture of the relations of the villagers. He observed, "no instances occur of a proprietor driven from the village by oppression or violence of one or any number of other shares; on the contrary, it is observable that they tender each other the most friendly and essential aides when in distress. They will supply cattle, till the lands themselves, contribute money when a sharer has been really unfortunate and they assist him in the disposal of his produce, in providing seeds, bullocks and implements should they be satisfied with them. This feeling ....is extended to the widow and necessitous family of a deceased sharer, and its effect scarcely surpassed.'[29]

Significantly, even during the course of struggle with the Mughal and Afghan rulers, the Sikhs did not entertain any enmity against the Muslims or their religion. Their struggle was against the Government and not against the Muslims. There is no instance on record of *Dal Khalsaji* or any of the *Misal* force having even attacked the Muslim village or their place of worship. If at any time mosques came to be attacked by them it was because they were the nerve centers of crusade (*Jehad*) against the Sikhs in those days. Otherwise there are instances when the Sikh Gurus and Sikh chiefs built mosques for their Muslim friends and subjects.[30]

As a ruler the Sikhs were very popular with their Muslim subjects due to their non-discriminating policies. For instance, when Ahmed Shah Abdali appointed Dadan Khan as governor of Lahore and retired to his country, Lehna Singh Banghi who had left Lahore on the approach of Abdali, came out of his retreat and came close to Lahore, the courtiers of Dadan Khan advised him to step down from his office and surrender it to Sardar Lehna Singh. Not only this, they advised the governor to see Lehna Singh and ask him for subsistence allowance which was graciously granted. It is also on record that Lehna Singh used to give turbans and bestow honours on *Qazis* and *Muftis* on the occasion of Id.[31] District Gazetteer Gujrat records : 'The names of Sardar Gujar Singh and Sahib Singh or often in the mouths of the people, who look back to their rule without the smallest bitterness. They seem indeed to have followed an enlightened policy, sparing no effort to induce the people harried by twenty years of constant spoliation to settle down once more to peaceful occupation."[32] It is interesting to note that when Sayid Ghulam Ghaus incharge of a theological seminary of Batala fled and sought asylum with Sardar

Mahan Singh, the Shukarcharia chief helped him in the restoration of his office.[33]

One of the peculiar features of the Sikh rule was the running up *Langar*. The institution of *Langar* had started with Guru Nanak Sahib at Kartarpur (Now in Pakistan) for the way-farers as well as the needy irrespective of caste, colour or creed. These *langars* of the Sikh rulers particularly during the time of famine or other natural calamities proved to be a great help to the Punjabis. District Gazetter Montgomny records that famine of 1783, occurred during the time of Budh Singh who is said to have 'sold all his property and to have fed the people with grain from the proceeds.'[34] Hundreds of people used to take their meals daily form the *Langar* of Jassa Singh Ahluwalia.[35] These *Langars* of the Sikh chiefs were so popular that the hearths where the *Langar* was cooked came to regarded as a sacred places of pilgrimage. For instance, Maharaja Ala Singh had started *Langar* which was supervised by his wife Fateh Kaur. The hearths where the *Langar* was cooked are still preserved at Barnala and considered as sacred places of pilgrimage by the people of the locality.[36]

Retrospectively, we may say that invariably all the Sikh rulers of the late eighteenth century kept the welfare of their subjects and dispensation of justice and service to the people upper most in their mind. They created a close identification with the people of the land, rejected the theory of the Divine Rights of the kings, adopted completely a non-communal policy in the conduct of state affairs. Appointments were not made on sectarian basis but on merit. As a result of their policies the peasantry which were predominantly Muslim, were contended and happy. There is no incident on record where the Sikh rulers destroyed any mosques or resorted to any kind of religious persecution. Also, we do not hear about any revolt during this phase of history by the Muslims against their Sikh rulers. If Maharaja Ranjit Singh is considered the most secular ruler of Indian history like Akbar the Great, he was inheriting this tradition from the late eighteenth century Sikh chiefs, who had evolved this tradition on the basis of Sikh ideals as enunciated by the Sikh Gurus and are enshrined in Sri Guru Granth Sahib.

REFERENCES

1. Bhagat Singh, *Sikh Polity in the Eighteenth and Nineteenth Centuries*, Oriental Publishers, New Delhi, 1998, pp. 121-22.
2. A.L.H. Polier, "The Siques", Ganda Singh (ed.), *Early European Accounts of the Sikhs*, Indian Studies Past and Present, Calcutta, 1962, pp. 61-62; James Browne, 'History of the Origin and Progress of the Sikhs', Ganda Singh, *ibid.*, pp. 14-17, 33; George Forster. *A Journey From Bengal To England*, Language Department Punjab, Patiala, 1970 (reprint-first published in 1808), 2 Vols. Vol. I, pp. 330-31; H.T. Prinsep, *Origin of the Sikh Power in the Punjab and Political Life of Maharaja Ranjit Singh*, Language Department, Punjab, Patiala, 1970 (reprint –first published 1834), pp. 17-29, John Malcom, *Sketch of the Sikhs*, London 1812, 114-123, 136; J.D. Cunningham, *History of the Sikhs*, Low Price Publication Delhi, 1990 (reprint – First published in 1849), pp. 85, 94, 95 fn.1 and 96.
3. N.K. Sinha, *Rise of the Sikh Power*, A Mukherjee and Co., Calcutta, 1960, pp. 57, 108–11 and 115.
4. Prinsep, *ibid*, p. 26, Cunningham, *ibid.*, p. 94, Sinha, *ibid.*, pp. 26, 108.
5. Bhagat Singh, *ibid.*, pp. 110–116.
6. Veena Sachdeva, *Polity and Economy of the Punjab, during the Late Eighteenth Century*, Manohar, New Delhi, 1993, p. 87.
7. Ganda Singh, *ibid*, pp., 15-16, 61; Forster, *Ibid*, p. 330; Malcolm, *ibid*, pp. 95-96 and 115, Prinsep, *ibid*, p. 71.
8. Bhagat Singh, *ibid.*, p. 109.
9. Malcoln, *ibid*, pp.120–23; Brown, *ibid*, pp. 14, 15, 16-17, 33-34; Polier, *ibid.*, pp. 61-62; Forster, *ibid*, pp. 329-32.
10. Ganda Singh, *ibid.*, p. 33; Prinsep, *ibid.*, 26; Cunningham, *ibid.*, p. 85, Sinha, *ibid.*, 108.
11. J.S. Grewal, "Eighteenth Century Sikh Polity', *From Guru Nanak to Maharaja Ranjit Singh; Essays in Sikh History*, Guru Nanak Dev University, Amritsar, 1972, p. 98.
12. Bhagat Singh, IInd, pp.77–79, H.R. Gupta, *History of the Sikhs*, Manshiram Manohar Lal, New Delhi, 1999, vol. II, pp. 73-132.
13. Bhagat Singh, *ibid.*, p. 79; Gupta, *ibid.*, pp. 82, 126–28

14. Ganda Singh, *ibid.*, p. 62.
15. *ibid.*, pp. 16,100.
16. George Campbell, *Memoirs of My Indian Career (ed.)* by C.E. Bernard, Macmillian and Company, London, 1892, 2001., vol. I, p. 180.
17. Forster, *ibid*, Vol. I, p. 321; Bhagat Singh, *ibid*, p. 107.
18. Kirpal Singh, *Life of Maharaja Ala Singh of Patiala and his times*, Khalsa College, Amritsar, 1954, p. 139.
19. Lepel Griffin, *The Punjab Chiefs: Historical and Biographical Notices of the Principal families in the territories under the Punjab Government*, Lahore, 1865, p. 468; Punjab Government records, Ludhiana Agency, 1808–15, II, 188-89
20. Bhagat Singh, *ibid.*, p. 108.
21. J.S. Grewal and Indu Banga, *Early Nineteenth Century Punjab*, Guru Nanak Dev University, Amritsar 1975, pp. 45, 57, 58, 93-94, 110; Veena, *ibid.*, p. 74.
22. Bhagat Singh, *ibid.*, p. 109.
23. Bhagat Singh, *ibid.*, pp. 133, 135; J.S. Grewal, *In the By Lanes of History*, IIAS, Shimla 1975, pp. 25-32; Documents, II, III, X, XIII, XV, XVIII and XXXII; The Qazi in the Pargaria', Histornians Punjab; Miscellaneous Articles, Guru Nanak Dev University, Amritsar, 1974; 38-74.
24. Veena Sachdeva, *ibid.*, pp. 117-18.
25. Kirpal Singh, *ibid.*, p. 139.
26. Indu Banga, *Agrarian System of the Sikhs : Late Eighteenth and Early Nineteenth Century,* Manohar No. 1978, pp. 138-39, 164-66, *Prinsep, ibid.*, pp. 27-29; Veena, *ibid.*, pp. 126-27.
27. Veena, *ibid.*, p. 117.
28. Hari Ram Gupta, *ibid.*, Vol. IV, pp. 528-29.
29. Punjab Government Records, Delhi Residency and Agency 1807–57, Vol. I, p. 22. Quoted in Bhagat Singh, *ibid*, pp. 129-30.
30. Bhagat Singh, *ibid.*, p. 73; Ganda Singh, *ibid.*, p. 58, f.n. 18.
31. Bhagat Singh, *ibid.*, pp. 107-8.
32. D.G. Gujrat, 1892-93, pp. 21-22.

33. Bhagat Singh, *ibid.*, 108.
34. D.G. Ludhiana, 1888–90, p. 72; *D.G. Montogomry*, 1883-84, p. 34.
35. Bhagat Singh, *ibid.*, p. 108.
36. Kirpal Singh, *ibid.*, pp. 147-48.

6

Jassa Singh Ahluwalia's Relations with Bharatpur State

We do not have any external evidence to devolve on the early life and social status of Ram Sukh Rao. From all the three historical works : *Jassa Singh Binod,* Ms. M/772, Punjab State Archives, Patiala; *Bhag Singh Chandaruday*, MS, Ml773, Punjab State Archives Patiala, and *Sri Fateh Singh Partap and Prabhakar* MS, M/774 Punjab State Archives, Patiala, which he produced during his life time, we can infer that he was very learned Brahmin. In his personal *Jagir* papers, he is referred as a *Jagirdar-i-a 'la* of the Ahluwalia Sardars. In these papers, both he and his son Harnam Dass are mentioned as *Bad-e-Firoshan i.e., bhat*. However, from his writings, it can safely be assumed that he was patronised and occasionally amply rewarded along with his son in the form of dresses and ornaments from Sardar Fateh Singh Ahluwalia. Also, his familiarity with various languages; Persian, Urdu, Sanskrit, Braj Bhasha and dialects of Punjabi spoken around Patiala and in the Jallandhar Doab shows that he was fairly an educated man. However, in his first work Jassa Singh Binod which contains the biographical account of Jassa Singh Ahluwalia, the founder of Kapurthala State, Ram Sukh Rao has provided a graphic account of Sardar Jassa Singh's relation with Bharatpur state. This manuscript contains 250 folios and was written during the reign of Fateh Singh Ahluwalia (1801-1837).[1]

Sardar Jassa Singh Ahluwalia, during his life time led several expeditions to Hindustan. Multiple reasons can be ascribed to take up these expeditions but prominent were : to crush the power of the Rohillas, to help the rulers of Bharatpur and to collect money from Rajput States; Bikaner, Jaipur and others.[2] In all these expeditions, Raja Gajpat Singh of Jind and Raja Hamir Singh the chief of Nabha personally participated in these expeditions with men and material to assist Sardar Jassa Singh Ahluwalia. Indeed, Raja Gajpat Singh was very trusted companion of the Ahluwalia chief in these expeditions who often served as his representative in delicate diplomatic missions.

However, in February 1764, Vakils of Raja Jawahar Singh came to Sardar Jassa Singh Ahluwalia and implored for assistance against Najib-ud-daulah to avenge the death of his father, Raja Suraj Mal, the Jat ruler of Bharatpur, while he was extending his domain towards South-West of Delhi through the territory of Mewat. In this region there were few settlements of Biloch chiefs such as Jhajhar, Tauru, Bahadurgarh and Farrukhnagar. These Biloch chiefs had sought Najib-ud-daulah's help against Jat expansion. However, in an action fought with the forces of Najib-ud-daulah, Raja Suraj Mal had been killed by Sayyid Muhammad Biloch on 25th December, 1763. Earlier Jawahar Singh had attacked the Biloch principality of Farrukhnagar where Sayyid Mohammad Biloch was then staying under the protection of its chief Mussavi Khan. Jawahar Singh mastered the town of Farrukhnagar and arrested Mussavi Khan. Najib-ud-daulah had made a protest to Raja Suraj Mal against this arrest and threatened to attack the principality of Bharatpur.

After Suraj Mal had been killed, Raja Jawahar Singh was left with two options; either to wait Najib's action against him or to attack Najib-ud-daulah in order to crush his power. He adopted latter course and started preparation to attack

Najib-ud-daulah to take revenge of his father's death. He sent Harji Mal Rababi to Sardar Jassa Singh Ahluwalia to enlist his help against Najib-ud-daulah. Harji Mal met the Ahluwalia chief and presented five horses and eleven thousands rupees on behalf of his master. During the interview Harji Mal acquainted Ahluwalia chief about the sad death of Raja Suraj Mal at the hands of the Afghans and requested for help on behalf of his master who wanted to avenge the death of his father. Sardar Jassa Singh told Harji Mal that he was very sorry to hear about the death of Rajaji (Raja Suraj Mal) and promised to help Raja Jawahar Singh in his expedition against Najib-ud-daulah. After Harji Mal two Musahib (courtier) of Raja Jawahar Singh : Madari Khan Mewati and Himatgir sanyasi appeared before the Ahluwalia chief and presented two horses of fine breed to the Sardar and acquainted the Ahluwalia chief that Raja Jawahar Singh had vowed not to sit on the throne of Bharatpur until he could kill Sayyid Muhammad Biloch, the killer of his father Raja Suraj Mal. The envoys further told to the Ahluwalia chief that if he agreed with the cause of Raja Jawahar Singh and wanted to help him against the Afghans then Raja Jawahar Singh would like to have an interview with the Ahluwalia Sardar. The Ahluwalia chief assured the envoys of his help. After, learning about the assurance of the Ahluwalia chief, Raja Jawahar Singh decided to meet him personally. However on Raja Jawahar Singh's approach to the camp of the Ahluwalia Sardar, the latter sent Raja Gajpat Singh of Jind along with other Sikh Sardars to receive Raja Jawahar Singh. In this interview, the Ahluwalia chief assured his help to Raja ji against Najib-ud-daulah. Before leaving his camp Raja Jawahar Singh presented rupees fifty one thousand to the Ahluwalia chief besides giving cash reward to other Sikh chiefs including Nihangs and Rababis. Ram Sukh Rao, asserts that the Ahluwalia Sardar decided to help the Raja of Bharatpur for three reasons: *(i)* because he was a Hindu; *(ii)* his father had been killed while fighting against the Mughal forces; and *(iii)* Najib-ud-daulah had paid less amount than agreed to in his previous expedition against him.[3] Ram Sukh Rao also opines that Marathas were invited on this occasion with the consent of Sardar Jassa Singh Ahluwalia.[4] However, all the three chiefs; the Marathas, the Ahluwalia and Raja Jawahar Singh deliberated on the political situation of the time and decided to attack Najib-ud-daulah in order to avenge the death of Raja Suraj Mal.[5]

When Najib-ud-daulah learnt about the alliance of the Marathas, the Sikhs and Raja Jawahar Singh against him, he immediately dispatched an envoy to Sardar Jassa Singh. The envoy, Dila Ram offered a hefty amount to the Ahluwalia Sardar and requested on behalf of his master not to help the Jat chief of Bharatpur. Sardar Jassa Singh convened a meeting of all the present Sikh Sardars to know their opinion about the proposal of Najib-ud-daulah. However, the Sardars unanimously decided to help the Jat Chief against the Afghan ruler. They told the envoy of Najib-ud-daulah that so long as the killer of Raja Suraj Mal is under his protection, they cannot think of any other option than to help Raja Jawahar Singh. They further told the envoy that peace can only be made if Najib-ud-daulah agreed to hand over Sayyid Muhammad Khan Biloch to them. Upon this Dila Ram, the envoy of Najib-ud-daulah presented Hundis of rupees three lakhs and again made a request not to help the Bharatpurias.[6] The Ahluwalia chief rejected this offer and reiterated his assurance to help the Bharatpurias. When Dila Ram informed Najib-ud-daulah about the conduct of the Ahluwalia chief he summoned other Rohilla chiefs to his aid and sent urgent entreaties to Ahmad Shah Abdali, informing him of the perilous situation. After making preparation, Najib encamped his troops outside Delhi to defend the capital.[7]

Joint forces of Raja Jawahar Singh, the Maratha Chief Malhar Rao and Sardar Jassa Singh Ahluwalia closely invested Delhi in November 1764. The Marathas were posted to the north of the city, and the Sikh to the north-west, while Jawahar Singh posted his army on the eastern bank of the river Jamuna and the rest before the Delhi and Ajmeri gates.

Ram Sukh Rao has given very detailed account of the battles which were fought between the two parties. Soldiers from both the sides fought every action with astonishing valour but the Jats proved more stronger than the Afghans in every action. For instance, on the first day there was a pitched battle between the Afghans and the Jats, the latter drove the Afghans back into the city. A thousand were killed and wounded from each side. According to Ram Sukh Rao, after the heavy loss on the first day of the war, the Najib sent envoy to Sardar Jassa Singh Alhuwalia and implored for peace on behalf of the Emperor of Delhi. Sardar Jassa Singh told the envoy that if Najib-ud-daulah was ready to submit to the terms already conveyed to him only then they could think of decampaing.[8] At the same time, the Ahluwalia Chief advised Raja Jawahar Singh to advance with his artillery. He, accompanied by Malhar Rao Holkar and other chiefs, crossed the Jamuna and plundered Shahdara and planted batteries on that side. Next day, the troops of Najib-ud-daulah owing to heavy cannonding of the Jats left the sandy plain below the fort and went inside; shells began to fall into the city. Ram Sukh Rao holds that when Jawahar Singh and Malhar Rao advanced their camp to the bank of river Jamuna east of Purana Qila, Najib-ud-daulah had taken position in Buland Bagh, at the foot of the Imperial fort. During this campaign, many actions were fought and in one of the action Nawab Aman Khan, the brother of Najib-ud-daulah was arrested. It so happened that during his tough fight with the enemy Aman Khan lost all his companions. But he continued to advance and create havoc among the ranks of the enemy. Eventually, he fell upon Sahib Singh, who was a close associate of the Ahluwalia Chief. Sahib Singh had lost his horse in an action and was standing on a side. When Aman Khan saw him standing alone without a horse, he attacked him with his sword. Sahib Singh clung to Aman Khan. Others came to Sahib Singh's rescue and arrested Aman Khan. He was put on an elephant belonging to the Marathas and was conveyed to the Maratha camp. At the end of the days battle, a council was called to decide the fate of Aman Khan. The Maratha wanted ransom while Raja Jawahar Singh wanted to kill him. However, Jassa Singh Ahluwalia was of the opinion that it was unethical to kill a war prisoner. Eventually, he prevailed upon both and Aman Khan was safely escorted to the camp of Najib-ud-daulah.[9] Nevertheless, Najib fought another battle with the Sikhs and the Jats near Paharganj and Sabjimandi. The action began with heavy musketry fire; a large number of men were killed and wounded. The Afghanas had to retire discomfited. The city had been closely invested; nothing was allowed to go inside the city. The Afghans were now left with no other choice than to starve or surrender. The inhabitants of the city started cursing the Nawab for placing them in a such a critical situation. They were demanding immediate peace with the Jats.[10] Consequently, Najib-ud-daulah sought an interview with the Jats and the Marathas. All the issues were discussed in detail with the allies. Ram Sukh Rao asserts that during this meeting Najib-ud-daulah offered rupees fifteen lakhs to the Maratha Chief. Thus, when the Afghans were on the verge of annihilation, the Maratha Chief went over to Najib-ud-daulah's side. In utter disgust, Raja Jawahar Singh was obliged to conclude peace with Najib-ud-daulah[11] Sardar Jassa Singh Ahluwalia too left the camp of the Jat ruler and started towards Punjab to measure sword with Ahmad Shah Abdali who had arrived near Lahore.[12]

REFERENCES

1. Ram Sukh Rao, *Jassa Singh Binod*, MS, M/772 Punjab State Archives Patiala, Punjab; see also Kirpal Singh *Catalogue of Punjabi and Urdu Manuscripts in the Sikh History Research Department*, SHRD, KCA, 1963, p. 30.
2. For instance, in the year 1760 Sardar Jassa Singh Ahluwalia led two expeditions to Hindustan, first was against Najib-ud-daulah and the second was to help Raja Suraj Mal, the Jat ruler of Bharatpur. In 1764-65, the Ahluwalia chief again went to that area to help Raja Jawahar Singh against Najib-ud-daulah. Again in 1765-66 he undertook another expedition to suppress the supporters of Najib-ud-daulah and collect money from the rulers of Bikaner and Jaipur states. In 1766-67 he again went

to that side to collect money from Najib-ud-daulah, the rulers of Bikaner and Jaipur. In 1768, he looted the outer suburbs of Delhi and his last expedition to Hindustan is dated 1772-73: Ram Sukh Rao, *ibid.*, Folio 102-a-b, 103 a-b, 110-b, 124-a, 131b, 132-135a, 164a-172a, 183a, 186b, 191-a, 205 ab.

3. Ram Sukh Rao, *Ibid.*, Folio 150-b and 151 a-b.
4. *Ibid.*, Folio 151b.
5. *Ibid.*, Folio 152 a-b.
6. *Ibid.*, Folio 152-a-b.
7. *Ibid.*, Folio 152b.
8. *Ibid.*, Folio 154a.
9. *Ibid.*, Folio 153b, 156b, 157a.
10. *Ibid.*, Folio 158a.
11. *Ibid.*, Folio 152a.
12. Ibid., Folio 158b.

7

Western Perception of Sri Harimandir Sahib During the Nineteenth Century

Sri Harimandir Sahib became a focal point during the reign of Maharaja Ranjit Singh who considered the city of Amritsar as his second capital. This relationship got special attention in the European travel literature. These travellers belonged to distinct nationalities having peculiar historical background. Their objectives to visit the Punjab varied as much as their nationalities. Their accounts depict many facets of life in the Punjab, during the reign of Maharaja Ranjit Singh. While travelling in the kingdom of Lahore, Sri Harimandir Sahib remained a focus of their attention. The present attempt is to analyse their perception on Sri Harimandir Sahib and to understand its historical position with the help of these evidences.

To understand the nature and significance of their observations, it is imperative to perceive their aims and objectives. For example William Moorcroft was a British veterinary surgeon to the Bengal Army.[1] His idea was to penetrate into Turkistan, to the country of a breed of good horses which it was his great ambition to domesticate in India. Coupled with this was the idea of exploring the possibilities of establishing commercial intercourse with the trans-Himalayan districts.[2] Victor Jacquemont was a naturalist. He was sent by the French Government to investigate the natural history of India in all its branches and to collect material to enrich the Royal Museum of Natural History at Paris in order to promote the progress of Science.[3] Purpose of Alexander Burnes was politico-commercial. Professedly, he was sent by the British Government to Lahore on a complimentary mission. He was to take from the ruler of England to the ruler of Punjab, five dray horses of a size never seen before in India. In fact, he was deputed to explore the countries upon the lower Indus, bordering upon the Oxus and Caspian; and to determine the navigability of the river Indus.[4] Baron Charles Hugel was a German. His primary concern was to know the greatness and power of the East India Company, the Maharaja's ally and the kingdom founded by Ranjit Singh.[5] Godfrey Thomas Vigne was an English. Before coming to India he had served in an infantry battalion. Later on he became a professional painter. He was travelling for amusement. He was neither professional author nor commissioned tourist. In his observations he was assisted by the possession of some knowledge of Science.[6] Charles Masson was a deserter from the ranks of the Bengal Artillery. His real name was James Lewis; a fairly educated English archaeologist. His interests appear to be in the antiquity and politics of Afghanistan.[7] A novelist traveller, Eden Emily, accompanied her brother George Eden Auckland to India. She remained with him till 1842 and was present at the time of signing the celebrated Tripartite Treaty.[8] Joseph Wolff was a Jewish missionary. He resolved to visit the eastern countries to prepare the way for missionary enterprises among the Jews, Mohammedans, and Christians who inhabited them.[9]

Amongst his contemporaneous, Baron Charles Hugel alone goes into the historical development of the Harimandir Sahib. The Harimandir has its own history. Fourth Guru Ram Dass got excavated the pool of nectar: Amrit-sarowar in 1573.[10] The fourth successor Guru Nanak, Guru Arjan Dev expanded and made it pucca in 1581. In the year 1589, he laid the foundation of Harimandir Sahib in the midest of Amrit-sarowar; which was completed during his ministry. Very soon, it became a place of pilgrimage for both, Sikhs as well as Hindus.[11] Interference of the Mughal administration, in the holy dipping of the Sikhs in the Amrit-sarowar, until the end of the fourth decade of the eighteenth century, is not known.[12] This attitude of the state, towards the Sikh bi-annual gatherings at the Harimandir, is attributed by Hugel to the poverty of the devotees who assembled here for ablution. He opines that places of pilgrimage are so numerous in India, that they are only noticed by the government for the sake of the tax levied on each pilgrimage; and here the assembled crowd being of the lowest classes, they had nothing from which any tax could be levied.[13]

By the turn of the fourth decade of the eighteenth century, Khan Bahadur Zakariya Khan, Governor of the Suba of Lahore, had seen clearly the importance of Harimandir Sahib and Amrit-Sarowar in the religious life of the Sikh community. The Mughal authorities were convinced that the very source of strength to the Sikh community was the Harimandir. They apprehended a political danger of its emergence. Consequently, they thought not only to destroy it but also aimed 'a fatal blow at the faith'.[14] Massa Ranghar with the orders of Khan Bahadur occupied the Harimandir. Four towers were erected at its corners to keep watch over the Sikhs; to check their gatherings at Harimandir on the days of Baisakhi and Diwali and to prevent them to have ablution in the holy waters of Amrit-Sarowar. Besides, the persecution of the Sikhs was made lawful. Hugel does not favour the policy of persecution. He observed that the persecutions are the very source of strength to a religion. Once a person adopt a faith whether right or wrong, no earthly event can tear it away from the soul.[15]

A number of battles were fought, during the eighteenth century, between the Sikhs and the Mughal state for the possession of the Harimandir. Inspite of their best efforts, the Mughal Governors of Lahore failed to supress the Sikhs. In their turn came the Durranis. Ahmad Shah Durrani decided to teach a lesson to the Sikhs. In his measures against the Sikhs, he went a step ahead of the Mughals and blew up Harimandir with gunpowder. The broad stones round the holly tank were torn up and flung into the water, which was chocked up with masonary and rubbish. Not being contended with this profanation, the Afghans, 'brought cows to the place, slaughtered them on the heaps of ruins, sprinkled the stones with their blood, and flung their entrails about.[16]

The importance of the institutions of *Sarbat Khalsa* and the *Gurmatta*, in the Sikh struggle for independence, becomes very clear in the observations of Baron Charles Hugel. During the eighteenth century, the cohesion of the Sikh community was preserved through these institutions. The institution of the *Gurmatta* made it possible for the Sikhs to select a common leader like Jassa Singh Ahluwalia, who carried the battle-axe of the people.[17] Furthermore, it made feasible for the Sikhs, to survive the state repression. Within two and a half decades, since the first profanation of Harimandir Ṣahib by Massa Ranghar, the Sikhs secured not only the Harimandir but also wrested sovereignty of the land of the five rivers. In fact, the Sikhs were attached to the Harimandir from the very core of their hearts and minds. Any attempt to detach them was bound to bring a more energetic response. Their love and sacrifice for this place was a reality. Even, immense losses of lives suffered at Kup Rahira could not demoralise them. After the Great Holocaust, when Ahmed Shah was yet to cross the Indus, they reassembled at Amritsar, to decide the line of action to be followed against the enemy. They emerged stronger than the Abdali had thought : through the *Gurmatta* they decided to avenge the profanation of their sacred place.[18] Consequently, their activities brought about, perhaps sooner than might otherwise have happened, the downfall of the Mohammedan power, in the north of India.[19] Commenting on the mood of the Sikhs towards the Muslims, Jacquemont says that 'when victory re-opened the gates of the Harimandir to the Sikhs, they carried out bloody reprisal and washed the steps of the sacred pool with blood of the Muslims'.[20] However, the Sikhs, within a very short period, could clean the desecrated tank and rebuilt the Harimandir. It was restored to greater splendour than ever before. These activities of the Sikhs, records Hugel, set 'a rare example for the Hindus'.[21]

To Hugel, Amrit-Sarowar appears to be a unique object on earth. It contains an immense body of water, 'as clear as a mirror', a rare occurrence in such places in India'.[22] It is 375 feet square.[23] Several stone steps lead the devotees to the holy water. The holiest place for bathing is on the eastern side. A devotee must have bathed outside it, before he/she is allowed to have ablution.[24] Amrit-Sarowar is surrounded by a pavement about 50 to 62(1/2) feet in breadth.[25] Around this stand some of the most considerable places belonging to Maharaja Ranjit Singh, his principal sardars and some of the holy buildings. Among these there is the place where Guru Ram Dass passed his whole life.[26]

Facing the gateway to the temple, stands Akal Bunga (Akal Takht). Here Guru Sahib (Guru Granth) rests during night hours. It is a repository of Guru's belongings; and baptistery of the Sikhs. Near the Akal Takht stands two large Sikh standards. Hugel describes these of red colour.[27] On one of these was written *Wah Gur Ji Ki Fateh* and on the other, the name of the excavator of the Amrit-Sarowar and founder of Ramdaspur—Ram Dass. Letters were in white colour. These flags were from 129 to 150 feet long; stretched on masts and confined with iron chains.[28]

Harimandir Sahib is a 'national temple' of the Sikhs.[29] It stands in the midst of a tank Amrit-Sarowar. It is a handsome building, built on an 'island', covered with burnished gold.[30] A narrow marble bridge, on the western side, connect it with the pavement around the Amrit-Sarowar, Its 'Mysterious and romantic' character appeals forcibly to the imagination of a visitor. It is far surpassed to the other Indian temples.[31] Its golden roof, designed very beautiful and skillfully, inlaid with marble, adds to its beauty. A large golden door opens into the temple. All the four golden doors are surrounded with little vestibules; the ceilings being supported by richly ornamented pillars.[32] Right in the centre of the temple is placed Guru Granth Sahib, under a canopy of gold cloth, quite stiff with pearls and small emeralds. The canopy cost 10,000 pounds. A granthi (who recites the Guru Granth), sits in presence of the Guru Granth. A *chauri-bardar* wave the *chaur* (fly-scarer), made of Tibet cow's tail, over the Guru Granth, to keep away the impurities. The lower portion of the interior walls were covered with Kashmir shawl stuff. Devotees sat in a circle around the Guru Granth, leaving an open space, which is never encroached upon, it being customary that the Guru (Granth Sahib) should be viewed from a certain distance with due reverence.[33]

Observations of these travellers communicate to the reader that politics was discussed at Harimandir Sahib, even during the reign of Maharaja Ranjit Singh. While making political decisions, guidance was sought from the Guru Granth. To illustrate this fact, we may turn to an incident narrated in this connection. When Lord Auckland came to sign the famous Tripartite Treaty, Eden Emily, an eye witness, observed that when all sat down, 'one of the priests made a long oration, to the effect that the two great potentates were now brothers and friends, and never could be otherwise. Then Governor-general made the speech to the same effect, and mentioned that the two armies had joined, and they could now conquer the whole world; and Ranjit Singh carried on the complement, and said that here the oracle had prompted him to make this treaty, and now they saw that he and the English were all one family. Such instances are multiple.[34]

These accounts give us to understand that Maharaja's control over the affairs of Harimandir was quite strong. When Lord Auckland refused to take off his shoes while entering into the Harimandir, he was admitted to the temple with his boots on, covering with a pair of dark stockings. The Sikhs remained quiescent..[35] However, visits of the Europeans to the temple were not liked by the Akalis. For instance Alexander Burnes, a state guest, while visiting the Harimandir wished to see the Akal Bunga. He offered rupees two hundred and fifty to the Akal Takht. But for fear of the Akalis, he was not allowed to go in. Desa Singh Majithia, who had been ordered by the Maharaja to make his visit secure, was so solitious about his safety that he led Alexander Burnes by the hand, which he grasped firmly through the assembled crowd.[36] Same happened with Jacquemont.[37] Before the Ropar meeting, when C.M. Wade visited the Harimandir, again for fear of the Akalis, Maharaja Ranjit Singh had to place a regiment of infantry.[38] Similarly when Lord Auckland and his party visited the Harimandir, Ranjit Singh made an elaborate arrangements for their security. Even, he had to make a general proclamation to the effect that 'he would put to death any body who maltreated any of the Governor-general's followers.[39]

Since these travellers were attached to peculiar cultural background! their incompetence to use proper words for Sikh customs and institutions is visible. For instance, Amrit-Sarowar appears 'a lake' to Alexander Burnes.[40] To Hugel, all the Sikh priests and other service performing personnel at the Harimandir are 'gurus'. The *ardas* (supplication) have been understood as 'a speech' and a *ardasia* (supplicator) as a master of the Guru's ceremonies. Furthermore, *mukhwak* is mentioned as 'a prayer' out of the Granth Sahib. The 'Siropa' (a robe of honour) is equated to a gift and a *Khilet* from the Guru (Granth).[41] Eden Emily could not visualize the holiness pinned to the custom of taking off shoes, before stepping into the holy shrine. For example, when Lord Auckland was admitted to the Harimandir with his boots on, covering with dark stockings, she viewed the Sikh custom of removing shoes as, that 'all they really care about is, that their sacred marble should not be defieed by shoes that have trodden the common streets'.[42]

Observations of these travellers carry certain limitations. These are due as to the purpose of visit as to the access of the foreigners to the Harimandir. For example, Charles, Masson, who himself never came to Amritsar, provides us misleading information about the beautification of the Harimandir by Maharaja Ranjit Singh.[43] However, these accounts shed much light on certain points and give us clues to their investigations. The roots of the religious practices, inharmonious with Sikhism, for which the Singh Sabhas in the late nineteenth and the Akalis in early twentieth century struggled, could be traced from the early nineteenth century.

REFERENCES

1. William Moorcroft and G. Trebeck, *Travels in the Himalayan Provinces of Hindus an and the Punjab, in Ladakh and Kashmir, in Peshawar, Kabul, Kundar, and Bokhara from 1819 to 1825*, 2 Vol. Punjab Languages Department, Patiala, 1970 (reprint-first published 1837), cited hereafter as Travels, I, XIX.

2. Moorcroft, Travels, I, xvi, xx, see also, *The Dictionary of National Biography* (ed.), Sir Leslie Stephen and Sir Sidney Lee Oxford University Press, London 1973, Vol. VIII (reprint-first published 1917) cited hereafter as *The Dictionary*, 784.

3. Victor Jacquemont, *Letters from India : Describing A Journey in the British Dominions of India, Tibet, Lahore and Kashmir during the year 1828, 29, 30, 31, under the order of the French Government*, 2 Vols., Edward Churton, London 1834,1, v; See also, H.L.O. Garrett (ed.), *The Punjab A Hundred Years Ago*, Punjab Language Department, Patiala 1971,1; M.F.O. 'Dwyer, "Jacquemont's Letters from India, Review", *Journal of the Royal Asian society*, XXIII, 1964 (reprint-first published 1936), 23; K.K. Khullar, *Maharaja Ranjit Singh*. Hem Publishers, Delhi 1980, 93.

4. Alexander Burnes, Travels into Bokhara : being the account of a Journeys from India to Cabool, Tartary and Persia, also, Narrative of Voyage on the Indus from Sea to Lahore, 3 Vols., Oxford University Press, Karachi (4th ed.), (cited hereafter as Travels), Vol. I, Preface, see also, The Dictionary, Vol. III, 389; Henry T. Prinsep, Origin of the Sikh Power in the Punjab and Political Life of Maharaja Ranjit Singh, Language Department Punjab, Patiala, 1970 (reprint-first published 1834), 121; Syed Muhammad Latif, History of the Punjab, Eurasia Publishing House, New Delhi, 1964, 443.

5. Baron Charles, Hugel, *Travels in Kashmir and the Punjab containing a particular account of the Government and character of the Sikhs,* Punjab Languages Department, Patiala, 1970 (reprint-first published 1845) (cited hereafter as *Travels,* 293; See also, V.S. Suri (tr.), *Umdat-ut-Tawarikh,* Daftar III, Pts (i-iv), Punjab Itihas Prakashan, Chandigarh 1974, 267.
6. *The Dictionary,* Vol. XX, 309, *Umdat-ut-Tawarikh.,* Daftar III, pp. 237, 242, 267, 269 & 270.
7. Charles Masson *Narrative of Various Journeys in Balochistan, Afghanistan and the Punjab,* 4 Vols. Oxford University Press, London 1974 (cited hereafter as *Narrative,* I, vii, viii, 3; 'Catalogue of European Manuscripts', *'India Office Library & Records,* Vol. 2, Pt. 2, pp. 1972-82.
8. *The Dictionary,* Vol. vi, p. 356.
9. *Ibid.*, Vol. XXI, p. 777.
10. Hugel has wrongly mentioned this event in the year 1581; *Travels,* p. 391. The excavation of the tank started on 6th November 1573 and was completed in 1577, and was made pucca in 1581 : Madanjit Kaur, *The Golden Temple Past and Present,* G.N.D.U., Amritsar 1983, pp. 8-10; Fauja Singh (ed), *The City of Amritsar—An Introduction,* Punjabi University, Patiala, 1977, p. 30.
11. Hugel, *Travels* p. 391; Rev. Jofeph Wolff, *Travels and Adventures,* Saunders, Otley & Co., London, 1861, p. 374.
12. Hugel, *Travels,* p. 391; In the 1740s, Zakariya Khan appointed Massa Ranghar in charge of Amritsar, to stop Sikh gathering at Amritsar at the days of Baisakhi and Diwali as well as not to permit any Sikh to bathe in the holy tank. He erected four towers at its corners to keep a strict watch on the approach of the Sikhs. He took his seat inside the Harimandir where he smoked hubble bubble and spat. Dancing girls gave performance of their craft in that sacred shrine; Hari Ram Gupta, *History of the Sikhs,* Vol. II, pp. 58-59.
13. Hugel, *Travels,* pp. 391-92.
14. *Op. cit.*
15. Hugel, *Travels,* p. 392.
16. Hugel, Travels, *op. cit.*, H.L.O. Qarrett, The Punjab. A of Hundred Years Ago, p. 27.

17. Hugel, *Travels*, p. 322.
18. Hugel, Travel, p. 392.
19. *Ibid*, pp. 392-93.
20. H.L.O. Garrett, The Punjab. A Hundred Years Ago, 27.
21. Hugel, *Travel*, p. 393.
22. *Op. cit.*
23. Hugels information is incorrect. Each sides of the tank at the bottom measures approximately 470 feet. The walls of the tank rise slantingly till the side at the top get broadened to 510 feet each: Madanjit Kaur, *The Golden Temple Past and Present*, G.N.D. University, Amritsar, 1983, p. 15.
24. Hugel, *Travels*, p. 393.
25. The Present *Parkarma* (marble pavement around the tank) is 60 feet wide : Manjit Kaur, *The Golden Temple*, 143.
26. H.L.O. Garrett, *The Punjab : A Hundred Years Ago*, 20; Eden Emily, *Up the Country*, Curzen Press, London, 1978 (reprint) p. 215; Hugel *Travels*, p. 393.
27. Hugel, S., Information is misleading, The colour of the Sikh standard is saffron.
28. The present Sikh standards at Akal Takht are one hundred and one feet long. Atma Ram (Singh) of Nerobi (Africa) denoted these standards. These were prepared by Deṣ Raj; who spent about two years to complete. These were installed on April 13th 1959. Around 1850s there existed about 60 feet long wooden standards. This information is based on an interview with a person who belongs to a family having the credit of stiching the rob of Sikh standard from the last one hundred and forty years, Gurdial Singh S/o Sohan Singh Kamboj of Amritsar.
29. Burnes, *Travels*, III, p. 176.
30. Hugel, *Travels*, p. 393, Eden Emily, *Up the Country*, 215-16, Burnes, *Travels*, III, p. 176.
31. Hugel, *Travels*, p. 394.
32. *Op. cit.*, Eden Emily, *Up The Country*, p. 216.
33. Hugel, *Travels*, p. 394; Eden Emily, *Up the Country*, p. 216.
34. Eden Emily, *Up the Country*, p. 215-16; Burnes, *Travels*, III, pp. 175-76; Hugel, *Travels*, 395.

35. Eden Emily, *Up The Country,* pp. 215.
36. Burnes, *Travels,* III, pp. 177-78.
37. *Jacquemont Letters* II, pp. 182-83.
38. *Loc. cit.*
39. Eden Emily, *Up the Country,* pp. 214-15.
40. Burnes, *Travels,* III, p. 176.
41. Hugel, *Travels,* pp. 394-95, Jacquemont, *Letters* II, p. 183.
42. Eden Emily, *Up the Country,* p. 215.
43. He says that the marble used at the Harimandar was brought from the famous Shalimar garden. *Narratives* 1,415. But we learn from the court historian of Maharaja Ranjit Singh that, The Maharaja issued an order for the preparation of a marble floor for the decoration of Darbarji and its *parkarma.* In continuation of this order Bhai Gurmukh Singh to fetch marble from that place and to prepare the floor in perfect beauty and grace, *Umdat-ut-Tawarikh,* Daftar III, p. 242.

8

Western Perspective of the Sikh Scripture

Nineteenth century western writings on the Sikhs and their past synchronise with the politics of British imperialists in the Indian sub-continent. This is obvious from the synchronization of a large number of important publications with important events. For instance, Captain Matthew's *Tour to Lahore* appeared in 1809, the year in which The Treaty of Amritsar between the East India Company and Maharaja Ranjit Singh was concluded. John Malcolm's *Sketch of the Sikhs* appeared soon after the conclusion of this Treaty. H.T. Prinsep and Alexander Burnes' works appeared after the conclusion of the Indus Navigation Treaty of 1832, in 1834 and 1835 respectively. Charles Masson's Travelogue appeared in 1842. Hugel's Travelogue was published in 1846. M.L. M'Gregor's *The History* of *The Sikhs* (1846) was meant to glorify the deeds of the British officers and justify the first Anglo-Sikh war. J.D. Cunningham wrote *History of the Sikh* (1849), to awaken the British Nation with the hope to influence the British policy towards the Sikhs. Travelogue of Baron Erich Von Schonberg was published in 1853. Emily Eden got her letters published in 1866. However, the nature of Western interest in the Sikhs changed after the annexation of the Punjab. Now their main concern was, how to handle them as subject people and to use their support and services for the extension and perpetuation of

British Raj. Since, religion was considered as the only source of inspiration and strength of the Sikh nation; the imperialists turned to know their beliefs and practices which eventually led them to the study of their scripture. Resultantly, Ernest Trumpp a trained Christian theologian was commissioned in 1869 by the Punjab Government to translate the Guru Granth, the fountain head of the Sikh beliefs and practices. Thus, the first major work which appeared after 1850s, was Dr. Ernest Trumpp's *Adi Granth*. Obviously, the Sikhs as an enemy and as a subject people remained important to the 19th century Western Scholars.

Dawn of the 19th century witnessed two major developments in the Indian sub-continent : sudden and rapid rise of Maharaja Ranjit Singh on the political scene of the land of the Five Rivers and British occupation of Delhi in 1803 which ended Maratha influence in northern India. The latter development pushed the British frontier to the Jamuna and made the East India company an immediate neighbour of the Sikhs, a 'singular nation' that inhabited the territories between the river Jamuna and the Indus. However, the Sikhs had already attracted attention of the British in the last quarter of the eighteenth century because of their incursions into the Doab. The changed situation made knowledge about the Sikhs still more imperative. The Director of the East India Company by their Despatch of the 5 June 1805, desired that all available information on the geography and history of India should be collected.[1]

Consequently a number of British civil and military servants in the garb of travellers, diplomats etc. were deputed to secure as much information as they could extract from various means about the Sikhs. Besides, several individual wrote at their own on the Sikhs, though not without specific purpose. They used the available information in the form of manuscripts, published works besides supplementing with their own observations on the Sikhs. However, to determine the nature of 19th century Western writing on the Sikhs we may place, though roughly, into four categories : *(i)* Travel literature, is an important gener of this phase. For, being brought up in a particular socio-cultural set up, the travelers observed those social institutions and religious practices which appeared to them peculiar and which were generally overlooked by the native chronicles. These accounts provide information on almost every aspect of the Sikhs life : social customs, beliefs and practices, fairs and festivals as well as social institutions like *Sati* amongst them. Though these accounts are sketchy and lack systematic presentation of the Sikhs, and their religion, yet, the significance of the evidence is due to the fact that it is based on personal observations and not on heresy. Also, these accounts were written away from the scene without fear or pressure of any kind; *(ii)* John Malcolm, H.T. Prinsep, Steinbach, M'Gregor and Cunninghan's works falls in the category of those works which make general survey of the Sikh history and treat Sikh beliefs and practices as a part of the Sikh history; *(iii)* accounts of William Ward, H.H. Wilson, Robert Needum Cust falls in the category of those works which were primarily concerned with Indian religions and treat Sikhism in a brief and sketchy manners; *(iv)* work of Ernest Trumpp falls in the category of those works which primarily deals with Sikh theology, for he was the only 19th century Western scholar who was commissioned primarily to the study of the Sikh theology on the pattern of Christian theology.

Since these scholars belonged to different cultural and religious traditions and could not grasp Sikh movement and Sikhism in its proper form; their inadequate understanding of Sikhism led to misinterpretation and misrepresentation of the Sikh tradition. For instance, majority of these writers have presented Sikhism as a response to the prevailing disorderly and chaotic religious condition in India : they emphasized the reformatory character of Sikhism. In their assessment, Sikhism aimed at synthesizing the positive elements from both Hindu and the Islamic traditions, having universal appeal and validity. Beyond this point they failed to perceive the originality of the vision and mission of Guru Nanak. However in their endeavor to elucidate the historical role of Sikhism, they have striven to determine the place and role of Sikhism among the Indian religions. The main issue which came to be discussed and elaborated in this context are the historical origin of the Sikh tradition, life history of the founder of the faith, relation of Sikhism to its historical background, development of Sikh religion, place of Sikhism among the religion of the world and analysis of the Sikh beliefs and practices in relation to the doctrines and practices of the preceeding religious traditions. Sikh beliefs and practices which have been discussed and deliberated in these writings are : the recitation of the name of the God, reverence to Guru Granth Sahib, emphasis on the active social life, service of the humanity, equality of the status of women, absence of untouchability, mode of initiation, dress and symbols of the community etc. The Sikh rejection of the doctrine of avtar, caste system, the practice of idolatry, practice of sati, sacrificial rituals, priest craft, ritualistic bathing at places of pilgrimages, have also been noticed by these scholars. Above all, the status, role message and use of the Sikh scripture has also found mention in these writings.

A close study of the 19th Century European writings on the Sikhs reveals that almost all are unanimous in attributing the origin of Sikhism to Guru Nanak. Doctrines preached by Guru Nanak proved to be a foundation of Sikhism and these are unquestionable.[2] In this context, Ernest Trumpp maintains that, "The doctrines once uttered by Baba Nanak were taken up by the following Sikh Gurus without any perceptible deviation; and after the volume of the Granth (Guru Granth) had been collected by (Guru) Arjan, they were never called into question, the Granth being held sacred as an immediate divine revelation.[3] Commenting upon the idea of God in Sikhism, Cunningham asserts that Guru Nanak invoked 'the Lord as one, the sole, the timeless Being; the Creator, the self existent, the incomprehensible and everlasting. He likens the Deity to Truth, which was before world began, which is, and which shall endure for even as the ultimate idea or cause of all we know and behold". 'Further he remarks that Guru Nanak, 'extricated his followers from the accumulated errors of ages, and enjoined upon them devotion of thought and excellence of conduct as the first duties. He left them, erect and free, unbiased in mind and unfettered by rules, to become an increasing body of truthful worshipper'.[4] Malcolm too describes Sikhism as a 'divine religion'.[5] To William Ward, God of Sikhism 'is an invisible spirit, and is to be conceived of as being active and passive with and without qualities.[6] H.H. Wilson have seen Divine unity as the basic tenets of the Sikh Gurus.[7] In short Sikhism is a revealed religion and the Sikhs believe in the unity of Divine Being. They worshiped God alone through the medium of Guru Granth Sahib.[8] They do not adore any idol or image. Their only from of worship is the repetition of the name of God, supreme-Being, eternal Truth, the creator of everything.[9] Malcolm observes that 'their Dharamsala, or temple of worship, are in general, plain buildings. Images are, of course banished. Their prescribed forms of prayer are, I believe, few and simple. Part of the writings of Nanak, which have since been incorporated with those of his successors, in the *Adi Granth* are read, or rather recited, upon every solemn occasion'.[10]

Most of the 19th century writers have enumerated Sikhs institution like *Sarbat Khalsa, Gurmatta* and *Dal Khalsa. Sarbat Khalsa* was generally held twice a year : on the occasion of *Bosakhi* (April) and *Diwali* (October), festivals, to decide the line of action to be followed against the common enemy, to pool the resources of the Sikh nation and to choose the common leader to lead the Sikh forces.[11] H.T. Prinsep have defined *Sarbat Khalsa* as 'an assembly of the chiefs' and *Gurmatta* as a 'special council' , 'where expeditions of importance, or any matter of more than ordinary moment were submitted to their united wisdom'. If the joint forces of several Misals took the field to collect *Rakhi,* the Sikh army assumed the denomination of *Dal of the Khalsa ji.*[12] These two institutions proved to be an important instruments for preserving the Sikh faith and enhancing political power in the 18th century, It also becomes clear how

Guru Granth Sahib through the institution of Gurmatta played a significant role in providing cohesion to the Sikhs and enabled them to wade through the pools of blood. John Malcolm says that the Gurmatta was convened by the Akalis who were in control of Sri Harimandir Sahib. He has described in detail the proceedings of the Gurmatta and its significance for the Sikhs. He maintains that, 'when the chiefs and principal leaders are seated, the *Adi Granth* and Dasama Padshah Ka Granth are placed before them. They all bend their heads before these scriptures and exclaim, Wai Guru'ji ka Khalsa! Wa Guruji Ki Fathe! A great quantity of cakes, made of wheat, butter and sugars, are then placed before the volumes of the sacred writings and covered with a cloth. These holy cakes, which are in commemoration of the injunction of Nanak, to eat and to give to other to eat, next receive the salutation of the assembly, who then rise, and the Akali's pray aloud, while the musician play. The Akalis, when the prayers are finished, desired the council to be seated. They sit down, and the cakes being uncovered are eaten of by all classes of Sikhs : those distinctions of original tribes, which are, on other occasions, kept up, being on this occasion laid aside, in token of their general and complete union in one cause. The Akalis then exclaim : "Sardars (Chiefs) this is the Gurumata" on which prayers are again said aloud. The chiefs, after this, sit closer, and say to each other : "The sacred Granth is betwixt us, let us swear by our scripture to forget all internal disputes and to be united."[13] Malcolm also assert that the first Gurmatta was assembled by Guru Gobind Singh himself.[14] Thus, Malcolm is the first and only Western Scholar who has given an elaborate procedure of performing *Gurmatta*, but his presentation contain contradictions so far as the presence of *Dasam Granth* along with *Guru Granth Sahib* is concerned. It is obvious from his above statement. For example, when the deliberation of the assembly starts Malcolm mentions the presence of two scripture, but when the Sikh chiefs resolve to act upon the *Gurmatta*, they swear by one scripture. Also, almost all the 19th century writers have mentioned the institution of *Gurmatta* and its role in the advancement of political power of the Sikhs but none has mentioned the presence of *Dasam Granth* in this context. However, collective decision taken in the presence of Guru Granth Sahib was considered as an order from the Guru which morally bound the Sikh chief to carry it out with all sincerity and diligence.

Almost all the 19th century writers under review are unanimous in describing *Khande-di-Pahul* as the only means to enter into the fold of Sikhism.[15] E. Samuel and Baron Charles Hugel refers to *Akal Takht* as a Baptistery of the Sikhs.[16] All of them delves on the initiatory rites in one way or the other. But few of them have described the mode of initiation, preparation of *Pahul*, injunctions to the neophyte and the *rehit* (code of conduct) of the Khalsa in detail. Malcolm describes the mode of initiation a follows: 'some sugar and water is put into a cup, and stirred round with a steel knife, or dagger.[17] About the *Banis* which were recited while preparing *Amrit* Malcolm say 'some of the first chapters of the Adi Granth and the first chapter of the Dasama Padshah Ka Granth are read'.[18] But Hugels observation suggests that Five Bani's were recited which also included sawayeas authored by Guru Gobind Singh.[19] Prinsep also appears to be subscribing to the views of Hugel.[20] Those 'who perform the initiation exclaim, *Wa! Guru Ji Ka Khalsa ! Wa! Guru ji ke Fateh* (success to the state of the Guru! Victory attended the Gúrú). After this exclamation has been repeated five times, they say, "This Sherbet is nectar. It is the water of life, drink it". The disciples obyes; and some Sherbet prepared in a similar manner, is sprinkled over his head and beard'.[21] Both Cunningham and Trumpp maintains that after Guru Gobind Singh had administered the *Pahul* to these five in this manner he took it likewise from them and became Gobind Singh.[22] In this way all the rest of his disciples were initiated to whom he gave the name of the Khalsa, adding to the name of each of them the epithet of Singh (lion)'[23] M'Gregor says that Guru Gobind Singh initiated ten men on the day of

Baisakhi of 1699. Obviously, he is referring to the Five beloved and the Five *muktas* who were initiated by Guru Gobind Singh himself immediately after the Five beloved.[24] Schonberg has referred to the distribution of *Karah Parsad* after the completion of the ceremony.[25]

These writers also delve on the question that at what age the neophyte could be initiated into Sikhism. For instance, Malcolm says that the *Pahul* may be taken at any time and at any age but, 'The children of the Singh's all go through this rite at a very early age'.[26] Whereas, Cunningham asserts that there is no authoritative rule regarding the age but the presence of the Five baptised Sikh is the basic requirement to perform initiatory rites.[27] Trumpp maintains that, 'The initiatory rites into the Khalsa is the *Pahul*. It is generally administered by five Sikhs and not before the attainment of years of direction; its administration is considered very meritorious and by instructing a disciple in the doctrine of the Guru, one will get final emancipation even while living'.[28] Both Cunningham and William Ward refers to the administering of Pahul to the women in the same manner as men.[29]

Next question relating to the initiation is the injunctions given to the Khalsa. Everyone of them has taken up this aspect of the *Pahul* ceremony in one form or the others. Some have described the DOS and Donts in detail while some has given only hint. In this context Malcolm says, 'After the ceremonies, the disciple is asked if he consents to be of the faith of Gúrú Góvind. He answers. "I do consent". He is then told, if you do, you must abondon all intercourse with the Minas, Dhirmalias, Masandias, Ramrayias, Kurimar and those who perferm *Bhadan*. Besides, they were instructed in some general precepts: 'He is told to be gentle and polite to all with whom he converses, to endeavour to attain wisdom, and to emulate the persuasive eloquence to Baba Nanak. He is particularly enjoined, whenever he approaches any of the Sikh temples, to do it with reverence and respect, and to go to Amritsar, to pay his devotion to the Khalsa and the State; the interests of which he is directed, on all occasion, to consider paramount to his own. He was also enjoined to read, the *Adi Granth* and 'whatever he has received from God', 'It is his duty to share with others' And after the disciple has heard and understood all these and similar precepts, he is declared to be duly initiated'.[30] Cunningham has put the injunction like this : 'All, he said must become one, the lowest were equal with the highest; caste must be forgotten, they must accept the *Pahul* and the four races must eat as one out of one vessel. The ways of the Hindus must be abandoned Brahman's thread must be broken, by means of Khalsa alone would salvation be attained, surrender to the faith and to him as their guide. Their words must be Kirtnash, Kulnash, Dharamnash, Karamnash'. They should worship one Invisible God and honour the memory of Nanak and his transanimate successors. They should rever none else than Guru Granth. They should keep unshorn hair and affix a epithet of 'Singh' with their names. They should wear arms and pay 'devotion to steel'. They should not have any social intercource with Dhirmalias, Ramrais, Masandias, Bhadnias (who shave their heads), Kurimar etc. They should refrain from the use of tobacoo and nor do they smoke drugs of any kind. To wear blue dress and 'Kach' (breeches) were other important injunctions.[31] However, Trumpp's views appears to be more relevant. He says that after the initiation ceremony, the Guru gave the order that, 'whoever desire to be his disciple, he must always have five things with him which all commence with the letter Kakka (*i.e.* K), *viz. Kes* (the hair), *Kanga* (a comb), *Karad* (a knife), *Kirpan* (sword) and *Kach* (breeches reaching to the knee, otherwise he would not consider him as his disciple'.[32] Furthermore, the Khalsa was instructed that, 'Temples Shrines and burning places are not to be worshipped, nor are other religions to be praised. The Vedas, Shastras, Puranas and the Quran are not to be minded, neither the Pandit nor the Mulla. All Hindu and Musalman rites are to be discontinued; the Hindu ceremonies at the time of birth, marriage and death should not be observed. No tilak should be applied to the forehead, nor should the sacred cord nor a rosary be worn, circumcision should not be practiced'.[33]

Amongst other observance, Trumpp describes, 'A Sikh is never to wear a cap, nor to shave his head or beard, nor to wear red clothes. He should bath in the cold water, comb his hair twice everyday and bind his turban after adjusting the tresses; he is never to take off his turban whilst taking his food.... He should always were breeches and have steel about his person, especially sword. The use of tobacco in any shape is prohibited. Gambling, especially the play of Chauppar and visiting prostitutes deserve severe punishment.'[34] These regulations were given to separate the Sikhs totally from the other communities and 'to form them into a distinct body, which as such should also be known by outward signs.'[35] However, like Cunningham and Trumpp, all other writers under analysis have mentioned one way or the other the observance of five Ks by the baptised Skihs and not five arms as has been wrongly mentioned by Malcolm and later on accepted by some of the 20th century historians like W.H. Mcleod and J.S. Grewal.[36]

Concerning the mode and object of worship all the writers under review are of the view that the Sikhs worship none else than Guru Granth Sahib. They do not admit any idol or image in places of their worship.[37] Their form of prayer are few and simple. Generally their places of worship were plain buildings where Guru Granth Sahib was recited in the morning and evening and every body irrespective of caste, colour or creed was allowed to attend'.[38] Except historic Gurdwaras any apartment in a house, where Guru Granth Sahib can suitably be installed, would serve as a place of Sikh worship. The building is not altogether important but the presence of Guru Granth. In this context observations of Charles Masson are quite significant. He observed that there were only two retainers of Sardar Hari Singh Nalwa at Dera Ismeil Khan. They had occupied a big house in the town and in one of their apartments was kept *Guru Granth Sahib* which they 'preserved with great care and approached with reverence' Further he observes that

Guru Granth Sahib is the 'only object of veneration for the Sikhs, because it contain the precepts of their Gurus. It was lodged on high pedestal in a spacious apartments in most of their villages. He says that many Banias (traders) used to visit Gurdwara and anyone qualified among them could also read Guru Granth Sahib.[39] Burnes observed similar situation at Multan where the Sikh population was confined only to an administrative staff.[40] Schonberg has very categorically revealed the advantage which the Sikhs have, as compared to other communities of India, particularly the Hindu, in regard to the form of prayer : 'Any one qualified, irrespective of caste, colour or creed could read *Guru Granth Sahib* and address his prayer to God, whereas in Hinduism, the privileged Brahmins are alone allowed to read the sacred books, they only enjoy the privilege of addressing the Almighty directly. But in Sikhism even the humblest man in society is taught to believe that his prayer is as acceptable before the throne of mercy as that of his more wealthy brethren.'[41] However, refering to the religious practices of the Sikhs William Ward observes : 'Seeking the company of the holy persons, loving attachment of God, repetition of the name of God, rejection of the idols worship and ceremonies connected with it .... reverence for the sacred compositions of the Gurus are some of the practices of the Sikhs'.[42] Besides, recitation of the hymns of Guru Granth Sahib (Kirtan) and performing *Ardas* are the major mode of worship of the Sikhs.

Although from the beginning of the 19th century onward, the original sources of Sikhism became accessible to the Europeans, yet like the 18th century European scholars, their ignorance of the language kept crippling their proper understanding of the Sikh scripture. This fact has been underlined by Ernest Trumpp too.[43]

Inspite of the fact that the language remained a main handicap yet the 19th century European scholars have commented upon the origin, status, teachings and role of the Sikh scripture in a very significant way. Almost all the writers are unanimous in attributing its origin to Guru

Nanak besides commenting upon its language. In this regard Malcolm holds : 'The Granth, the whole of the first part of which is ascribed to Nanak, is written, like the rest of the books of the Sikhs in the Gurumukh (Gurmukhi) character.'[44] Commenting upon the religion of Guru Nanak and the nature of Sikh scripture Ward maintains that Guru Nanak propagated the doctrine of the Divine unity and to promote the sipirt of devotion amongst his followers 'Nanukh composed a number of sacred hymns in praise of the Deity which have a place in the *Adee-Grunthu* : in which work repeating the names of God is enjoined on the Sikhs'. The God of Guru Nanak is 'an invisible sipirt'. 'He is truth, the Creator and Governor of all the things, Omnipresent, free from fear and from enemies, Immortal, Everlasting, Self-existant. He is Truth; He existed in this form before the foundation of the world, and He remains the same while the world exists and after it shall be destroyed : He is to be known by means of a spiritual guide'.[45] Wilson also maintains 'the divine unity as the basic tenets of Sikh Gurus' enshrined in Guru Granth Sahib.[46] However, the Sikh scripture is a revealed literature having Divine origin and status. Its compilation provided 'consistent form and order to Sikh religion. It gives 'fixed rules of religious and moral conduct'. Above all, it is the very fountain of Sikh beliefs and practices.[47] Cunningham is very categorical in observing the significance of the canonization of the Sikh scripture by Guru Arjan Dev : Guru Arjan was the first who clearly understood the wide import of Guru Nanak's teachings or who perceived how application to every state of life and to every condition of society'. Further he say 'he (Guru) declared the '*Granth*' or book; and gave to his followers their fixed rules of religious and moral conduct, with an assurance that multitudes even of divine Brahmans had wearied themselves with reading the *Vedas* and had found not the value of an oil-seed.[48] Commenting upon the purpose of compiling the Adi Granth, Trump remarks : 'Purpose of Guru Arjan was to give a sacred code to the Sikhs, in order to unite them more closely by one common religious tie and to separate them from the mass of Hindus'. Also, he wanted to provide an authenticated text to the Sikhs, which supplanted the authorities of Vedas by enabling a common man to read it in his own mother tongue.[49] However, it is fully installed in all the Sikh places of worship with due reverence and ceremonies. It is the only object of worship.

Most of the writers agrees that personal Guruship ended with Guru Gobind Singh. They also agree that Guru Gobind Singh appointed Guru Granth as the 'Guru' of the Sikhs before his demise at Nander.[50] For example Cunningham says that when the Sikhs assembled around the Guru, whose end was approaching 'asked in sarrow who should inspire them with truth and lead them to victory when he was no more. Gobind bade them be of good cheer; the appointed Ten had indeed fulfilled their mission, but he was about to deliver the Khalsa to God, the never dying. 'He who wishes to behold the Guru let him search in the *Granth* of Nanak. The guru will dwell with the Khalsa; be firm and be faithful : wherever five Sikhs are gathered together there will I also be present'.[51] Trumpp appears to be more apt when the says that the Guru Sahib instructed the Khalsa as, 'After me you shall everywhere mind the book of the *Granth Sahib* as your Guru : what ever you will ask it, it will show to you. Whoever be my disciple, he shall consider the *Granth* as the form of the Guru, and whichever disciple wishes to have an interview with me, he shall make for one Rupee and quarter, or for as much as he is able, *Karah Parsad*, then opening the book (Guru Granth) and bowing his head he will obtain a reward equal to an interview with me'.[52] Thus it is obvious from these observations that the doctrine of *Guru Granth* and *Guru Panth* was widely prevalent during the 19th Century.

The Sikhs regarded Guru Granth Sahib as an embodiment of Sikh Gurus for it contains their precepts. They respected and venerated it as they used to venerate the Sikh Gurus while they were living in this world. However, according to E. Samuel it is 'a book of laws' for the Sikh code of conduct. It was lodged with great care under 'a silken canopy' in Sri Harimandir Sahib, the 'House of

God'.[53] To Malcolm it (Guru Granth) became the sole object of veneration after the death of Guru Gobind Singh. The Sikhs do not allow any other object than *Guru Granth Sahib* in their places of worship.[54] About the status of the Sikh scripture Alexander Burnes remarks are very apt. During his visit to Multan, he observed that 'we found him (the priest) seated on the ground, with a huge volume in front of him, and a place covered with cloth, like an alter, at one end of the apartment. He opened the book at my request and repeating the words '*Wa gooroo jee ka fattee*' touched the volume with his forehead, and all the Sikhs in attendance immediately bowed to the ground'. Furthermore he says that I need hardly mention, that the volume was the *Granth* or the holy book of the sikhs the reverence for it amounts to veneration, and the priest wave a *Chury* or Tibet cows tail, over it, as if he were fanning an emperor'.[55] Hugel's observation about the veneration and the status of the Sikh scripture are quite appropriate. While visiting Sri Harimandir Sahib he recorded that right in center of the temple 'Sat the first Guru of the Sikh faith on the masnad, or throne of cushions, the walls of the building being ornamented with a handsome carpet worked out in gold, while before him lay another of Kashmir Shawl stuff. A circle of devotees and followers has formed around him, leaving an open space which is never encroached upon, it being customany that the Guru should be viewed from a certain distance with due reverence'.[56]

Guru Granth Sahib is the only guide in spiritual as well as temporal matters. Not only an ordinary Sikh but Maharaja Ranjit Singh himself used to seek guidance from Guru Granth Sahib before making vital political decisions. Prinsep has very aptly described the method through which the Maharaja used to seek guidance from Guru Granth Sahib before taking vital political decisions. He states that, 'It is no uncommon practice of Ranjit Singh, when he contemplates any serious undertaking, to direct two slips of paper to be placed on the *Granth Sahib* or sacred volume of the Sikhs. On the one is written his wish, and on the other the reverse. A little boy is often brought in, and told to bring one of the slips, and whichever it may happen to be, His highness is satisfied as it were a voice from heaven'.[57] Emily Eden too have recorded a deep faith of the Maharaja in the Oracle of *Guru Granth Sahib*.[58] Similarly Burnes have also noticed a deep faith of the Sikhs masses in an Oracle of their scripture. He refers to an oration of a priest in which he acknowledged before Guru Granth Sahib that what ever the Sikhs enjoyed on this earth was the bountry of the Guru. When he enquired about the secret of their increasing power from a venerable Sikh chief, the old man replied : 'it had been predicted in their Granth....'.[59] Similar views have been expressed by Charles Masson, when he says : The *ardas* was 'concluded with a vociferous invocation to the Guru Granth for victory and extension of the faith.[60] However, regarding the status of the Sikh scripture all the 19th century Western scholars under review, except Malcolm, agree that *Guru Granth* is the only scripture to which Sikh accord the status of the Guru. These writers do not observe any preference to *Dasam Granth* over *Guru Granth* as has been done by Malcolm. In fact Malcolm through his *sketch of the Sikhs* wanted to promote Imperial interests which he did by creating a dichotomy between the followers of Guru Nanak and the followers of Guru Gobind Singh by introducing *Dasam Granth* to provide justification to the mission of Guru Gobind. Any way a recent study reveals that presently published Dasam Granth did not exist in the 18th century.[61] Neither E. Samuel, who published his work a year before the *Sketch of the Sikhs* nor the subsequent visitors like Burnes, Hugel, Schonberg, Emily Eden etc. mention about the existence of this Granth at Harimandir Sahib. Cunningham too has found Malcolm as contradictory and does not attribute the entire *Dasam Granth* to Guru Gobind Singh. According to him only the first five chapter and a part of the sixth was written by Guru Gobind Singh and the rest is the work of the four scribes.[62] Trumpp also asserts that Guru Gobind Singh did not write the entire Granth.[63] Thus, Malcolm, who is otherwise regarded as the founder of Sikh historiography have misinterpreted and misrepresented the facts regarding the Sikh history and faith. For instance, his claim that John Lyden translated for him the Punjabi manuscript is also false. John Lyden translated only Bachiter Natak for him and not the so called *Dasam Granth.* Similarly he translated only 11 pauris of 41 var attributed to Bhai Gurdas; Bhagat-Ratnavali, biographies of mythical and historical Bhagats and Gian Ratnavali (1st var of Bhai Gurdas) and a *Kurkha* of Guru Gobind Singh in Duggar dialect.[64] Thus many of the misconception having their origin with Malcolm have been taken as established facts by many historians.

Commenting on the message of the Sikh scripture Malcolm holds Guru Nanaks' mission was 'divine' which, according to Ward, teaches 'devout attachment to God and the harmless behaviour towards all creatures.'[65] Cunningham have very aptly summed up the message of Guru Nanak embodied in Guru Granth Sahib : He maintains that inventive genius of Guru Nanak retained all positive elements of earlier efforts and rendered them more definite and practicable. Thus he rendered his mission applicable to all time and places.[66] Basic principles enunciated by the founder of Sikhism was that God is above every human creature, be he a Pandit, a Dervish, a Saniyasi or a Mulla. He tells plainly 'that virtures and Charities, heroic acts and gathered wisdom are not of themselves, that the only knowledge which availeth is the knowledge of God'.[67] Favour of God and salvation can be sought "in good works and uprightness of conduct."[68] According to Cunningham, the core message of Guru Granth Sahib is :'God is to be worshipped in spirit and in truth, with little reference to particular form, and that salvation is unattainable without grace, faith and good works.' On the basis of the ideas presented in Guru Granth Sahib, Cunningham, has tried his best to elucidate the Sikh ideas about God, avtars, saints, image worship, miracles, transmigration, grace, predestination, asceticism, caste, food, infanticide etc.[69] Referring to the philosophy of Guru Granth Sahib, Hugel assert that, it contains the maxims of the Sikh faith, the faith which made no discrimination on the basis of caste, creed or colour and did not allow any sort of image worship'.[70]

Captain Matthew has striven hard to show the influence of the teachings of Guru Granth Sahib which changed their way of life and distinguished them from the rest of the communities of the world. He asserts that the Sikhs are more hospitable and kind to stranger than other communities. They 'disclaims to distinctions of religion or complexion.' They generally marry one wife and the practice of *sati* is rarely practised. Unlike the other communities the Sikh ladies were not confined to their houses and they bore the general reputation of chastity. Perhaps for this reason, he noticed that the syphilistic complaints were very few as compared to the inhabitants of other regions or communities. Summing up the Sikh character, he maintains that, 'they are just and amicable in their social intercourse, and affectionate in their domestic relations. One quality particularly raises the character of the Sikhs above all other Asiatics and that 'is their higher veneration for truth'. Both as a people and as individuals, they may be considered as much less addicted to the low artifices of evasion, lying, or dissimulation, than any other race of Asiatics. Implicit dependence may be placed upon their promise, in all matters either of public or private concern, and if a Sikh declares himself your friend, he will not disappoint your confidence : if, on the other hand, he bear enimity to any one, he declares it without reserve-upon the whole, they are a plain, manly, hospitable, and industrious people, and by far the best race I have ever met in India.'[71] Similar views have been expressed by Burnes, Masson, Hugel etc. In short the Sikh way of life, their dress, food habits and general conduct too find mention in these writings. For instance, *Pagri* (turban) was an integral part of the Sikh apparel."[72] Maharaja Ranjit Singh used to reward those soldiers who kept long beard.[73] Masson has mentioned the wearing of 'bulky trousers terminating at the knee, the legs from the knee being naked'.

Further he says, ' they allow the hair of their heads to attain its full growth and gathered up into a knot at the crown'.[74] According to Burnes, 'these seiks are tall and bony men, with every martial carriage : the most peculiar part of the dress is a small flat turban which becomes them well; they wear long hair and from the knee downward do not coverlegs.' Undoubtedly, Burnes describes the Sikhs as 'the most rising people of India.'[75] Their form of salutation is *wahe guru ji ka khalsa* and those who respectfully address them salute them as *Khalsa ji*.[76] However, Schonbergs description of the Sikh priest is an enunciation of the true Sikh character or Sikh identity in the 1850s. For instance, he observed that the 'appearance of Sikh priest is exactly what one might expect in the minister of war like people. The tall blue turban, bound with an iron head piece, the sabre always close girded to his side, his shield slung upon his back, and the long beard descending to his breast, gives to this warrior-priest a highly picturesque aspect.[77]

Retrospectively, an analysis of the 19th Century Western writings reveals that almost all the important aspects Sikhs Panth have been touched upon in one way or the other. One can easily surmise the origin and development of Sikh faith, beliefs and practices; social and religious, mode and object of worship besides, the origin, status, philosophy and role of Guru Granth Sahib both in the acquisition of political power and in transforming the Sikh society.

However what emerges from their observations is that Guru Granth Sahib is the only object of veneration for the Sikhs. These writes do not observe any preference to *Dasam Granth* over *Guru Granth* as has been purposely done by Malcolm and later on accepted by Mcleod and Grewal. The Sikh admit none else than Guru Granth Sahib into their places of worship (Gurdwaras). They venerate it as an Emperor, for it embodies the precepts of their Gurus. Each word of it is considered as an order from the Guru. It is the only guide in spiritual as well as temporal matters. The Sikhs firmly believe in its teaching, for their application can transform human lives and thereby can create a better social order. Its role in the transformation of the Sikh Social world and perpetuation of Sikh identity has been amply noted by these writers. For instance higher veneration for truth universal philanthropy, equality amongst human beings, toleration towards other religion, non-existence of forceful conversion, conspicuous absence of the practice of Sati, encouragement to widow re-marriage observance of chastity etc., have been described as the major traits of the ideology of Guru Granth Sahib. However, it also becomes clear from their observations that five *banis* were recited while preparing *Khande-di-Pahul*. Also, we find mention of five Ks in one way or the other rather than the five weapons and initiation of women in the same manner as men. Come what may, these writings shed much light on the status and role of the Sikh scripture in the advancement and transformation of Sikh society. For example, observations of Prinsep, Burnes Hugel, Emily Eden etc. suggest that the authority of Guru Granth Sahib was recognised by the Sikhs in every sphere of life. Also, general character of Sikhs and Sikh priests as described in these writings speaks of the higher spiritual advancement of the Sikhs. Above all, Schonberg's description of the Sikh priest gives us to understand that the Sikh identity was not created and established during the Singh Sabha but it was very much intact prior to the annexation of the Land of the Five Rivers.

REFERENCES

1. G. Khurana, *British Historiography on the Sikh Power in the Punjab*, Allied Publishers, New Delhi, 1985, p. 16.
2. John Malcolm, *Sketch of the Sikhs*, London, 1812, pp. 169, 172-73.
3. Ernest Trumpp, *The Adi Granth or the Holy Scriptures of the Sikhs*, Munshiram Manohar Lal, New Delhi, 1997- first 1877, xciii.
4. J.D. Cunningham, *History of the Sikhs*, Low Price Publication, New Delhi (1990-first 1849), pp 38, 41.
5. Malcolm, *Ibid.*, pp. 144-46, 165.
6. William Ward, *The Hindus (History, Literature and Religion,*

Publication Service, New Delhi, 1981 (first Serampore 1815) 2 Vols., pp. 343, 346 qouted in *Western Perspective on the Sikhs Religion,* by Darshan Singh.

7. H.H. Wilson, Civil and Religious Institutions of the Sikhs, The Sikh Religion : A Symposium, p. 56.
8. Robert Needum Cust, *Sikh Land or the Country of Baba Nanak, Linguistic and Oriental Essays*, London, 1880, p. 55.
9. Cunningham, *Ibid.*, pp. 38, 39, 329-36; Charles Masson, *Narrative of Various Journeys in Balochistan, Afghanistan and the Punjab*, London 1842, 3 Vol., Vol. I, pp. 46, 424; Malcolm, *Ibid.,* pp. 168, 188
10. Malcolm, *ibid.*, p. 168.
11. Baron Charles Hugel, *Travels in Kashmir and the Punjab*, Language Deptt., Punjab, Patiala 1970, p. 272
12. H.T. Prinsep, *Origin of The Sikh Power in The Punjab and Political Life of Maharaja Ranjit Singh with an account of the Religion, Laws and Customs of the Sikhs,* Language Department Punjab, Patiala 1970, pp. 26,
13. John Malcolm, *ibid.*, pp. 120-22.
14. *Ibid.*, 123
15. Captain Matthew, '*Tour To Lahore*', *Asiatic Annual Register*, 1809, p. 422; Malcolm, *ibid.*, 181-82; Ward, p. 172; Prinsep, *ibid.*, p. 2; W.L.M. Gregor, *History of The Sikhs*, London, 1846, 2 Vol., Vol. I, p. 74; Cunningham, *ibid.*, 63; Trumpp, *ibid.*, pp. xci, Hugel, *ibid*, 281-82; Baron Erich Von Schonberg, *Travels in India and Kashmir*, London, 1853, 2 Vols., Vol. II, pp. 156-57.
16. Matthew, *ibid*, p. 422; Hugel, *ibid.*, p. 282.
17. Trumpp describes it as two–edge-dagger, *ibid.*, p. xci.
18. According to Trumpp, the Bani used at the time of the preparation of *Pahul,* from the Dasam Granth was *Akal Ustat; ibid*; p. xc; while Prinsep and Hugel have quoted sawayias from the Dasam Granth which were recited while preparing the *Pahul*; Prinsep. *ibid*, pp. 171-72; Hugel, *ibid.,* p. 282.
19. Hugel, *ibid.*, p. 282.
20. Prinsep, *ibid.*, pp. 171-72.
21. According to Trumpp, 'Sherbet' was sprinkled on the body of the neophyte and not on the beard : *ibid.*, p. xci.

22. Cunningham, *ibid.*, p. 65; Trumpp, *ibid.*, p. xci.
23. Cunningham, *op. cit*; Trumpp, *op. cit.*
24. M'Gregor, *ibid.*, Vol. I, p. 75.
25. Sehonberg, *ibid*, Vol. II, pp. 157-58.
26. Malcolm, *ibid.*, p. 186.
27. Cunningham, *ibid.*, p. 65.
28. Trumpp, *ibid.*, p. *cxiii.*
29. Ward, *ibid.*, p. 172; Cunningham, *ibid.*, pp. 314, 315.
30. Malcolm, *ibid.*, pp. 183-85.
31. Cunningham, *ibid.*, pp. 63-64; 66-317, 318, 321.
32. Trumpp, *ibid.*, p. xc
33. *Ibid.*, p. xciv
34. *Op. cit.*
35. *Ibid.*, xci.
36. W.H. McLeod, *Sikh if the Khalsa : A History of Khalsa Rahit*, Oxford 2003, pp. 40, 204, 206-07, 209, 212, 249; J.S. Grewal and S.S. Bal, *Guru Gobind Singh : A Biographical Study*, Punjab University, Chandigarh, 1967, pp. 187-88.
37. Hugel, *ibid*, p. 282; Malcolm *ibid.*, p. 168.
38. Masson, *ibid.*, I. p. 424, Malcolm, *ibid.*, p. 168., Schonberg, *ibid.*, Vol. II, p. 156.
39. Masson, *ibid.*, Vol. I, pp. 46, 424.
40. Burnes, *ibid.*, Vol. I, pp. 101-102.
41. Sehonberg, *ibid.*, Vol. II, pp. 156-57.
42. William Ward, *ibid.*, p. 343, quoted in *Western Perspective.*
43. Trumpp, *ibid.*, p. xcii.
44. Malcolm, *ibid.*, pp. 168-69.
45. William Ward, *ibid.*, pp. 343-346, quoted in *Western Perspective.*
46. Wilson, *ibid.*, p. 56, quoted in Western prospective.
47. Cunningham, *ibid.*, p. 46; Malcolm, *ibid.*, p. 36, M'Gregor, *ibid.*, Vol.-I, p. 44.
48. Cunningham, *ibid.*, pp. 46-47.
49. Trumpp, *ibid.*, pp. ixxx-xi.

50. M, Gregor, *ibid.*, Vol. I, pp. 76, 89; Masson, *ibid.*, I, p. 424. Malcolm *ibid.*, pp. 196-97.
51. Cunnigham, *ibid.*, p. 74.
52. Trumpp, *ibid.*, p. cxi.
53. Mathews, *ibid.*, pp. 430-31.
54. Malcolm, *ibid.*, pp. 76, 89, 168, 169, 196.
55. Alexander Burnes, *Travels* into Bokhara, John Murray, London, 1835, 3 Vols., Vol. I, pp. 101-02.
56. Hugels, *ibid.*, p. 394.
57. Prinsep, *ibid.*, p. 153.
58. Emily Eden, *Up the Country*, London, 1866, 2 vols. I, pp. 7-8.
59. Burnes, *ibid.*, Vol. I, p. 151.
60. Masson, *ibid*, Vol. I, p. 424.
61. Jasbir Singh Mann, *Fresh Look at Dasam Granth : Analysis of its Text and History*, Guru Nanak Memorial Lecture Dec. 2003. Punjabi University Patiala. Unpublished paper.
62. Cunnigham, *ibid*, pp. 325-329.
63. Trumpp, *ibid.*, p. cxi.
64. J.S. Mann, *ibid.*, p. 48.
65. Malcolm, *ibid*, pp. 144, 165; Ward, *ibid.*, pp. 171-72.
66. Cunnigham, *ibid.*, p. 38.
67. *Op. cit.*
68. *Ibid.*, p. 39.
69. *Ibid.*, pp. 329-36.
70. Hugel, *ibid.*, pp. 281-82.
71. Matthew, *ibid.*, pp. 422-24, 431.
72. Masson, *ibid.*, I, pp. 432, 433; Hugel, *ibid.*, p. 285.
73. Cunningham, *ibid.*, p. 152.
74. Masson, *ibid.*, Vol. I, pp. 434, 443.
75. Burnes, *ibid.*, *Vol.* I, pp. 45, 76; II 39, 285, 286; III 101, 140.
76. Masson, *ibid.*, Vol. I, pp. 425; Hugel, 339-394.
77. Schonberg, *ibid.*, Vol. II, p. 157.

9

The Kingdom of Lahore in the 1830s

By the end of the third decade of the nineteenth century, the kingdom of Lahore was at the zenith of its glory. The work of consolidation was almost complete. All the civil and military institutions, whether innovated or revived, were functioning well. The might of Maharaja Ranjit Singh was felt all around. He was, by this time, thinking to have control over Sind and thereby an outlet to the sea. At the same time, the East India Company, which had practically controlled the whole of India, was thinking to acquire 'the natural line of defence—the Indus. To fulfil this task, Alexander Burnes was deputed, professedly, on a complimentary mission to Lahore.[1] In reality, he was ordered to collect sufficient information not only about the land and water routes but also about the power and attitude of the people and rulers of different countries occupying this region towards the British government.[2] Under such a specific scheme of the British government for conducting a survey of political and geographical nature, the kingdom of Lahore received Burnes' attention because of its power and strategic importance.

Burnes' objective to know the power of the kingdom of Lahore, made him interested in the army of Maharaja Ranjit Singh. He considered it one of the instruments which enabled the Maharaja to conquer and maintain such a powerful kingdom. According to Alexander Burners, the regular infantry, cavalry and artillery amounted to 25,000, 5000, and 150 guns respectively.[3]

Five regiments of regular infantry were paraded before Alexander Burnes.[4] It was trained as a European Infantry. Its contingents were 'fully equal' to the troops of the East India Company. They were well accoutred and manoeuvered with regularity and precision. However, they were destitude of the most essential quality of a soldier, *i.e.*, discipline.[5] Burnes suggested two measures to improve this short-doming : *(i)* by increasing the power of the native officers, *(ii)* by removing a just ground of discontentment which arose from the inequality of pay of the individuals of the same rank.[6] Without commission, these men did not possess a respect for themselves, nor were they respected by their soldiers.[7] The dress of the contingents of the regular infantry was white, with black cross belts. They bore muskets which were the manufactures of Kashmir or Lahore and had a cost of Rs. 17 per piece. There was a curious' mixture of Hindustanis and Sikhs in every corps. The words of command were given in French.[8]

Burnes had a very high opinion of the Maharaja's artillery but not of the cavalry.[9] The guns were well cost and the carriages were in good repair. The guns were made at Lahore costing the state Rs. 1,000 each.[10] However, the horses and equipment were inferior. The average cost of a gun was 5,000 rupees. This sum included the pay of the officers and men and up keep of the horses. The Maharaja had hundred pieces of field artillery, exclusive of battering guns and mortars.[11] He evinced a keen interest in shell practice. But his army was unacquainted with the mode of fusing iron and the shells were constructed of brass.[12]

The irregular troops consisting of cavalry fell little short of 50,000 men. They were denominated as *ghorcharhas*, meaning horsemen. As a native soldiery, they were an efficient, well mounted and serviceable body. However, they were superior to their neighbouring enemy—the Afghans.[13]

A regular muster of these forces was exacted, with a few favoured exceptions. The *ghorcharahs* were paid by assignment of land.[14]

The pay of the regular troops of the Maharaja was higher than that of the Company's troops.[15] Sometimes, but surely not regularly, the officers were paid in Kashmir shawls.[16] The troopers of the regular army were clothed by the State. The Sikh contingents had have messes attached to their units and the food was supplied at a deduction of two rupees a month for each man.[17] However, the irregularity of payments had caused unrest in the army.[18] For this inattention of the Maharaja towards his army, Burnes has given two reasons which do not withstand the facts. For instance, the Maharaja's growing friendship with the British Government and 'the increasing avarice of age.'[19]

Burnes entertained doubts that if some change for the better did not take place in the administration of the army, the regular forces of the Punjab would either get in 'a state of mutiny or they would be greatly diminished'.[20] Furthermore, he doubted the viability of the system too. The new system was strongly disliked by the Sikh Sardars.[21] 'The French officers,' observed Burnes, 'when deprived of their patron, would find it necessary to stand aloof from motives of personal safety; and if they left the country, the wreck of their labour would soon perish in the general tumult.[22]

After consolidating his conquests, Maharaja Ranjit Singh implied his mind to those improvements which spring only from great minds. He evolved a system of government 'far beyond the native institutions of the East, though far from the civilization of Europe.' His despotism was benevolent.[23] However, Burnes was incredulous about the viability of the civil institutions evolved by the Maharaja. He opined that 'a well-stored treasury with an army in arrears and clamouring for pay, increasing duties on merchants and traders, exorbitant taxes on the husbandman, with embezzlement of public revenues, and a general corruption in the higher officers of the state, are not the signs favourable to the durability of a government.'[24] Notwithstanding this observation, Burnes found Ranjit Singh's government rather vigorous and well consolidated. But this vigour was sufficient only 'for a native state.'[25]

Composition of the ruling class in the kingdom of Lahore was of special interest to Burnes. He was keenly interested in knowing the extent of the influence which the Lahore nobility could exercise over the actions of the Maharaja. The power of most of the members of the original Sikh principalities had been neutralised or subverted by the Maharaja. The void was filled by new creation. A number of individuals rose to prominence by the favour of the Maharaja namely *Jamadar* Khushal Singh, the *Faquir* brothers, the brothers etc. Being his own 'minions', this newly created aristocracy did not have any influence on the actions of the Maharaja[26] but somehow, these persons, particularly, the Jamwal brothers, had managed to instil this belief in the minds of the people. Therefore, they were making every use of their supposed influence 'to fill their coffers, and nourish the art of corruption.'[27] Hira Singh, the young son of Dhian Singh, was a favourite of the Maharaja. Dhian Singh too, being the Prime Minister, was exercising his art in the court. He was 'fortifying his native home, in the vicinity of Bhimber, which he had strengthened by guns taken from Lahore, a fact which no one disclosed to the Maharaja.' He was judiciously preparing himself with an eye on the future.[28] Gulab Singh was managing the salt mines ar.d holding a large portion of territory towards Jhelum.[29] Hence, the old Sikh aristocracy was jealous of the power of the Dogra family. But, Maharaja Ranjit Singh's power made them afraid of giving any offence. Also, the liberality of the Maharaja in bestowing large Jagirs on the old Sikh Sardars, secured their conciliation to his rule.[30]

Burnes' concern with the health of the Maharaja and internal condition of the royal house appears to be a part of the British imperialistic designs. As the Maharaja's health was deteriorating, Burnes surmised that his life was not very long. Since everything in his dominions revolved around his genius, the demise of such a man would have much greater political implications. Therefore, he turned with due interest 'to speculate on the probable termination 'of this kingdom'.[31] It was believed by Burnes that Maharaja Ranjit Singh had only one son named Kharak Singh. He possessed none of the qualities of his father. Therefore, he was incapable to follow his father's footsteps even at the remotest distance. Being 'imbecile, illiterate and inanimate' he had a few favourites or enemies. He did not take any share in the State politics. Consequently, he had no faction which might have rendered him help in the hour of difficulty,[32] Prince Naunihal Singh, the grandson of the Maharaja, though intelligent, was yet a minor. Prince Sher Singh was 'unquestionably the most rising person in the Punjab.' He possessed most generous disposition. A 'brave and frank' soldier, he was respected by the people, particularly, the soldiery. He had equally secured the friendship of the French gentlemen in his father's service. Without much difficulty, he could succeed to the extensive realm of his father. Burnes professed that 'if Sher Singh does not secure a supremacy, this kingdom will probably relapse into the former state of anarchy and small republics; or be reduced to subjection by some neighbouring power'.[33] However, inspite of his ability to secure the throne and run a good administration, opines Burnes, it is to be remembered that he was 'a spurious child, and with many friends, he has some enemies, and will have to contend with the legitimate son, and, perhaps, treasures of his adopted father.'[34]

The revenue receipts of the kingdom of Lahore in the 1830s was about two and a half crores of rupees per annum including the revenue due from lands alienated in *jagirs* and *dharmarth*.[35] The province of Kashmir, which formed 'a kingdom' in itself, yielded rupees thirty six lacs; exclusive of ten lacs which were spent on its defence.[36] The chief of Peshawar paid a yearly tribute about sixty thousands, excluding bara rice.[37] The revenue from Multan amounted to ten lacs of rupees a year.[38] The salt mines yielded eighteen and a half lacs of rupees including two and a half lacs levied as duties.[39] In tune with other Indian states, the collectors of the Maharaja too worked arbitrarily. At the outset, they were presumed to be dishonest; they worked on the assumption that they would 'be rifled' and 'rifled the peasant.' However, the exactions as regulated by the State were mild.[40]

The Punjabi peasant produced food grain, pulses, oil seeds as well as cash crops, including fruits. Wheat, barley, pulses and oil seeds were cultivated in the Punjab plains. In the sub-mountain, rice was grown. The cane thrived well and sugar was manufactured. In the Doab, between the rivers Satluj and Beas, a considerable quantity of cotton was produced. Indigo was reared from Multan and eastward of Lahore. Multan was also famous for its tobacco. All kinds of vegetables, common to India, were produced everywhere. Abundance of fruit grew in the province of Kashmir as well as in the rest of the Punjab.[41]

Numerous horses, mules and camels were found in the Punjab. These were of a superior description. The land of *Majah* (a tract between the rivers Beas and Ravi) was celebrated for the breed of its horses. So was the *dhanni* horses, found between the rivers Jhelum and Indus. The mules reared on the banks of Jhelum and the camels in southern parts of the Punjab, were equally strong and serviceable. However, the cattle, though numerous, were small and not of good description.[42]

Mineralogically, the Punjab was not very poor. The range of hills, extending from Jhelum to Indus, had an extensive deposits of rock-salt. Towards Mandi, in the foot-hills, mines of salt too were found. Eight-hundred thousand maunds of salt was annually extracted from the salt range at Pind Dadan Khan. It was an article of export; it brought considerable profit to the state.[43] Depositories of coal and iron too were found in the foot-hills.[44] Alum, sulphur and antimony were found in the salt range and other high lands of the Punjab.[45] Gold was found in the sands of Chenab. The Punjab plains yielded a considerable quantity of nitre. A best quality of charcoal was made from 'tooree' or milk-bush; it provided a necessary ingredient for manufacture of gun powder.[46]

Manufactures of the Punjab were varied and plenty. The range of the craftsmen, of the kingdom of Lahore, was from big guns for the army to a sickle for the peasant; from esteemed Kashmiri shawls for aristocracy to a coarse cloth khadar for a layman. Cotton cloth of various texture, was manufactured at Hoshiarpur ar.d Rahon.[47] Multan produced *Mas* (satin), '*kais*' (a silk manufacture), and chintses in plenty. Its '*kais*' was famous for 'the strength of its texture and the brilliance of its colours'. The silk scarfs and shawls were extensively used in the court of Ranjit Singh and by the aristocracy of the Punjab.[48] The Multani carpets were inferior to those made in Persia; but the Kashmiri carpets were certainly superior to the Persian manufacture,[49] '*Lungis*' were made at Bahawalpur and Peshawar; the Bahawalpuri '*lungis*' were celebrated for the fineness of their texture.[50] The Punjabi brocade was not superior to the Bengali and Gujrati.[51] However, the most celebrated article, the manufacture of the Kingdom, was shawls, particularly the shawls of Kashmir, The value of shawls and shawl goods manufactured in Kashmir in the 1830s was nearly Rs. 70.000.[52]

Numerous trading centres in the Punjab were observed by Alexander Burnes. But 'the mart of Punjab trade' was Amritsar. Its bazars exhibited much greater appearance of wealth than Lahore.[53] Trade of Multan was much the same as at Bahawalpur but on larger scale. Within a decade, a trade of ten lacs of rupees was driven in chints from Bombay to northern parts of India.[54] However, trade in this article was on the decrease with Persia. The Multani chints could not compete with the British manufacture. The price of the Multani chints remained same in 1830s what it was in 1820s. But the British chints could be purchased at one sixteenth of its value, what it was in the 1820s, when the British produce first entered into the Persian market. Also, it had ceased to be a rarity.[55] The silk article of Multan 'Kais' was exported to India (comprising British and Mughal territories) and to Central Asian countries.[56] The finer white cloth of the Punjab was sent to the south of Satluj, Bokhara and Turkistan.[57] Cotton '*lungis*' were exported to Afghanistan and Central Asia.[58] Sugar and Indigo were exported to Bokhara and other Muslim countries.[59] Kashmiri shawls were extensively exported to India (comprising British and Mughal territories), Afghanistan, Persia, Rusia and Central Asian countries.[60] A store of shawls worth about 50 lac of rupees was run at Amritsar by the State. In the year 1832, shawls worth two lacs of rupees were sent to Russia alone; the Kashmiri shawls was a craze for the nobility.[61]

Imports of the Punjab were fewer as compared to the exports. The chief article of imports to the Punjab was horses and a great quantity of both fresh and dried fruits. Horses came mainly from Turkistan.[62] Although Peshawar, Ghazni and the valley of Belabagh (near Jalalabad), exported pears, plums and pomegranates to the Punjab but the chief exporter in fruits was Kabul.[63] Madder was imported from Ghazni and Kandhar.[64] Pashm (wool) for shawls came from Tibet, Jurkistan and Bokhara.[65]

Restrospectively, the Kingdom of Lahore in was a most vigorous and well consolidated state. Its military resources were immense.

It could produce everything which was sufficient not only for its own inhabitants and army but also it could export to other countries. The road from one extremity of the country to the other could admit of wheeled carriages, except in the mountains. All the rivers of the Punjab, including the Indus, were navigable.[66] If the royal house was not enough competent to defend its possessions, after the demise of the great Maharaja, the Sikh masses were strong enough to do so. They formed 'a healthy and vigorous body.' No other race was 'equal to their power.' Hence, Burnes admits that they were 'certainly powerful people' and 'better constituted to uphold their government'.[67]

REFERENCES

1. Alexander Burnes, Travels into Bokhara : Being the account of a journey from India to Cabool, Tartary, and Persia, also, narrative of Voyage on the Indus from sea to Lahore, 3 Vols., O.U.P., Karachi (4th ed.) (cited hereafter as Travels), Vol. I, viii—ix ; The Dictionary of National Biography (ed.), Sir Leslie Stephen and Sir Sidney Lee, London, 1917, Vol. III, p. 389; Syad Muhammad Latif, History of the Punjab, New Delhi, 1964, p. 443.
2. Burnes, *Travels*, I, preface , III, ix-xi, Latif, *op. cit.*, p. 444.
3. Burnes, *op. cit.*, II, pp. 286-87; III, p. 296.
4. *Ibid.*, HI, p. 156.
5. *Ibid.*, II, pp. 286-87 ; III, pp. 102, 155-56, 296-297.
6. *Ibid.*, II, p. 287.
7. Loc. cit.
8. *Ibid.*, III, pp. 102, 155-56.
9. Burnes inspected a train of fifty one pieces of artillery. They were brass 6-pounds each drawn by six horses. These were commanded by a native officer who put them through the movements of horse artillery, and formed line and column in every direction. The evolution was not rapidly performed; but the celerity was considerable; and no accident in over-turning or firing occurred throughout the morning, *Travels*, III, p. 165.
10. *Ibid.*
11. *Ibid.*, III, pp. 156,165-66.
12. *Ibid.*, I, p. 16.
13. The superiority of the Sikh cavalry men consisted in being easily rallied; while the Afghans terminated a battle with the first discomfiture, Burnes, *op. cit.*, II, p. 287.
14. *Loc. cit.*
15. *Lac. cit.*
16. Maharaja Ranjit Singh told Burnes : 'As I have a chief, who may be entitled to a balance of 300 rupees, shawls to the value of 500, he is well pleased,' *Travels*, HI, p. 164. 17. *Ibid.*, II, p. 287. J8. Burnes has mentioned that the garrison at the fort of Attock had mutinied because of the arrears of pay, *Travels*, I, p. 78.

17. *Ibid.*, II, p. 287.
18. *Ibid.*, II, p. 288.
19. *Ibid.*, II, p. 288; Burne's assumption is wrong. The system of keeping the army in arrears had long been known to India, and the Maharaja had followed his predecessors in this instance to ensure the fidelity of the troops. Not with standing the system of arrears, payment was made more or less, regularly, after every two months. Fauja Singh, Military System of the Sikhs, Delhi,]964, pp. 166-67.
20. Burnes, *op. cit.,* II, p. 288.
21. Burnes observed that the Maharaja had a disciplined army consisting of infantry, with due proportion of cavalry and artillery, but the system was unpopular in the country, and 'the Sikh Sardars viewed with distrust the innovation and anovator,' *Travels*, HI, p. 296.
22. *Loc. cit.*
23. *Ibid.*, II, p. 282.
24. *Ibid.*, II, p. 283.
25. *Ibid.*, p. 294.
26. *Ibid.*, II, p. 284.
27. *Loc. Cit.*
28. *Ibid.*, II, p. 285, Burne's observations do withstand the facts. See Fauja Singh, *op. cit.*, p. 68.
29. Burnes, *op. cit.,* II, pp. 284-85.
30. *Ibid.*, III, p. 124 and 297.
31. *Ibid.*, II, pp. 283, 285-86.
32. *Ibid.*, II, p. 296.
33. *Ibid.*, II, pp. 297-98.
34. *Ibid.*, II, p. 297.
35. *Ibid.*, II, p. 288; III, p. 297.
36. *Ibid.*, 11, p. 288; HI, pp. 156, 297.
37. *Ibid.*, II, pp. 293, 319, 321, 325; III, p. 298.
38. *Ibid.*, JIT, p. 303.
39. *Ibid.*, I, p. 55.
40. *Ibid.*, III, pp. 297-98.

41. *Ibid.*, II, pp. 402-04; III, pp. 303-04.
42. *Ibid.*, I, pp. 10-11 ; II, p. 289; III, p. 299.
43. *Ibid.*, I; pp. 51-55 ; II, p. 401.
44. *lbid.*, n, p. 401.
45. *Ibid.*, I, pp. 52,-II, P. 402.
46. *Ibid.*, II, pp. 401-402.
47. *Ibid.*, II, pp. 400-01, 406.
48. *Ibid.*, II, pp. 399-400; III, p. 111.
49. *Ibid.*, II, P. 400.
50. *Ibid.*, II, pp. 293-94, 419.
51. *Ibid.*, II, p. 400.
52. *Ibid.*, II, pp. 418, 435.
53. *Ibid.*, II, p. 415; HI, p. 159.
54. *Ibid.*, II, p. 405,- III, p. III.
55. *Ibid.*, II, p. 407.
56. *Ibid.*, II, p. 399.-HI, p. 111.
57. *Ibid.*, II, pp. 400-01, 434-35.
58. *Ibid.*, II, p. 419.
59. *Ibid.*, II, pp. 167, 435-36.
60. *Ibid.*, II, pp. 399, 428, 34-35.
61. *Ibid.*, II, pp. 398-99, 435.
62. *Ibid.*, II, p. 275.
63. *Ibid.*, I, pp. 223, 253, 255; II, p. 416.
64. *Ibid.*, II, p. 416.
65. *Ibid.*, II, pp. 175, 440.
66. *Ibid.*, U, pp. 288, 89; III, pp. 288, 99.
67. *Ibid.*, II, pp. 285-286.

10

Maharaja Ranjit Singh's Rule : Western Perception

To understand Maharaja Ranjit Singh and his times, European travel Literature is a significant genre. Being outsiders and having varied objectives to visit the kingdom of the Maharaja, These travellers made observations about those aspects of the polity, economy and society of the Kingdom of Lahore which were generally ignored by the non-European chroniclers. However, the present paper is based on the observations of six travellers. Four of them are English, one French and One German. Like their nationalities, their purpose to visit the Sikh dominion too varied. There is a marked dichotomy in their explicit and implicit purpose which was maintained persistently for diplomatic reasons. In fact, the purposeful dichotomy served as a device to keep the hidden motives ambiguous. For instance, the English travellers were exploring information which was needed by their masters for the advancement of their imperialistic design, while both the non-English travellers were writing to gratify the curiosity of their countrymen about the polity of an Asian ruler in close contact with the expanding Western colonialism. Therefore, all the six reflect some common interest in Maharaja Ranjit Singh and his Rule.

Although, Maharaja Ranjit Singh owed his elevation to his ability and energy, yet number of causes favoured his rapid rise to political ascendency. These were : the unshaken confidence of the Maharaja in his own resources; the factionalism amongst the chiefs; both in the Punjab plains as well as in the hills; the absence of the most powerful chiefs, who had carried the battle-axe of the people against the Mughals and the Afghans, due to death or old age; rapid fall of the Durrani's Power coupled with the subjection of the Kabul Court to factional intrigues and counter intrigues; preoccupation of East India Company's Government in their own affairs in India etc.[1] However, the process of acquisition and consolidation of political power by the Maharaja can broadly be marked by three phases : from the occupation of Lahore (1799 A.D.) to the year 1809 A.D.; from this date to the year 1818 A.D.; and from the death of Fateh Khan Barakzai, a powerful Wazir of Kabul in 1818 A.D. onward till his advance towards Sind, Chinese territory and Kabul was checked by the British.[2]

However, by the end of the third decade of the nineteenth century, the Kingdom of Lahore was at the zenith of its glory. The work of consolidation was almost complete. All the civil and military institutions, whether innovated or revived were functioning well. The might of the Maharaja was felt all around. It is significant to note here that except William Moorcroft, all other travellers under perusal visited the Kingdom of Lahore between 1830-40.[3] Thus when Alexander Burnes, an English diplomat visited the dominions of the Maharaja in the 1830s, he found it as, 'one of the few countries on the globe', which had both, 'political and natural limits defined.' On the north it was bounded by the Himaliya, westward by the Indus, and on the South East by the river Satluj. Watered by the five rivers, 'the territory of the Maharaja was compact and his hold over it was strong.' His government was most vigorous and well consolidated. But for Burnes, this vigour was sufficient only for 'a native state.'[4]

To comprehend this vigour of the domain of the Maharaja, these travellers have discussed his position as a Ruler, his ascendency over his nobles, jagirdars and vassals, his relations with his political rivals; the Afghans and the East India Company besides counting his resources in terms of revenue, armed forces etc. and civil administration. However, from the observation of these travellers, the position of the Maharaja appears to be very strong. For instance, Jacquemont observed that Ranjit Singh was a monarch absolutely independent, and possessing the greatest power in Asia after the British. He was better obeyed by his subjects than the Mughal emperors at the zenith of their power.[5] Hugel states that Ranjit Singh ruled undisturbed over both Hindus and Muslims. His Kingdom being exclusively his own, nothing took place throughout its whole extent without his express commands. In fact, Maharaja was the soul that animated the entire body.[6] None of his countries or grandees had influence on his actions. The foreigners in his service too had no influence over him. Their advice was followed when it was good, but it was never accepted without a trial of its value.[7] Burnes was much impressed by the way Ranjit Singh conducted the state affairs. He says that 'he never quitted the presence of a native of Asia with such impression as he left Ranjit Singh 'without education and without a guide, he conducted all the affairs of his kingdom with surpassing energy and vigour, and yet wields his power with moderation quite unprecedented in an Eastern Prince.' As a ruler, he had no equal from Constantinople to India.[8] He was a despot in the true sense of the word.[9]

Both, the splendour and the composition of the Lahore Durbar has drawn much attention of these travellers. The court of the Maharaja was a 'singular one' for, the Maharaja did not sit on the throne. Although he had not taken any title for himself and was content with his own name, Yet he had have a complete ascendency over his nobles.[10] For, the power of most of the members of the original Sikh principalities had been neutralized or subverted by him. The void was filled by new creation; number of individuals rose to prominence by the favour of the Maharaja, namely, *Jamadar* Khushal Singh, the Faquir brothers, the *Jamwal* brothers etc. Being his own 'minions' this newly created aristocracy did not have any influence over the actions of the Maharaja.[11] However, both, Burnes and Hugel sensed a danger to the Sikh monarchy from the power and activities of the Jamwal brothers, after the demise of the Maharaja. They were busy in filling their coffers and nourishing the art of corruption.[12] The young son of Dhian Singh, Hira Singh, was a favourite of the Maharaja. Being Prime Minister, Dhian Singh too was exercising his art in the court. He was fortifying his native home, in the vicinity of Bhimber, which he had strengthened by guns taken from Lahore, a fact which no one disclosed to the Maharaja. He was judiciously preparing himself with an eye on the future.[13] Gulab Singh was managing the salt mines and holding a big estate towards Jhelum.[14] Hence, the old aristocracy was jealous of the power of the Dogra family. But being afraid of Maharaja's power, they did not give any offence. Also, the liberality of the Maharaja in bestowing large *jagirs* on the old Sikh Sardar, secured their conciliation to his rule.[15]

Writing towards the end of Maharaja's reign, Hugel underlined Maharaja's hold over his *jagirdars*. A word form his lips could reduce a noble to a begger. Transfer of jagirs was quite usual. Confiscation of property after the demise of a sardar was a common practice. Even in case of hereditary jagirs, the right of the heir to secure his property dependent on the will of the Maharaja. Under any circumstances, of course, he had to pay a large sum by way of nazrana for the investiture of the turban in the court. The 'fiefs' granted by the Maharaja were worth revenue of 1,09,28,000 rupees, and could be withdrawn at any time by his arbitrary will or command. These grants of lands were given in perpetuity.[16]

To increase his political power and eventually to expand his dominions, Maharaja Ranjit Singh made an effective use of the institution of Vassalage. In the assessment of these travellers, the Maharaja appears to be a successful suzerain. For instance, Sansar Chand, once a powerful ruler in the hills, had to go to his court once a year. Though, he was never asked to pay tribute, yet he had to render military service whenever required.[17] The Raja of Mandi was so frightened of his Sikh master that he did not allow William Moorcroft to pass through his territories, unless he secured permission from the Maharaja.[18] The Raja of Kulu was fined rupees 80,000 for having facilitated Shah Sujah's retreat to Ludhiana, and rupees 50,000 for giving cooperation to the British against the Gorkhas.[19] Hugel observed that between Baramulla and Muzzafrabad, all the petty chiefs, rajas and Khans were tributaries of the Maharaja. Each one of them had, at least one family member as hostage in Kashmir. Even, if there happened to be no male child, their wives and daughters were kept as security for their good behaviour.[20] This hold was equally strong over the far off regions of the Kingdom of Lahore. For example, the chief of Ladakh requested Jacquemot to use his influence with the Maharaja to get his areas clear due to the treasury of Lahore.[21] The Afghan chiefs of Peshawer were allowed to retain their territory on payment of tribute and placing their sons as hostages in the court of Lahore. Masson found them very impatient under the Sikh yoke, but every manifestation of countimacy only tended to reinforce their subjection.[22] However, non-Muslim chiefs were no exception in this respect.[23]

As a rule the Maharaja never approved of strong forts in the territories of his vassals. Even Fateh Singh Ahluwalia, 'a brother of the turban' to Ranjit Singh, was instantly summoned by the Maharaja when he heard of the construction of a fortress by him.[24] The Dogra brothers seems nonetheless to have an exception in this regard.[25] Unlike Jacquemont and Hugel, Moorcroft and vigne had given an impression that the vassals of Ranjit Singh were so tired of his high handedness that almost all of them wanted to come under the British protection whenever they could find a suitable chance.[26]

To ascertain the acceptance and appreciation of Maharaja's authority by the masses, these travellers have discussed his administration of justice. Next to the Maharaja, the court of the *Qazi* was in operation. For instance, General Ventura was functioning as *Qazi* of Lahore.[27] Moorcroft who visited Kashmir soon after its annexation refers to the *kotwal* of Srinagar as chief officer of justice.[28] Muhammad Afzal was functioning as chief judge of Kashmir.[29] Besides, *Shariat* for the Muslims, *Sustomary* laws were prevalent. Punishments were not severe, for the Maharaja was always unwilling to inflict punishment of death or mutilation. Hanging was heard only in case of lawless tribal people and a slayer of cow. A homicide was rarely put to death.[30] Unlike Hugel, both Jacquemont and Moorcroft does not present a happy picture of the administration of justice in the province of Kashmir.[31] However, Hugel informs us that people of Kashmir were contented with the justice dealt out to them. For, the dreadful crualities perpetrated by their earlier rulers, who far the smallest offences punished them with the loss of their noses and ears made them well satisfied with their present, comparatively, mild government. In truth, he observed, 'there is a little oppression on the part of the governors and thanadars.'[32]

Commenting upon the law and order situation, Hugel observed that the Punjab was much safer than Hindustan.[33] This was possible, perhaps, due to an efficient police and spy system introduced by the Maharaja. Jacquemont observed a chain of informers from a ward of a city or from a village or a district to the Maharaja in person. For example, all the posts established, for collecting the duties of all description, were also meant for collecting information. These custom officers were 'the first link in an immense chain of intelligence, which converged to the Governor of the province and to Ranjit Singh himself, information on all details which his prudence or his avarice might desire.' Comparing Maharaja's police and intelligence system with those of France, Jacquemont asserted that 'Our Paris Police Know nothing in comparison with those of Kashmir and the Punjab.' Thus, the Governor of Kashmir was certainly better informed than the prefect of police in Paris.[34]

Both the non-English travellers observed the contrast between the resources of the Maharaja and the East India Company. In Jacquemont's assessment Maharaja Ranjit Singh was the only ruler in India 'who could possibly withstand the British, but even his resources were meager as compared to the British Government.' He states that Ranjit Singh's revenue was only three millions sterling while the Company's was twenty six millions sterling.[35] Hugel states that, 'Ranjit Singh is considered altogether independent of British Indian Government, and in truth is as much so, as his position as a weaker neighbour can admit of.'[36] In the assessment of these travellers, the revenue receipts of the Kingdom of Lahore was about two and half crores of rupees per annum, including the revenue due from lands alienated in jagirs and *dharmarth*.[37] The province of Kashmir which formed 'a Kingdom' in itself, yielded rupees thirty six lacs; exclusive of ten lacs which were spent on its defence.[38] The chief of Peshawar paid a yearly tribute about sixty thousands, excluding *bara* rice,[39] The revenue from Multan amounted to ten lacs of rupees a year.[40] The salt mines yielded eighteen and a half lacks of rupees including two and a half lacs levied as duties.[41] In tune with other Indian states, the collectors of the Maharaja two worked arbitrarily. At the out set, they were presumed to be dishonest; they worked on the assumption that they would 'be rifled' and 'they rifled the peasants.' However, the exactions as regulated by the Maharaja were mild. The peasantry was in a most prosperous condition and did not have any complain about the state exactions.[42]

Armed forces of the Maharaja were of special interest to these travellers, yet, none of them have given a systematic account of its evolution. All of them made observations about those wings of the army which they saw at the time of their visit or which were paraded before them on a particular occasion. However, on the basis of their observations, the army of the Maharaja can broadly be divided into three categories : the French Legion or the model brigade; regular troops : infantry, cavalry and artillery and the irregular troops. With minor differences, Burnes, Jacquemont, Hugel and Masson agrees that the army of the Maharaja was around 80000 in number. The disciplined troops amounted to 25000 infantry, 5000 cavalry and 150 guns. The irregular troops which were all cavalry (*gorcharas*), amounted to 50000.[43] Besides, pay of the troops, modes of payment, irregularities in payment, rules of promotion and leave, dress and equipments, drill and words of command and mess system have been noted and appreciated.[44]

Burnes was highly appreciative of the infantry and artillery of the Maharaja. The infantry was commanded by General Ventura. Every corps contained a mixture of Hindustanis, Sikhs and Gorkhas. Every contingent was 'neatly dressed in white, with black cross belts and bore muskets.' The brigade manoeuvered under a native general officer with 'an exactness and precision.' Commenting upon the artillery, Burnes observed that 'evolution were not rapidly performed; but the celerity was considerable; and no accident in overturning or firing occurred. The guns were 'well cost' and carriages in 'good repair.' In his estimation strength of this wing of the army was 100 pieces of field artillery, exclusive of battering guns and mortors.[45] Moorcroft formed a very favourable opinion of the cavalry of the Maharaja.[46] Jacquemont found Maharaja's troops better than his expectations in every respect.[47] Burnes found them as drilled as European, fully equal to the troops of the Indian army, but destitute of the most essential quality of a solider - discipline.[48] However, in Hugel's assessment the army of the Maharaja was 'superior to any coming across the Indus, but not of coming from the east of his dominion.'[49]

Both the non-English travellers felt certain that the viability of the kingdom of Lahore rested on the nature of its relation with the British. They felt sure about the innate potentialities of the Maharaja to withstand the British, but for his merger resources as compared to the East India Company. This led them to peep into his relations with the British.[50] Hugel viewed the treaty of 1809 A.D. signed between the Maharaja and the East India Company as 'a great set-back to Ranjit Singh's cherished desire to command the whole Sikh nation, but he felt bound to sigh it. The Maharaja resisted the British demands so long as he could afford it. But when he found himself too weak to act against their wishes, he yielded.'[51] The treaty, however, obliged him to increase his power towards North and West. But this was not necessarily what the British had wanted. If they did not interfere, it was only because they had many weighty affairs on their hands.[52]

Jacquemont explicitly states that the British Government wished to extend its frontier from the Satluj to the Indus and frustrate Ranjit Singh's designs over Sind. In accordance with the instructions from the Court of Directors, the of Amirs Sind were pressed hard to sign a treaty affording every facility and protection to the commercial and military navigation of the British on the Indus. However, the fear of the Sikh danger made the Sindis to comply the British proposals.[53] This was done without any reference to the Maharaja. In Hugel's assessment, it was an act of disgrace on the part of a power like the British.[54]

Commenting upon the meeting of Governor-General with the Maharaja at Ropar in 1831 A.D., Jacquemont observed that explicitly it was intended to cement the friendship between the two powers. In reality, the British Government wanted to know Maharaja's views about the British scheme of Navigtion of the Indus. Also, it was meant to frighten him with a show of the superiority of the British arms rather than to solicit his willing consent to the British proposals.[55] Besides, the supposed Russian danger was also made a point.[56] Eventually, the Maharaja submitted to the British proposals, though unwillingly and half-heartedly.[57] However, Jacquemont was convinced that 'someday or other (but not for some year), the company will extend its empire from the satluj to the Indus.'[58] Hugel opined that an offensive and defensive treaty with the British Indian Government could only ensure the integrity of the dominion of the Sikhs. But, he felt certain that 'the British will not sign such a treaty which would have prevented them from taking immediate advantage of any sudden occurance which might fall out.'[59]

In retrospect, the evidence presented in the European Travelogues on Maharaja Ranjit Singh and his Rule are sketchy in nature and lacks systematic presentation. This can be explained due to the scope and nature of their interests in the dominions of the Maharaja. The need of the British policy maker was to know the then state of the Kingdom of Lahore. Therefore, they evinced more interest in the working of certain institutions. For instance, Burnes was keen in noting the composition of the nobility, besides counting the strength of the armed forces. By doing this, perhaps, he was trying to single out those chiefs which could easily be pursued against the Maharaja. These examples are multiple, However, personally brave, the Maharaja was a skillful diplomate, a wary politician and a good administration.[60] He was an acute observer of manners and 'a better judge of horses, swords, and matchlocks, than the sciences of Europe.'[61] As a sagacious and skillful architect, he had formed one majestic fabric from many insignificant and unpromising fragments.[62] In the sphere of administration, he had applied his mind to those improvements which sprang only from great minds. His despotism was without its 'rigours' and 'cruelity.' His system of government was far beyond the native institutions of the East, through it was far from the civilization of Europe.[63]

REFERENCES

1. Charles Masson, *Narrative of Various Journeys in Balochistan, Afganistan and the Punjab*, 4 vols., Oxford, Karachi 1974, I, pp. 403, 416-17, 427–73 (hereafter Journeys); Baron Charles Hugel, *Travels in Kashmir and the Punjab containing a particular account of the Government and Character of the Sikhs (1845)*. Punjab Languages Department Patiala 1970, pp. 212, 77–79; 84; 364-65, 68, 69, 79, 92 and 403; (hereafter Travels) Alexander Burnes, *Travels into Bokhara; being the account of a Journey from Sea to Lahore*, 3 Vols., Oxford, Karachi, 1973, II p. 314 (hereafter *Travels*); G.T. Vigne, *Travel Kashmir, Ladak, Iskardo, the countries adjoining the Mountain*

Course of the Indus and the Himalayas, North of the Punjab, 2 vols. Henery Calburn, London, 1842, I, 107 (hereafter *Travels*).

2. Masson, *ibid.*, I, 416-17.
3. William Moorcroft visited the Dominion of the Maharaja in 1820s. while Alexander Burnes, Charles Masson, G.T. Vigne, Victor Jacquemont and B.C. Hugel visited it between 1830–40.
4. Burnes, *ibid.*, II, 264.
5. Victor Jacquemont, *Letters from India : Describing a Journey in the British Dominions of India, Tibet, Lahore and Kashmir during the years 1829, 1830, 1831 under the orders of the French Government*, 2 vols., London, 1834, I, 399; II 244 (hereafter *Letters*).
6. Hugel, *ibid.*, 348, 404 and 410.
7. *Ibid.*, 388.
8. Burnes, *Travels*, I, 33.
9. Hugel, Travels, 330; Jacquemont, *Letters* I, 342; II, 87.
10. Jacquemoent and Solty Koff, *The Punjab : A Hundred Years Ago* (tr. & ed.), H.L.O. Garret, Languages Department, Punjab, Patiala 1971; 42 and 49 (hereafter *Journal*); Jacquemont, *Letters*, II, 15; Hugel, *ibid.*, 288.
11. William moorcroft and Trebeck, *Travels in Himalayan Provinces of Hindustan and the Punjab in Ladak and Kashmir, in Peshawar, Kabul, Kanduz and Bokhara from 1819 to 1825* (1837), Languages Department Punjab, Patiala 1970; 5, 56, 58, 62, (hereafter Travels); Hugel, *ibid.*, 287-88, 92; Burnes, *ibid.*, II, 285, III, 144–148, 150; Vigne, *ibid.*, II, 73-74; Masson; *ibid.*, I, 440; Jacquemont, *Journal*, 42, 50.
12. Burnes, *ibid.*, II, 284-85; Hugel, *ibid.*, 288; Vigne, *ibid.*, II 422.
13. Jacquemont, *Letters*, II, 166; *Journal*, 61-62; Hugel, *ibid.*, 288; Burnes, *ibid.*, II, 285, 94, 337; Vigne, *ibid.*, I, 183, 84, 218-19; II, 107-8, 196, 392.
14. Burnes, *ibid.*, II, 284-85.
15. *Ibid.*, III, 124 & 297.
16. Hugel, *ibid.*, 158, 193, 330, 404; Jacquemont, Journal, 73.
17. Moorcroft, *ibid.*, 76,78; Vigne, *ibid.*, I, 107-8.
18. Moorcroft, *ibid.*, 26-27; Vigne, *ibid.*, I, 79-80, 85-86; Jacquemont, *Letters*, II, 184-85.

19. Moorcroft, *ibid.*, 107.
20. Hugel, *ibid.*, 83-84, 116, 186, 188-09, 196; Vigne, *ibid.*, I, 182-83, 192-93, 195; II, 181-82; Burnes, *ibid.*, I, 293-94, II, 292; Jacquemont, *Letters*, II, 150; *Journal*, 85.
21. Jacquemont, *Letters*, II, 140-41.
22. Masson, *ibid.*, I, 132.
23. Vigne, *ibid.*, I, 33,156-57, 158, 192-93; Moorcroft, *ibid.*, 9,18,41; Hugel, *ibid.*, 40, 53, 61, 83-84, 174, 384-85.
24. Hugel, *ibid.*, 74, 397.
25. Burnes, *ibid.*, II, 284-85, 94,337; Vigne, *ibid.*, I, 183-84, 218-19, 238-39, 245; II, 107-8, 196, 392, 488; Jacquemont, *Letters*, II, 166; *Journal*, 61-62; Hugel, *ibid.*, 288.
26. Moorcroft, *ibid.*, 79, 104, 107; Vigne, *ibid.*, I, 85-86,145-46, 156-57, 179-80, 188, 192-93.
27. Hugel, *ibid.*, 397.
28. Moorcroft, *ibid.*, 345.
29. Vigne, *ibid.*, II, 37-38, 72.
30. Jacquemont, *Letters* II, 25, 58, 67,156; *Journal*, 65; Hugel *ibid.*, 317; Vigne, *ibid.*, II, 37-38; 72; Moorcroft, *ibid*, 345.
31. Moorcroft, *ibid.*, 442, Jacquemont, *Letters* II, 156.
32. Hugel, *ibid.*, 156.
33. *Op.cit.*, 316, 339, 340; Masson, *ibid.*, 426.
34. Jacquemont Journal, 73; Vigne, *ibid.* II, 247, 266.
35. Jacquemont, *Letters*, II, 118.
36. Hugel, *ibid.*, 116, II.
37. Burnes, *ibid*, 288, 297, 316; Masson, *ibid.*, I, 430-31; Jacquemont, *Journal*, 10; Hugel, *Ibid*, 403-4.
38. Burnes, *ibid.*, II, 288; III, 156, 297.
39. *Ibid.*, II, 293, 319, 321, 325; III, 298.
40. *Ibid.*, III, 303.
41. *Ibid.*, I, 55.
42. *Ibid.*, III, 297-98.
43. *Ibid.*, li 286-87, Hugel, *ibid.*, 305, 368 and 404; Masson, *ibid.*, I, 431-32; Jacquemont, Letters, *ibid.*, II.

44. Jacquemont, *Journal*, 24-28, 31-32; 43,51-52, 58-59, 67 and 68; *Letters*, I, 222; II, 193; Burnes, *ibid.*, I, 16,78; II, 287-88; III, 102, 155-56 & 164; Masson, *ibid.*, I, 432–37, 39 & 43; Hugel, *ibid.*, 198-99, 241, 84, 85, 89, 305, 30F 31, 39, 46 & 47; Vigne, *ibid.*, I, 70; II, 119-20; Moorcroft, *ibid.*, 27, 28, 329.
45. Burnes, *ibid.*, I, 32; III, 155-56, 165,66.
46. Moorcroft, *ibid.*, 58-59, 60.
47. Jacquemont, *Letters*, II, 183, 217.
48. Burnes, *ibid.*, II, 286; III, 102, 155-56, 296.
49. Hugel, *ibid.*, 289, 334-35.
50. Jacquemont, *Letters*, II, 118; Hugel, *ibid.*, 16.
51. Jacquemont, *Journal*, 20; Hugel, *ibid.*, 277.
52. Hugel, *ibid.*, 284.
53. Jacquemont, *Journal*, 37, 39; *Letters*, II, 221.
54. Hugel, *ibid.*, 324-25.
55. Jacquemont, *Letters*, II, 112.
56. *Ibid.*, 276.
57. *Ibid.*, 290.
58. *Ibid.*, I, 232, II, 221, 255-56; *Journal*, 39.
59. Hugel, *ibid*, 335-36.
60. Jacquemont, *Letters* I, 383-399; II, 168.
61. *Ibid*, I, 298; II, 228.
62. Hugel, *ibid.*, 294 & 366.
63. Burnes, *ibid.*, I, 282.

11

Charles Masson's Account of the Sikhs

Charles Masson's (1800-1853 A.D.) real name was James Lewis. He was fairly educated. He enlisted himself in the East India company's Army on 5th October, 1821 A.D. and served in the Bengal Artillery till 4th July 1827 A.D. He deserted the Army while his regiment was stationed in the vicinity of Bharatpur. He spent next twelve years of his life, he spent in travelling through different part of Asian countries. During these travels, he spent six and a half year at Kabul and its dependencies. However, he spent nearly a year in the dominions of Maharaja Ranjit Singh. In 1842 A.D. he got published his travelogue into three volumes. In his work, he has devoted a good number of pages to the Sikhs and their rule.[1]

Like his contemporary European travellers, Masson too was interested in the political power of the Sikhs as augmented and consolidated under the able leadership of Maharaja Ranjit Singh. To understand the process of acquisition of political power by the Sikhs, he delved into the historical development of the Sikh nation as well as Sikhism. Though he has devoted only few pages to the history of the Sikhs from Guru Nanak, the founder of the Sikh faith, to the establishment of an independent Sikh rule, yet he provides very interesting insights into the historical development of the Sikhs from a 'Seet' to a 'nation.'[2] Masson saw no serious threat being posed by the Mughal rulers to the Sikh faith for nearly two centuries from its inception. Thus, he asserts, that from the times of Guru Nanak Dev to the times of Guru Teg Bahadur, the Sikh enjoyed these two Gentries of 'repose' for the development of their faith as to the augmentation of their number. He is of the view that before the times of Aurangzeb's rule, the Sikhs were considered an 'object of contempt but not of persecution.'[3]

A qualitative dichotomy between the followers of Guru Nanak and Guru Gobind Singh, tenth and last master of the Sikhs has been underlined. Masson holds that the followers of Guru Nanak were 'harmless free-thinker', while the measures of the tenth Guru had made them 'a nation of infuriated fanatics.'[4] This change has been attributed to the repressive measures of Emperor Aurangzeb against the Sikhs. Consequently, the Sikhs were compelled to arm themselves. Thus, they revealed their 'strength' and power of resistance and effected 'an entire change in the constitution of their community.'[5] However, the anarchy which followed the death of Aurangzeb provided an opportunity to the augmentation of their number.' Although in the fifties of the eight tenth century, when Ahmad Shah Abdali invaded India, the position of the Sikhs was not better than 'banditti.' Yet they were able to resolve into a multitude of little 'bands' under various leaders and 'had established strongholds and places of repose without number. In spite of the ruthless measures taken by the Burrani monarch the number of the Sikhs 'increased prodigiously. Eventually, in their struggle against the Durranis, they emerged all powerful. By defeating and slewing the Durrani governor of Lahore, they became its master in 1765 A.D.[6] Inability of the Durranis to assert their claims over the Punjab coupled with Ranjit Singh's 'ability and energy, enabled the Sikhs to assume a regular form of Government and to erect 'a powerful kingdom' from the wreaks of the states and principalities around them.[7]

Masson asserts that majority of the Punjabis, particularly the Sikhs welcomed the ascendancy of Maharaja Ranjit Singh. Though, during the process of acquisition of political power the Maharaja had to encounter strednuous opposition from the old Sikhs and non-Sikh chiefs, but he proved himself enough powerful to subvert them. However, after consolidating his position, he created a new class of chiefs and leaders, generally from the lover classes. This ushered a new era, an era of societal change in the history of the Punjabi society. To notice this change brought about by the political ascendency of the Sikhs, Masson became interested in the Sikhs as people.

Masson is very appreciative of physical traits of the Sikhs. 'Their limbs', he comments 'are musculor and well proportioned and they have a stoutness of legs and calf, seldom seen in the Hindustani.' Though instances of very tall stature were there, but gnerally they attained height 'a little above the middle size.'[8] Sikh women were attractive and well dressed.[9] They were rarely permitted to go abroad.[10] However, the Sikhs were exclusively a military and agriculturist people. They were very fond of rearing horses and horned cattle. There was hardly a Sikh family who did not have one or two brood mare and several horned cattle.[11] So much so, in the irregular cavalry of Maharaja Ranjit Singh nearly every man's horse was bonafied his own property, and even in the regular cavalry a very trifling proportion of the horses belonged to the Maharaja.[12]

The Akalis amongst the Sikh counterpart of the Punjabi society, appeared a singular entity to Masson. They dressed themselves in dark blue or black clothes. They were always armed in a most profuse manner, some of them had half a dozen swords, pistols and other arms struck about them and their horses. They carried round the top of their pagri (turban) a circular disc, with a rim an inch broad, with a very sharp edge. It was an offensive weapon which was thrown by the hand. Masson was astonished when he was assured that the Akalis 'could eject it with such force that they could divide the leg of a horse or even of an elephant.'[13]

Apparel of the Sikhs, though, appeared peculiar to Masson yet it was graceful. It consisted of a *pagri* (turban), a *jacket* and large bulky trousers terminating at the knee; the legs from the knee were naked. The chiefs occasionally wore full trousers. A scarf was usually thrown over the shoulders. It was usually trimmed with a coloured border and sometimes scarlet shawls or other showy fabrics were also worn by them. Generally speaking, these articles of dress were white. However, the Sikhs were very clean in their dress.[14] Amongst both higher and lower strata of Sikh society, men as well as women were very fond of ornaments. Masson observed that the courtiers, attendants and domestic servant of the Maharaja were splendidly clad and displayed a profusion of gold and jewelled ornaments.[15]

Both the sexes allowed the hair of their body to attain its full growth. Men gathered hair of the head into a knot at the crown. By pressing it tightly back from the forehead they sometimes elevate the upper part of the face which impart a peculiar cast to their countenance.[16] They were not restricted to certain food and drinks. But they were forbidden to eat beef and smoke tobacco in any form. However, *jhatka* (to sever the Head of animals employed for food with one stroke of sword) was eaten by them.[17] Their customary way of exclamation was *Wah Guru Ji Ki Fateh*. The superiors, whoever, were addressed as *Khalsa* Ji *i.e.* a member of the *Khalsa Panth*.[18]

Their reverence for Guru Granth Sahib was great. Almost every village in the Punjab had a Gurudwara where in a spacious apartment it was lodged on a table under a canopy with great respect. All the Sikh inhabitants of the village used to come and make obeisance to it. It was very peculiar to Masson to note that the Sikhs did not have a particular priest to perform religious ceremonies. He observed that any one qualified amongst the visitors could open Guru Granth sahib and read aloud a portion of it. Also, they were not enjoined upon to observe many forms or prayers, usually, in the morning and evening they offered up a short prayer, 'which in conformity to the military complexion thrown over all their acts, they repeated, firmly grasping with both hands their swords and which concluded with a vociferous invocation to their Guru for victory and the extension of their faith. Here Masson is referring to the Sikh *Ardas* (Supplication).[19]

However, the Sikhs were not free from rituals inconsistent with Sikhism. Caste prejudice among them was not less strong than the Hindus. Also, they were not free from *Brahmanical* influence. The *Brahmins* were held in high esteem. Almost all the Sikh chiefs had kept a family priest in their establishments. For instance, Masson observed Takur Singh, son of Sardar Sham Singh Attariwala, repeating some prayer over a basin of wanted *ghee* (clarified butter) produced by the *Brahman*, who alike mumbled something, and at the conclusion of the ceremony dropping a copper coin into the fluid.'[20] Ordinarily, though, the low caste Hindus, particularly, the banais did not receive much courtesy.[21] Yet, they felt themselves at liberty under Sikh rule to display their wealth whereas under the Mohammedan masters they were studious to conceal it. The Sikh rulers did not interferes in any way in their religious matters. They were at liberty to worship to whomsoever they liked. Celebration of Hindu festivals was not only allowed but some of them like *Diwali, Dussehra, Holi* etc., were also celebrated by the Maharaja himself.[22]

Their attitude towards Muslims was too not harsh. Masson observed that 'the cruelties practised against the Mohammedans in the countries they (the Sikhs) have subdued ought not, I think, to be alleged against them as proof of their ferocity. Haven knows the fury of the bigoted Mohamadans is terrible and the persecuted. Sikhs, in their day, were literally hunted like beast of the field. At present. flushed by a series of victories, they have zeal and buoyancy of spirit amounting to enthusiasm and with power of taking the most exemplary revenge, they have been still more lenient than the Mohammedans were ever towards them.'[23]

Masson has referred to the 'free use of wine' and practice

of Polyanding amongst certain sections of the Sikhs.[24] But he justify their conduct by saying that 'such customs must not be imputable to them as Sikhs, they are rather the remains of an ancient and rude state of society. It must also be observed that trespasses on the rules of decency must be made by themselves, and amongst themselves; liberties taken by strangers would be held as crimes, and resented, accordingly. He wished that should the Sikhs continue as independent nation, it may be supposed that increased civilization will gradually remove these traces of barbarism.'[25] However, He paints them as frank, generous extremely hospitable, social and lively but lacking, in general knowledge. They were 'certainly a fine race of men, particularly the better classes.'[26] Nevertheless, Masson's understanding of Sikhism and its founder seems to be inadequate and therefore at places misleading.[27] But his account of the Sikhs as people is very vivid and animated. He has diligently observed vices and virtue of the early nineteenth century Sikhs.

REFERENCES

1. Charles Masson, *Narrative of various journeys in Balochistan, Afghanistan and the Punjab, including a residence in those countries from 1826 to 1839*, 3 Vols., OUP. Karachi, 1974 (first 1842, hereafter *Narrative*.
2. Masson, Narrative, I, pp. 417-27
3. Masson, *ibid.*, I, 421
4. *Ibid.*, 417-18
5. *Ibid.*, 417-18,21
6. *Ibid.*, I, 422, 426-07
7. *Ibid.*, I, 422-23
8. *Ibid.*, I, 433.
9. *Ibid.*, I, 404, 447.
10. *Ibid.*, I, 447.
11. *Ibid.*, I, 434, 38, 48.
12. *Ibid.*, I, 434.

13. *Ibid.*, I, 436-37, 451.
14. *Ibid.*, I, 65, 433-34.
15. *Ibid.*, I, 443.
16. *Ibid.*, I, 434
17. *Ibid.*, I, 419, 424
18. *Ibid.*, I, 425, 451
19. Masson, *ibid.*, I, 424.
20. *Ibid.*, 424, 450-51.
21. *Ibid.*, 436, 474.
22. *Ibid.*, I, 30, 47, 182-83, 98, 445-46.
23. *Ibid.*, 435.
24. *Ibid.*, I, 433, 435, 437.
25. *Ibid.*, 435-36.
26. *Ibid.*, 433-34, 435, 452.
27. *Ibid.*, 419.

12

John Malcolm's Perception of the Sikh Scripture

British interest in the Sikh past was actuated by their imperial designs. Changed political scenario in the 1800s made knowledge about the Sikhs more imperative for the East India Company. For instance, dawn of the 19th century witnessed two major developments in the Indian sub-continent: Sudden and rapid rise of Maharaja Ranjit Singh on the political scene of the land of the Five Rivers and British occupation of Delhi in 1803 which ended Maratha influence in northern India. The latter development pushed the British frontier to the river Jamuna and made the East India Company an immediate neighbour of the Sikhs, a 'singular nation' which was in the control of the territories between the rivers Jamuna and Indus. However, the Sikhs had already attracted attention of the British in the last quarter of the 18th century due to their incursions into the Gangatic Doab. Resultantly, the Directors of the East India Company by their dispatch of the 5th June, 1805, desired that all available information on the geography and history of India should be collected.[1]

Resultantly, a number of British civil and military servants in the garb of travellers, diplomats etc. were deputed to collect as much information as they could extract from various means about the Sikhs. However, John Malcolm came to the Punjab in 1805 as British official.[2] He was accompanying Lord Lake who too came to the Punjab in pursuit of Jaswant Rao Holkar. Malcolm's official duty was to persuade the Sikh Chiefs not to render any help to Holkar.[3] Malcolm availed of this opportunity to collect both written as well as oral information about the history, manner and religion of the Sikhs.[4] Besides, he was in possession of 18th Century English writings on the Sikhs but these to him were 'sufficient only to excite than to gratify curiosity".[5] Towards the end of 1806, he visited Calcutta and stayed there for six months. During this period, he wrote his *Sketch of the Sikhs*. Initially, he thought of writing a detailed history of the Sikhs but the active nature of his public duties did not allow him much time and leisure for it.[6] Eventually, he produced this sketch in haste with the explanation that, "it will be useful at the moment when every information regarding Sikhs is of important," and with the motive that, "it may, perhaps, stimulate and aid some person, who has more leisure and better opportunities to accomplish that task which I once contemplated."[7] Verlly, Malcolm through the *Sketch of the Sikhs* wanted to make the British Administrators aware from the religion and customs of the Sikhs for better governance. Notwithstanding, the publication of the *Sketch of the Sikhs*, provided new dimension to the British historiography on the Sikhs which later on came to be regarded as the foundation of Sikh Studies.[8]

Malcolm attributes the origin of Sikhism to Guru Nanak. Doctrines preached by Guru Nanak proved to be a foundation of Sikhism and these are unquestionable.[9] Commenting upon the idea and nature of God in Sikhism, Malcolm asserts that Guru Nanak's 'God is true, eternal, creator of the universe. He is supreme. All other created beings, even the Devtas, are inferior to Him. And those who elevate deities to God are ignorant.[10] Above all, Guru Nanak entirely grounded his religion on principles of pure deism.'[11] Furthermore, the Sikhs worshipped God alone through the medium of Guru Granth Sahib. They do not adore any idol or image. Their only form of worship is the repetition of the name of God, Supreme-being, eternal Truth, the Creator of the universe. Malcolm observes that 'their Dharmasala, or temple of worship, are in general, plain buildings. Images are of course banished. Their prescribed form of prayer is, I believe, few and simple. Part of the writings of Nanak, which have since been incorporated with those of his successors, in the Adi Granth is read, or rather recited upon every solemn occasion."[12]

Malcolm is very categorical in observing the significance of the canonization of the Sikh Scripture by Guru Arjan Dev ji. Its compilation provided 'consistent form and order' to the Sikh religion and 'united the Sikh nation more closely' which in due course helped in securing more converts to the Sikh faith. However, Adi Granth owes its origin to Guru Nanak. It is written in Gurmukhi script. It is a revealed literature having Divine Origin and status. It gives fixed rules of religious and moral conduct. Above all, it is the very fountain of Sikh beliefs and practices. The Sikhs do not allow any other object than Guru Granth Sahib in their places of worship.[13] Quite interestingly, Malcolm does not accord Guru Granth Sahib the status of Guru.[14] He does refer to the commandment of Guru Gobind Singh to the Sikhs, before his demise at Nander, to read 'the Granth' and live according to its Philosophy, yet he keeps the identity of the 'Granth' ambiguous. Also, unlike other 19th century, European writers he accords equal status to Dasam Granth with Guru Granth Sahib and asserts that "This volume (Dasam Granth) which is not limited to religious subjects, but filled with accounts of his own battles, and written with a view of stirring up a spirit of valour and emulation among his followers, is at least as much revered, among the Sikhs, as the Adi Granth of Arjunmal".[15] In fact Malcolm through his *Sketch of the Sikhs* wanted to promote Imperial interests which he did by creating a dichotomy between the followers of Guru Nanak and the followers of Guru Gobind Singh by introducing Dasam Granth to provide justification to the mission of Guru Gobind Singh which is contrary to the historical facts and Sikh traditions. A recent study reveals that Dasam Granth did not exist in the 18th Century.[16] Neither Captain Matthew, who published his work a year before the *Sketch of the Sikhs* nor the subsequent visitors like Jacquemont, Burnes, Hugel, Schonberg, Emily Eden etc. mention about the existence of this Granth at Harimandir Sahib. Cunningham too has found Malcolm as contradictory and does not attribute the entire Dasam Granth to Guru Gobind Singh. According to him only first five chapters and a part of the sixth was written by Guru Gobind Singh and the rest is the work of the four scribes.[17] Earnest Trumpp also asserts that Guru Gobind Singh did not write the entire Dasam Granth.[18]

Perhaps to provide more plausibility to his argument, Malcolm unlike his predecessors, Polier, Brown and Forster, describes the proceedings of the institution of *Gurmata* and its significance for the Sikhs in detail. He observed that, 'when the chiefs and principal leaders are seated, the Adi Granth and Dasama Padshah Ka Granth are placed before them. They all bend their heads before these scriptures and exclaim, Wah Guru Ji Ka Khalsa! Wah Guru Ji Ki Fateh! A great quantity of cakes, made of wheat, butter and sugar, are then placed before the volumes of the sacred writings and covered with a cloth. These holy cakes, which are in commemoration of the injunction of Nanak, to eat and to give others to eat, next received salutation of the assembly, who then rise, and the Akalis pray aloud, while the musicians play. The Akalis, when the prayers are finished, desired the council to be seated. They sit down, and the cakes being uncovered are eaten by all classes of Sikhs : those distinctions of original tribes, which are, on other occasions, kept up, being on this occasion laid aside in token of their general and complete union in one cause. The Akalis then exclaim : "Sirdars! (Chiefs) this is the Guru-Mata!" on which prayers are again said aloud. The chiefs, after this, sit closer, and say to each other : "The scared Granth is betwixt us, let us swear by our Scripture to forget all internal disputes and to be united". [19] Clearly, thus he has confused the institution of *Gurmata* with the institution of *Sarbat Khalsa*.

However, he asserts that the Gurmata was always convened by the Akalis at Amritsar. On this occasion the Sikh chiefs used to decide the line of action to be followed against the common enemy, to pool the resources of the Sikh nation and to choose a common leader to lead the Sikh forces.[20] He also asserts that the first *Gurmata* was convened by Guru Gobind Singh himself and the last was called in 1805 when the British army came to the Punjab in pursuit of Jaswant Rao Holker.[21] On this occasion, he maintains : 'It was attended by few chiefs; and most of the absentees, who had any power, were bold and forward in their offers to resist any resolution to which this council might come...[22] Thus, Malcolm is the first and only British scholar who has not only given an elaborate procedure of performing *Gurmata* but has also commented upon its significance for the Sikhs. But his presentation contains contradictions as well as misrepresentation of facts. For instance, at the commencement of the deliberations of the assembly (Sarbat Khalsa) Malcolm mentioned the presence of two Scriptures, but when the Sikh chiefs resolve to act upon the *Gurmata*, they swear by one Scripture. Interestingly, he does not disclose the identity of this Scripture too. Also, almost all the 18th and 19th century writers have mentioned the institution of *Gurmata* and its role in the advancement of political power of the Sikhs but none has mentioned the presence of Dasam Granth in this context. Furthermore, his assertion that when the armies of both : Marathas and the British in 1805, were present in the Punjab a *Sarbat Khalsa* was called which was attended by very few, is wrong. For instance, he has not disclosed who convened the *Sarbat Khalsa* and on which date. The court historian of Maharaja Ranjit Singh does not mention it.[23] The fact is that Maharaja Ranjit Singh invited all the Trans-Satluj Sikh chiefs to join him at Amritsar. None of them responded to his call for almost all of them were in direct communication with Lord Lake. Interestingly even Bhag Singh of Jind, maternal uncle of Maharaja Ranjit Singh, was in the camp of Lord Lake and he was deputed by Lord Lake to dissuade his nephew from joining the Maratha Chief.[24]

Khande-di-Pahul is the only means to enter into the fold of Sikhism, more properly, according to Malcolm, into the commonwealth of the Khalsa.[25] He has commented upon the mode of initiation, preparation of the Pahul, injunction to the neophyte and rahit of the Khalsa. He holds that 'some sugar and water was put into a cup, and stirred round with a steel knife or dagger.' Malcolm asserts while that preparing *Pahul,* the *Bani* was recited from the Guru Granth Sahib as well as from the Dasam Granth. But he neither enumerate the *Banis* and normention which *Bani* was recited from which Granth.[26] Amongst the observances; the Khalsa was asked to devote himself to arms for the defence of the commonwealth and the destruction of its enemies, these enemies to Malcolm are the Muslims, to keep hair and wear a blue dress.[27] Khalsa was further asked to abondon all intercourse with the Minas, Dhirmaliyas, Ramrayias, Masandias, Kurimars and those who perform bhadan.[28] Besides, the Khalsa was instructed in some general precepts : 'He is told to be gentle and polite to all with whom he converse, to endeavour to attain wisdom, and to emulate the persuasive eloquence of Baba Nanak. He is particularly enjoined when ever he approaches any of the Sikh temples, to do it with reverence and respect, and to go to Amritsar, to pay his devotion to the Khalsa and the State; the interest of which he is directed, on all occasions, to consider paramount to his own.' He was also enjoined to read Adi Granth and share his earnings with others. And after the disciple has heard and understood all these and similar precepts, he is declared to be duly initiated. Any one belonging to any race or creed could come into the fold of Sikhism by going through initiatory rites. Also the neophyte could be initiated at any time and at any age but 'the children of the Singh's all go through this rite at a very early age.' However, the presence of Five Baptised Sikhs is the basic requirement to conduct initiatory rites.[29]

Malcolm thought no other source better than Guru Granth Sahib for the understanding of Guru Nanak and his philosophy. Very interestingly, he is the first British scholar to realize the need to translate Guru Granth Sahib.[30] But he attributes the origin of Sikhism to the prevailing disorderly and chaotic religious conditions in India, and emphasizes the reformatory character of Sikhism. In his assessment, Sikhism aimed at synthesizing the positive elements from the Hindu and the Islamic traditions, having universal appeal and validity. In this way, he fails to percive the originality of the vision and mission of Guru Nanak.[31] He further asserts that the Khalsa Panth was composed of the Khulasa (unbatised) and the Khalsa (baptized) Sikhs, the former being the devotees of Guru Nanak and the latter of Guru Gobind Singh.[32] To substantiate his argument, he chooses Guru Granth Sahib to denote the philosophy of Guru Nanak and the Dasam Granth for the philosophy of Guru Gobind Singh. Thus, he treats the Sikh movement as two separate streams based on two different ideologies; the ideology of Guru Granth Sahib which teaches benevolence and peacful co-existence of mankind and the philosophy of Dasam Granth which perpetuate militancy and enjoin upon its votaries to arm themselves, as Malcolm puts it, against the Muslims.[33] Thus his understanding of the mission of Guru Nanak and Guru Gobind Singh is inadequate and therefore misleading. Not only this, he has misinterpreted and misrepresented many facts regarding the Sikh history and faith, and at places contradict his own thesis. A few glaring example would suffice to understand his notion. For instance, he, to start with communalizes the sources by denominating these as; Sikh sources and Muslim sources to assert. He was the first British writer to assert Kabirs that Amritsar was not founded by Guru Ram Das. It was very ancient town, known formerly under me name of Chak. Guru Ram Das only added to its population and built Amrit Sarovar. Furthermore, he was the first to use Bachitar Natak for the re-construction of Guru Gobind Singh's biographic to denominate it as *Dasam Padshah Ka* Granth and accord to it an equal status to the Adi Granth; amongst the observances by the baptized Sikhs to mentioned five arms instead of five K's to assert that Guru Gobind Singh took military service under Emperor Bahadur Shah; to mention the difference between the Banda Singh Bahadur and the Akalis on account of introduction of certain changes in diet, dress and salutation by the former. Surprisingly, he was the pioneer to think of introducing certain changes in the Sikh dieting through 'the Nirmala and Shahid.'[34] Similarly his claim that John Lyden translated for him the Punjabi manuscript is also false. John Lyden translated for him only Bachittar Natak and not the so called Dasam Granth. Besides, he translated only 11 pauris of 41 var attributed to Bhai Gurdas, Bhagat Ratnavali (biographies of mythical and historical Bhagats) and Gian Ratnawali (Ist Var of Bhai Gurdas) and Kurka of Guru Gobind Singh in Duggar diet.[35] Thus many of the misconceptions and mis-representations having their origin with Malcolm have been taken as established facts by many modern historians of the Sikhs.

REFERENCES

1. J.S. Grewal, *Muslim Rule in India : The Assessment of British Historians*, Calcutta, 1970, p. 110; G. Khurana, *British Historiography on the Sikh Power in the Punjab*, Mansell Publishing Ltd., London, 1985, p. 16; Darshan Singh, *Western Perspective on the Sikh Religion*. Sehgal Publishers Service, New Delhi, 1991, pp. 13-14.
2. John Malcom, *Sketch of the Sikhs*, John Murrary, London, 1812, p. 1.
3. G. Khurana, *ibid.*, p. 18.
4. Malcolm collected large number of manuscripts including a copy of the *Adi Granth, The Dasam Padshah Ka Granth, the Vars of Bai Gurdas, the Janam Sakhi of Bhai Buta*, etc. Besides John Leyden, a trained surgeon and a man of great learning and having command over oriental languages, translated a few passages from Punjabi and Duggar dialects for him dealing with the Sikh history and religion. He also availed of the services of Sikh priest of Nirmala Order (Atma Ram) who explained to him the ceremonies of their religion in a very free and open manner : Malcolm, *op.cit.*, 1-3 (int); Darshan Singh, *op.cit.*, p. 15.
5. Malcolm, *op.cit.*, p. 1.
6. Khurana, *ibid.*, p. 18.

7. Malcolm, *ibid.*, p. 1&4.
8. Darshan Singh, *ibid.*, p. 15; Khurana, *ibid.*, pp. 17-34.
9. Malcolm, *ibid.*, pp. 169, 172-73.
10. *Ibid.*, p. 21.
11. *Ibid.*, p. 171.
12. *Ibid.*, p. 168.
13. *Ibid.*, p. 168,188.
14. *Ibid.*, p. 196.
15. *Ibid.*, p. 51-52.
16. J.S. Mann, *A Fresh lookat Dasam Granth : Analysis of its Text and History*, unpublished paper.
17. J.D. Cunningham, *History of the Sikhs*, Low Price Publication, New Delhi, 1990, pp. 30-41.
18. Ernest Trumpp, *The Adi Granth*, Munshi Ram Manohar Lal, New Delhi, 1997, p. cxi.
19. *Ibid.*, pp. 120-22.
20. *Ibid.*, p. 21.
21. *Op., cit.*
22. *Ibid.*, p. 107.
23. Sohan Lal Suri, Umda-ut-Tawarikh, (ed. J.S. Grewal & Indu Banga), G.N.D.U., Amritsar, 1985, Daftar II, pp. 67-68.
24. *Op.cit.* see also. H.R. Gupta, History of the Sikhs, Munshi Ram Manohar Lal, Delhi, 1999, Vol. V, pp. 207-208.
25. Malcolm, p. 180.
26. *Ibid.*, p. 183.
27. *Ibid.*, p. 180.
28. *Ibid.*, p. 183-85.
29. *Ibid.*, p. 186.
30. *Ibid.*, pp. 22, 169-72.
31. *Ibid.*, pp. 1-76, 144-196.
32. *Ibid.*, p. 183.
33. *Ibid.*, pp. 41-76.
34. *Ibid.*, pp. 29-30, 54-63, 71, 89, 145, 182, 185,195-96.
35. *Ibid.*, pp. 1-5; J.S. Mann, *op.cit.*

13

Early Nineteenth Century Punjabi Society in European Travel Literature

European travel literature contains evidence on almost all the sections of the early 19th century Punjabi society : aristocracy, traders, artists, peasants, workers, slaves, and dancers etc. The travellers keenly observed the change which political ascendancy had brought about in the Sikh way of life. Being brought up in particular socio-cultural setup, they observed those social institutions and practices which appeared to them peculiar and which were generally overlooked by native chroniclers. However, the purview of the present paper is to understand the early 19th century Punjabi Society in the light of the evidence presented by the European Travellers.

In the 1830s Alexander Burnes, a British diplomat travelling in the dominion of Maharaja Ranjit Singh, enumerated the population of the Punjab as 30,00,000. The Muslims and the Hindus were predominant, for the 'Khalsa' population was about 5,00,000.[1] The Muslims were composed of mainly two sects : the Sunis and the Shias. The ratio in which these sects existed is not known exactly.[2] The Hindu social order was marked by traditional system of varna. However, many sub-castes did exist and the most superior of these were the Pandits (Brahmins).[3]

Occupationally, the peasantry constituted the bulk of the Punjabi society. It was composed of all the three communities : the Muslims, the Hindus and the Sikhs. However, the Jats were predominant among them.[4] A considerable number of artisans living in the cities, towns and large villages belonged to the Mohammedan and Hindu faiths. Labourers, both in the urban and in rural areas, however, were mostly chamars or Hindus of low caste.[5]

The life style of the chiefs or aristocracy was not different from the life style of the Maharaja. One may find a difference of degree but certainly not of kind. They went about attended by a large retinue. Their apparel were gorgeous and dwellings like mansions. They kept, a *zenana*, though small, consumed much spirituous liquor and listened to the *nach* girls.[6]

Dwellings of the upper classes were good enough to suit their status and the aristocracy had houses which corresponded to 'baronial castles'. These were built of bricks plastered with mud.[7] Both, Burnes and Jacquemont observed that though the houses of the Sikh chiefs were the best' and had at a distance 'an imposing and respectable appearance', yet they were inferior to the fortified dwellings of the Rajput chiefs of Mewar.[8] Jacquemont found their houses at Amritsar 'much inferior in design and construction to those at Benaras'.[9] However, it was common among the wealthy as well as the poor to whiten their houses and cover the front with coarse mythological pictures.[10]

The cost of living and the wages earned by the people engaged in different trades are suggestive of the general condition of the masses. For example, a good copyist used to make three annas a day, a calligrapher three and half annas, a carpenter four annas a cutter eight annas, a gun-smith and a bow and arrow maker one rupee, a pen-case maker four annas, a good journeyman tailor two to four annas and a potter about nine annas a day.[11] A filed labourer in Kashmir was a gainer of about two rupees a month, after feeding himself and his family out of his wages.[12] Both

Burnes and Hugel observed that the inhabitants of the kingdom of Lahore were well fed and healthy, well-clad and happy and not wanting even in ornaments.[13] However, the expenses of a poor man in the Punjab were about three large rupees or 6s, a month, but the provisions on which he subsisted were six or eight times cheap as those eaten by an English peasant. The expenses of his counterpart in the valley of Kashmir did not exceed more than two Hari Singh rupee or 25. 8d. a month.[14]

The rich bankers and merchants had houses three to four storeys high where as the common people in the plains lived mostly in *kacha* houses, made of sun-dried bricks. In the mountainous regions, the houses were usually a group of two or three cottages built of loose stones, wood, bamboo and the interior being plastered with mud. In some places, these were flat-roofed while in others thatched with rice straw.[15] Near and on the river banks, the habitation was of temporary nature being mostly of pastoral tribes who never built any shelter beyond 'a movable hamlet'.[16]

Turban, jacket and trouser or tunic formed the common apparel. However, the Muslims wore skull caps under the turban while caps were used for head dress in the hills.[17] The chiefs or wealthy people wore turban, jacket, *angraka* (coat) and a large bulky trouser. A scarf was usually kept over the shoulders. It was usually trimmed with a coloured border. Sometimes, scarlet shawls or other showy fabrics were used for this purpose. At times over the whole apparel a mantle, lined with skin, was thrown. Even the attendents of the Maharaja used to clad splendidly and displayed a profusion of gold and jewelled ornaments.[18] However, the common people in the plains usually adorned themselves with home made *khadar* while in the mountainous and sub-mountainous regions woollen garments were mostly used.[19]

Like Hindus, the Sikhs were not restricted to certain food and drinks. However, they were forbidden to take beef.[20] The Muslims were rather more prone to animal diet than the Hindus who were mostly vegetarian.[21] Not much is known, about the food habits of the common Punjabis. However, common food items of the Punjabis were *chapattis* made of wheat flour, varieties of boiled rice, pulses, meat, chickens, eggs, milk, butter, ghee, fruits, sweatmeats, *sharbats* etc.[22] However, very sumptuous meals were taken by the upper classes.[23] Tea and coffee was mostly used in the hills, particularly the black tea made the best beverage in the mountainous regions.[24] We learn from W. Moorcroft that around 1820s the tea was becoming popular in the Punjab too.[25] For cold drinks, *sharbats* of different kinds were used.[26]

Opium, *bhang*, liquour, tobacco etc. were the main intoxicants. Opium was largely consumed by the rich section of the society, particularly the aristocracy. A narcotic preparation of the juice of hemp or infusion of poppy heads and hemp was mostly used by the poor.[27] Inspite of the prohibition of liquor in Sikhism, the Sikhs used it indiscriminately. The Maharaja himself was very fond of liquor and the Sikh aristocracy made no exception. No function, celebration of an event or a festival could pass without the introduction of a bout.[28] The commoners too used it. Vignue observed that 'the Oriental have no idea of drinking unless they can drink too much.'[29]

Majority of the people did not relish the idea of educating their children. This feeling was rather strong amongst the agricultural and labourer classes. For instance, while travelling in the Rachna Doab in 1830s, when A. Burnes suggested to an agriculturist to send his boy to school, he replied that 'education was rather useless to a cultivator of the soil,[30] With few exceptions, this notion did prevail in the higher quarters of the punjabi society too.[31]

The Muslim ladies observed parda more strictly than the Hindus and the Sikhs.[32] However, the women of the hill tribes did all outdoor work and even followed the plough.[33] Victor Jacquemont makes us believe that slavery as an institution did exist in the Punjabi society. In the *Zenana* of General Ventura, he observed, the ladies were guarded and attended by female slaves. They were bought for rupees sixty to eighty from the dealers, who brought them from the hills. Interestingly, Slavery was uncommon among the men.[34]

The practice of *sati* was not peculiar to the inhabitants of the kingdom of Lahore.[35] However, in the Punjab proper and in the valley of Kashmir, it was practised very rarely.[36] But in the submountainous regions it was commonly performed.[37] Child marriage and prohibition of widow remarriage appears to be the root cause of this social evil.[38] Even this horrible custom embroiled the Sikh portion of the Punjabi society so far as the upper classes were concerned.[39]

Prostitution was not an irrespectable profession. Jacquemont tells us that in Amritsar the prostitutes had their separate quarters. They were never exposed to insult and it would have been a grave lack of good manner not to return their salutation which they never omit to give to a respectable passerby. Jacquemont's description of their apparel and physique is vivid and bold.[40]

The dancers were under the surveillance of the ruler and were little better than slaves. They were generally not allowed to sing or dance without an adequate permission.[41] However, they always moved in covered vehicles drawn by oxen, escorted by a party of armed police whom they pay for fear of being robbed of costly jewels with which they were commonly adorned.[42]

The sale of female children, in the hills, was considered a good source of income by their parents. The female child who promised, to turn out pretty was sold at the age of about eight.[43] Jacquemont has underlined the import of Kashmirian pretty faces to the Punjab, to adron the harms of the chief and nobles, irrespective of their religious creed. However, the prettiest of the dancing girls were from the wattal tribe.[44]

The practice of polyandry appeared to Jacquemont, a destitude of 'reason and moral sense'.[45] Masson tells us that it was common among the Sikhs to have one wife shared between brothers. The wife was considered to be an impure creature for her husband. He hardly considered her as being, of the same-species with himself. However, Masson argues that this custom was not imputable to them as Sikhs, for 'they were the remains of the ancient and rude, state of society'.[46] He hoped that 'should they continue as an independent nation, it may be hoped that increased civilization would gradually remove these traces of barbarism' and 'in the course of time they would grow enlightened and become superior people.'[47]

Fairs and festivals' had an important role to play in the emotional life of the Punjabis. *Dussehra, Diwali, Lohri, Basant, Holi* etc. were celebrated with great enthusiasm.[48] On the day of *Dussehra*, the Maharaja used to hold the annual review of his forces.[49] Though, originally *Diwali* was a Hindu festival, the Sikhs celebrated it with great noise and splendour. On that day Golden Temple was lighted with lamps which presented 'the image of pandemonium'.[50] Festival of *Lohri, Basant* and *Holi* too were celebrated with similar zeal. The way Maharaja Ranjit Singh used to celebrate these festivals gives the impression that these were the state owned festivals.[51]

Besides festivals, annual or bi-annual visits to religious places on a particular occasion, the annual fairs on the temples, tombs and the confluence of the rivers, was a great source of joy to the people. For instance, an annual fair was held at the temple of Katas around 10th or 12th of April in which the Hindus and the Sikhs participated alike.[52] A tomb of a Mohammedan saint at Katas and of Bahawal Haq at Mullan attracted numerous visitors annually.[53] Similarly, visit to Haridwar on the occasion of *kumb* was a great source of joy.[54]

Watching and listening to the dancers was another source of recreation. In the courts of the rulers, irrespective of their means, it was the general practice of having dancing girls. It was thought necessary to have a proper reception of a guest to the court. The Maharaja had the 'rarest beauties' in his Court.[55] Dancing as a profession was in vogue in the kingdom of Lahore. However, by some people it was looked down and the dancers were generally called *kangri* by the rustic.[56] The Maharaja had a regiment of the Kashmirian amazons, who could drink an incredible quantity of spirituous liquor without becoming intoxicated.[57] In fact, observed Hugel, they were 'so completely deadened by their course of life that they appeared to be no longer alive to any excitement'.[58]

Another source of amusement was gossip. Referring to the passion for amusement Hugel found much truth in the proverb that, 'you can take away the wife and children of a Sikh while he is listening to the adventures of Rustam and Surabs, and he would not miss them.'[59]

The evidence on the Punjabi Society does not reflect a serious concern of the Travellers. Their major concern appears to be with the Sikh portion of the Punjabi Society, yet the description is cursory and lacks depth. Only those aspects are discussed which come under direct observation like dress, dwelling, festivals, amusements etc. Also, they do not make serious attempt to understand the Punjabi Society and its social dynamism. For instance, social order, social institutions and forces of change are not taken up adequately. In the name of the Sikh society only the aristocracy is discussed. On the other hand, evidence related to Kashmir deals with the common men. The Muslims and the Hindus have drawn little attention. However, with the rise of the Sikhs to power, their social position underwent a change. Now they were at the top of the social hierarchy. On the other hand the social position of the Muslims went down. Most of the information on the Sikhs suggests that they were discussed as a ruling class and not the Sikh masses.

REFERENCES

1. Burnes does not make it clear what he meant by the term 'Khalsh'. Does it include the whole population professing the Sikh faith or the Singhs of Guru Gobind Singh alone? *Travels into Bokhara : Being the account of a Journey from India to*

Kabul, Tartary and Persia, also, Narrative of Voyage on the Indus from Sea to Lahore, 3 Vols., Oxford University Press, Karachi (4th ed.). (hereafter as Travels), II, 286.

2. G.T. Vigne, Travels in Kashmir, Laddak, Iskardo, *The countries adjoining the mountain course of the Indus and the Himalaya, North of the Punjab,* 2 Vols., Henry Colburn, London, 1842, (hereafter Travels), II, 137, 139.
3. Baron Charles Hugel, *Travels in Kashmir and the Punjab containing a particular account of the Government and character of the Sikhs,* Punjab Language Department, Patiala, 1970 (reprint - first published 1845) (hereafter Travels), 185; Victor Jacquemont, *Letter from India : Describing A Journey in the British Dominions of India, Tibet, Lahore and Kashmir during the year 1828, 29, 30, 31 under the Order of the French Government,* 2 Vols, Edward Churton. London 1834 (hereafter *Letters*), II. 59, 66; Charles Masson, *Narrative of various journeys in Balochistan, Afghanistan and the Punjab,* 4 Vols, Oxford University Press, London 1974 (hereafter Journeys), I, 424, 450-51.
4. Burnes, *Travels,* I, 3-4.
5. V. Jacquemont and A Soltykoff, *The Punjab : A Hundred Years Ago* (ed. H.L.O. Garrett), Language Department, Punjab, Patiala, 1971, (hereafter *Journal*), 4, 25.
6. Burnes, Travels, I, 13-14; III, 101-146; Jacquemont, *Letters,* I. 393-94; 396, 401; II. 71-72, 163; *Journal,* 34, Vigne, *Travels,* II, 102-03; Hugel, *Travels,* 115, 191.
7. Burnes, Travels, I, 13-14; Jacquemont, *Travels,* II. 16, Journal, 26. 28, 57-58; Vigne, *Travels,* I. 220, 236-37; 246, II, 187-88; Hugel, *Travels,* 207.
8. Burnes, Travels, I, 14.
9. Jacquemont, *Journal,* 26.
10. *Ibid.,* 26, 57-58.
11. Vigne, *Travels,* II, 121. 126, 127; Jacquemont, *Journal,* 69.
12. Vigne, *op. cit.*
13. 13 Burnes, *Travels,* I 3-4; Hugel, *Travels,* 38, 68, 332.
14. Vigne, *ibid.,* II. 120.
15. Jacquemont, Journal, 61; Burnes, *Travels,* I, 146; W. Moorcroft, *Travels in the Himalayan Provinces of Hindustan and the*

Punjab, in Laddak and Kashmir, in Peshawar, Kabul and Kanduz and Bokhara from 1819 to 1825. Language Department Punjab, Patiala 1970 (reprint first published 1837) (hereafter *Travels*) 409; Vigne, *Travels*, I, 174-75. 205; II, 189.

16. Burnes, *Travels*, III, 287-88, 307.
17. Vigne, *Travels*, II, 140; Jacquemont, *Journal*, 25; Moorcroft, *Travels*, 108.
18. Masson, *Journeys*, I, 433-34; Jacquemont, Journal, 25, 40; Hugel, *Travels*, 380; Burnes, *Travels*, I, 61; III, 102, 136; Vigne, *op. cit.*
19. Moorcroft, *op. cit.*
20. Hugel, *Travels*, 283.
21. Masson, *Journeys*, I, 424; Burnes, *Travels*, III, 141: Jacquemont, *Journal*, 21; *Letters*. II, 59; Vigne, *Travels*, II, 140-41.
22. Burnes, *Travels*, III, 136, 166; Vigne, *Travels*, I, 72, 181.
23. Jecquemont was served with a splendid dinner by M. Allard by a host of servants richly dressed in Silk : *Letters*, I, 394-95.
24. Burnes, *Travels*, III, 166.
25. Vigne, *op. cit.*, I, 72.
26. Moorcroft, *Travels*, 197.
27. *Ibid.*, 53, 108-09; Jacquemont, *Journal*, 9.
28. Hugel, *Travels*, 311; Burnes, *Travels*, I, 27-28.
29. Vigne, *Travels*, II, 102.
30. Burnes, *Travels*, I, 44.
31. Hugel, *Travels*, 221, 281; Burnes, *Travels*, I, 44; III, 140-41.
32. The Muslim ladies concealed their body in such a way that one could not see even their countenance. They could be seen throwing white robe over their entire body leaving netted orifice before the face and the mouth; Burnes, *Travels*, I, 62, III, 82, 85, 146.
33. *Ibid.*, II, 212-13.
34. Jacquemont, *Journal*, 34-35.
35. *Ibid.*, 56; *Letters*, II, 12, 151.
36. Vigne, *Travels*, I, 83-84, 86: II, 12, 151; Jacquemont Journal, 55-56, *Letters*, II. 207.

37. Jacquemont, *Journal*, 55.

38. Amongst the Hindus marriages usually took place before the girl child get puberty and it often happened that a little girls of the age of 8 or 10 became a widow by the death of the child to whom she had been married and to whom she had never seen, was condemned to celibacy for the rest of her life: Jacquemont, *Journal*, 9, Vigne, *Travels*, M, 11-12.

39. *Ibid.*, I, 83-84; 86; II, 151; Jacquemont, *Letters*, 207.

40. He found them squatting neatly and tastefully dressed usually in white, pink or red muslin and adorned heavily with gold ornaments. They were 'fair enough: that is to say of a deep pallor with no more colour in their cheeks than in the rest of their faces. They are all very small, with good features and breasts, but their arms are too thin, their thigh thinner still, and their legs so thin as to be actually unsightly; their eyes, naturally beautiful, have an added brightness and softness from the custom of slightly darkening the lower eye-lid with a preparation of antimony", *Journal*, 27.

41. Hugel, *Travels*, 146.

42. *Ibid.*, 311.

43. These were sold from twenty to three hundred Franks but average rate was fifty to sixty franks : Jacquemont, *Letters*, II, 65.

44. *Ibid.*, II, 74-75; Vigne, *Travels*, II, 144-45.

45. *Ibid.*, II, 91. 98; *Journal,* 73.

46. Masson, *Journeys*, I, 435.

47. *Ibid.*, 436.

48. Hugel, *Travels*, 283, 310-11, 338-40; Masson, *Journeys*, I, 445-46; Jacquemont, *Letters*, 329; II. 198, 182-83; Vigne, *Travels*, I, 43; II, 94; Burnes, *Travels*, I, 26-28.

49. Masson, *Journeys,* I, 445-46; Jacquemont, *Letters*, I, 329.

50. Jacquemont, *op. cit.,* II, 182-83, 198.

51. Hugel, *Travels*, 283; 310-11, 338-40; Burnes, *Travels*, I, 26-28, Masson, *Journeys* I., 47; Vigne, *ibid*, I, 43.

52. Vigne, *Travels*, I, 55; Jacquemont, *Journal*, 62; Hugel, *Travels*, 42, 45-46.

53. Jacquemont, *op. cit.*, Burnes, *Travels*, III. 111-12.

54. Burnes, *Travels*, I, 69.

55. Hugel, *Travels*, 310; Jacquemont, *Letters*, I, 391; II. 16, 55-56, 65-66; *Journal*, 44-45.

56. Hugel, *Travels*, 146, 309.

57. *Ibid.*, 309-10, Jacquemont, *Letters,* II, 313-14.

58. Hugel, *Travels*, 309.

59. *Ibid.*, 145-46; 339.

14

Liberation of Sri Darbar Sahib Tarn Taran

The *Sarovar* (sacred tank) and the city of Tarn Taran was founded by Guru Arjan Dev in 1590 A.D.[1] In 1597, Guru Arjan Dev himself laid down the foundation of the shrine of Tarn Taran.[2] However, during the British regime the management of the shrine was entrusted to *Sarbrah* of Sri Harimandir Sahib (Golden Temple), Amritsar. His control over the *pujaris* (priests of the shrine) was lax. Consequently, the *pujaris* indulged in shockingly immoral and un-Sikh-like practices. The Reformists under the leadership of Singh Sabha, Tarn Taran persuaded the *pujaris* to desist from such practices which were not in consonance with the Sikh ethos and traditions. But of no avail, resultantly, there started a struggle between the *pujaris* and the Reformists. Eventually, the Reformists were able to secure possession of the shrine but not without sacrificing their lives.

From the foundation of the shrine of Tarn Taran till the end of Sikh rule (1849 A.D.), the management of its affairs remained satisfactory and acceptable to the Sikh masses. But after the annexation of the kingdom of Lahore, the British Government assigned its management to the *sarbrah* of Sri Harimandir Sahib, Amritsar. He was a puppet of the British Government. He was not attentive to the affairs of the shrine. Consequently, the *pujaris* of Tarn Taran became unaccountable and social evils and un-Sikh-like practices commenced.

The most disturbing and painful scene could be seen on the day of every *amavas*. During the times of Guru Arjan Dev only two *amavas* were celebrated.[3] In 1622 A.D., the Sixth Guru, Guru Hargobind commanded the Sikhs to celebrate all the twelve *amavas*.[4] With the passage of time and passing of the control of the shrine into the hands of the *pujaris*, the day of *amavas* used to be celebrated like a fair and unheard of social evils were while entering into the Darshani Deori, they would shout "Hey Guru Arjana! Ae the Jo Assni Marji Kareep Tun Nahi Sanu Varzana.'[5] practised. For instance, Bottles of liquor were placed in the holy sarovar to be consumed after these were chilled; groups of rogues used to move around the parkarma singing cheap and dirty doggerel, forcibly entering into women's bathing places, mischief monger used to fill their laps and bags with berry, sugarcane cutlets (ganeris) and ladoo (sweetmeat), coins, Kaudian (small shall used as coin in olden dang) etc. to be thrown at young women sitting in the Bungas or on the floors. Roguishness surpassed every limit when, shaping their hands like a bowl, they should "piss piss in it so that they could taste their urine". Rowdy young used to move about the Parikarma carrying clubs on their shoulders, challenging each other, there used to be many skirmishes with many injuries. If a woman happens to stray into the crowd, she used to be pushed around and insulted by such hooligans; even they were kidnapped. Many shops operated within the *parikarma* and rubbish was thrown in the *parikarma* itself. *Bungas* were generally occupied by gangsters. Dancers and prostitutes used to visit the fair and their dances were held in front of the *Darshni Deori*.[6] These heart-rending malignances were unbearable for the true followers of Guru Nanak.

Idols of Hindu deities were established and worshipped in the parikarma. For instance, idol of Bhairon was placed in a corner of the southern side of the sacred tank. Another idol of Mata Sheranwali (mother goddess sitting on the lion) was too placed in the parikarma. Before worship, these idols were washed in the water of the Holy tank. Red lead (*sandur*) was offered to deity of Bhairon and the same was carried home by the devotees as it was considered very efficacious in diseases. Tonsure rites were openly performed in the parikarma.[7]

The moral character of some of the priests was most shocking. Some of them often came drunk to the shrine. Some of them were seen sitting before the Holy Guru Granth Sahib with quails in their hands. Besides shaving, they snuffed tobacco and consumed *Kutha* (meat of animals slaughtered as prescribed by Islamic law). There was no limit to theft. Incidents of kidnapping the children of the devotees were common. Purses of the devotees were lost while paying obeisance to Guru Granth Sahib. No one could dare to complain. If any one opposed, he/she was pushed out of the shrine and threatened with dire consequences. Penniless devotees had to borrow money to return to their destination.[8]

No woman's honour was safe; mockery with women and passing of obscene remarks to young girls was a routine. One younger daughter of Bhai Sant Singh was mocked at by a priest by calling her *bhabi* (sister-in-law). A priest attempted to rape a young girl of Babu Sita Ram in the shrine itself. Somehow, she managed to escape and narrated the incident to her parents. When leading citizens protested against such an in human behaviour of the priest, they were frankly told by the *pujaris* that the shrine was their shop; and they would treat the visitors as they liked. After this women of respectable families stopped visiting the shrine.[9] Above all, the pujaris divided the whole income of the shrine among themselves, while most of them were following other professions in the city. Nothing was spared for the daily devotional music service and the lightening of the *parikarma*. The condition of the shrine was as bad as that of Sri Harimandir Sahib, Amritsar before it was liberated from the *pujaris*.[10]

However, with the establishment of Singh Sabha Tarn Taran in 1885 A.D. a systematic campaign was launched by the reformists to restore pristine Sikh practices. They were backed by several organizations and individuals.[11] To eradicate aforesaid pernicious practices, they used all possible means; platform, press and petitions. All the malignances were brought into the notice of the Government officials as well as the *sarbrah*. Also, they started holding weekly and annual *Diwans* (religious congregations) in the *parikarma* near the shrine, where Sikh doctrines were preached. Dismayed by this move, the *pujaris* approached the *sarbrah*. With his connivance, the Deputy Commissioner of Amritsar, banned holding of *Diwans* by the Reformists in the parikarma.[12]

Elated with this success, the *pujaris* became more arrogant in their behaviour. Bhisop Gilford was allowed to preach gospel in the *parikarma*, near *Bunga Majhbian*, on the day of every *amavas*. A Ramgarhia Sikh was not allowed to pay his respects on the pretext that he had been rebaptised by Bhai Sant Singh, the secretary of Tarn Taran Singh Sabha. *Karhaparsad* (sacred food) offered by Bhai Aya Singh Nihang was not accepted by the *pujaris* on the plea that he had been baptizing women. The members of the Singh Sabha were not allowed to recite *Assa di Var* in the shrine. In 1911 A.D. Son of Bhai Sant Singh was murdered. His dead body was found in the sacred tank after six days. When towards the end of 1920 A.D., S. Lachman Singh Dharowali came with the girls of his school to pay his respects at Tarn Taran, the *pujaris* prevented the girls from singing hymns in the shrine and drove them out as they belonged to the Singh Sabha.[13]

On 11th January, 1921, *the Khalsa Sewak Jatha* of Tarn Taran was not allowed to perform *Kirtan* in the shrine. Other bodies of reformists were similarly treated.[14]

Such was the condition of the Shrine of Tarn Taran when, the Shiromani Gurdwara Parbandhak Committee was formed on 15th November, 1920 A.D. By that time control of several shrines including Sri Harimandir Sahib and Sri Akal Takhat had been wrested by the Akalis. Seeing the fate of these Gurdwaras, the *pujaris* of Tarn Taran instead of reforming themselves approached Mr. C.M. King, the Commissioner of Lahore on 18th December, 1920 A.D. and sought his favour against the impending encounter with the Akalis. Mr. King who inspite of his long experience of this distinct and probable knowledge of the doing of these *pujaris*, instead of telling them to realize the true significance of this movement of reform told them that if need be they might apply to the Almighty *Sarkar* for support.[15] Bhai Mohan Singh Vaid, a highly respectable leader of Tarn Taran, wrote to Mr. King on 3rd January and asked him to publicly contradict these rumours, which were detrimental to public peace. No reply was ever vouchsafed to Bhai Mohan Singh, not even an acknowledgement.[16] However, encouraged by the assurance of the Commissioner, the priests of Tarn Taran assumed a very truculent attitude towards the panth. They started making arrangement to teach a lesson to the Akalis, if they ever come to the shrine. Professional ruffians were hired. Each one of them was to receive rupee two daily along with a quota of liquor as much as one could consume. Weapons like axes, chopper, hatchet, clubs etc. were collected and deposited in a big box in the treasury room. Even manufacturers of fireworks were asked to supply explosive balls.[17]

On 24th January 1921, while members of the Shiromani Gurdwara Parbandhak Committee were deliberating on the third floor of Sri Akal Takhat, wife of Bhai Sant Singh of Tarn Taran stood up from the Diwan in front of Sri Akal Takhat. She related the suffering of her family; they had undergone at the hands of the priests of Tarn Taran. She said, her son had been thrown into the sacred tank with stones tied around his neck. Her daughter had been harassed in the shrine. She also described how a Hindu girl had been kissed within the holy of the Holies. How devotees particularly the Akalis were insulted. Several other examples of missconduct of the *pujaris* were cited.[18] She implored the leaders of the *Panth* to take suitable action against the wrongdoers as early as possible. Her speech created a great sensation in the audience. Eventually, the jathedar then and there addressed prayer to the Almighty, asking for guidance as how to reform the shrine. The decision was conveyed to the leaders of other organization they were asked to reach Amritsar on 25th January. However, 40 of them assembled at Manji Sahib on 26th January at 4 A.M. They took ablution in the Holy Tank and under the leadership of Bhai Teja Singh Bhuchar proceeded to Tarn Taran by the morning train. They reached Tarn Taran at about 6 A.M. First they stopped at Bunga Bhuchran where 30 more Akalis belonging to other organizations joined them. All the 70 offered prayer to the Almighty for the success in their mission.[19] However, they entered the precinct of the shrine around 8 A.M. The morning service was still going on. After paying respects to the holy Guru Granth Sahib, they sat to listen to the devotional music. As they had been premonished about the accumulation of weapons in a treasury room, six of them were posted to guard the room, while each door of the shrine was guarded by two Akalis. To prevent the incoming of mischievous priests some Akalis took positions in the *Darshani Deori*. Seeing some excitement among the priests, the leader of the jatha tried to allay their fears by telling them, that the jatha, had come not to disturb their possession but to induce them to remove the public grievances amiably.[20]

However, after the morning service was over, the youthful among the priest, tried to provoke a fight by abusing and attacking the Akalis. But the latter kept quite. The older priests among whom were Bhai Nihal Singh and Gurbaksh Singh, spoke calmly, welcoming the Akalis and promised to do their best to bring about a peaceful settlement. In fact, the priests wanted to gain time to inform their supporters in the city and in the adjoining villages. Eventually, it was mutually agreed to meet in a small conference at 4 P.M. The priests named their rcspresentatives : Bhai Nihal Singh, Gurbaksh Singh, Gurdit

Singh, Sewa Singh, Sunder Singh and Teja Singh. The Akali Jatha nominated Jathedar Teja Singh Bhuchar, S. Balwant Singh of Kulla, S. Dan Singh Vachova, S. Kartar Singh Jhabar and Hakim Bahadur Singh. The following citizens of Tarn Taran and its neighbourhood were also asked to participate in the conference—Bhai Mohan Singh Vaid, Sant Singh, Mehtab Singh Headmaster, Master Ishar Singh, S. Bishan Singh, S. Sunder Singh Karkhanewale, S. Bishan Singh Lambardar, Bhai Jassa Singh, Gian Singh Mandiwala, S. Dharm Singh Ries of Usma and some other respectable persons from Amritsar.[21]

The *pujaris* in the meantime sent their men to the neighbouring villages to call their supporters and themselves began to make secret arrangement for attacking the Akalis. Amongst other things, they ordered a manufacturer of fireworks to supply explosive balls.[22] The Akalis too sent their men to inform the Sikh *sangat* in the surrounding villages.[23]

In the meanwhile the Sikh resident had brought articles of food for the jatha. They dispersed to different *Bungas* and other places in the vicinity to cook their food and take rest.[24] Around 2 P.M. Jathas of Sikh *sangat*, chanting hymns, started coming to the shrine from adjoining villages. *Langar* (free kitchen) was opened and *Diwan* was organized in front of the shrine.[25]

At 4 P.M. the representative of both the parties met in *Bunga Dhotian* and the following five conditions were laid before the pujaris for their acceptance :

1. That the management of the shrine of Tarn Taran be carried on according to the rules laid down by the Shromani Gurdwara Parbandhak Committee;
2. That a provisional local committee affiliated to the Shiromani Committee be formed to supervise the management;
3. That all the existing defects be removed and in future no chance of any complaint be given to the panth.

4. That all those among the priests who have broken the religious law would accept any punishment imposed by the sangat, and
5. That only those be appointed *granthis* who conform strictly to the rules of baptism.[26]

By 5.30 P.M. the representative of the priests agreed to these demands. But they proposed to inform about their confirmation by 10 A.M. on 27th January, as they wanted to consult other fellows whose number according to them was 300.[27] They went into the shrine and members of the jatha came to join the Diwan. While Bhai Kartar Singh Jhabbar exhorted the Sikh *sangat* to give time to the priests, Sardar Dan Singh pointed out that certain rough men were collecting in Gurdit Singh *pujari's* building adjoining the Jhanda Bunga. On the left of the main entrance, two women were going up and down repeatedly with lamp and seemed to be storing something in the upper storey. The gas lamp in front of the shrine also began to grow dim for want of oil. The jathedar gave instructions to all Sikhs present to remain firm and not to retaliate under any circumstances.[28]

At about 8.30 P.M. two *pujaris*, Teja Singh granthi and Gurbaksh Singh *granthi* came to the *Diwan* and announced that all had agreed to accept the terms of reform and asked S. Dan Singh and S. Kartar Singh to bring a fair copy of the document to be signed by the *pujaris* who were sitting in the shrine. Their number at that time was 70. At this S. Dan Singh said that the appearances were suspicious and that they should come out.[29] But the representatives laughed at the suspicion as baseless, and said that as all the priests were collected inside, their signature could be taken at once. However, Bhai Mohan Singh was sent out to copy out the terms of the agreement; and he informed of it to the Tehsildar, the Circle Inspector and other Government officials who were present outside the main gate of the shrine.[30]

The representatives of the *pujaris*, in the meanwhile, had agreed that the priest who performed the duty of *granthi* was by character unfit for the post, and that, until a better man was appointed in his place, Bhai Saran Singh of the jatha should be allowed to perform the service. Accordingly, Bhai Saran Singh accompanied by S. Balwant Singh of Kulla went into the shrine which was full of *pujaris* and their hench men. Many more Akalis followed them. A moment later, as Bhai Bahadur Singh Hakim was addressing the *Diwan* outside, an explosive ball burst near him. Then four or five more balls fell and burst in different places among the audience, wounding several with the small pieces of iron and nails. These balls and bricks fell from the roofs of Gurdit Singh *pujari's* house and other *bungas* close to it.[31] It was a signal for the beginning of an attack on the Akalis who had gone inside.

Inside the shrine, when the recitation of *Rehras* was over, as agreed earlier, Bhai Saran Singh wished to perform service but the *granthi* incharge refused. When Sardar Balwant Singh was bowing his head before Guru Granth Sahib, a blow fell upon him and his arm was almost severed from his shoulder. Bhai Hazara Singh of Aldinpur who bowed next, received a mortal wound in the belly and fell prostrate on the ground. As he was receiving blow after blow he was heard to say, "Brothers, you may kill me; I will not attack brother." Bhai Hukam Singh of Vasaukot got four *chhavi* blows on his head. Bhai Tota Singh Peshawari got six inches cut on his arm, inspite of his wearing an overcoat. Others who got badly hurt were Bhai Gurbaksh Singh, Labh Singh, Bela Singh and Ishar Singh. The whole attack lasted only for few minutes and in all about 17 members of the Jatha were wounded.[32]

The *pujaris* had thrown down the door screens and had blown out the lamp before commencing attack. Due to the confusion caused by the explosion outside nothing was known to the people in the *Diwan* about the tragedy until the wounded Akalis tottered out and hastily told the tale of the calamity. The jathedar ordered all the outlets to be guarded at once. When the horrified Sikhs entered the shrine they found the sacred place full of blood and two of their men lying on the ground. The *pujaris* were drunk and looked wild. Many of them had already fled, some swimming away across the tank. The remaining were caught and bound down with their own scarfs or turbans. After a few minutes it was considered wiser to let them off. They went away on their own legs. The Akalis admitted the wounded to the hospital, where they were attended by Dr. Sunder Singh and Dr. Harnam Singh. The Tehsildar and the Police Inspector came at about 10 P.M. and went into the shrine to see what had happened. The Naib-Tehsildar asked the *pujaris* if anybody belonging to their party had been wounded. But none complained of any injuries received. However, on 27th January, on the advice of the police the priests brought 13 men on *charpais* as wounded to the hospital. Most of them had blue marks, which could have been got by tying wet cloth round the spots.[33]

The blood stained shrine was washed and cleaned by the Sikhs on the 27th of early morning. Countless tears mingled with the water used to remove the blood. The usual morning service was held and pristine Sikh traditions were restored; Langar was opened to provide food to all visitors irrespective of caste colour or creed.[34] A provisional local committee of 15 members was formed to control the affairs of the shrine until the Shiromani Gurudwara Parbandhak Committee made another arrangement.

The district Magistrate and the Superintendent of Police came from Amritsar and interviewed the leaders of both the parties. They expressed their sympathy with the Akalis for their sufferings and asked them to file suits against the *pujaris* for attacking and wounding them. However, the reply of the Akali leader's was typical, 'we have yet to reform many Gurdwaras and might suffer the same fate everywhere. Instead of taking cases from us give us our temples.'[35]

Bhai Hazara Singh who had been severely wounded succumbed to his injuries on 27th in the afternoon. His funeral took place at 2 P.M. on 28th. It was attended by

20,000 men and women from far and near including several journalists from Amritsar and Tarn Taran. Almost all the villagers of Aldinpur came with the martyr's mother, who felt proud of her son and blessed him. The people, too, who formed a long procession, showed a remarkably calm and orderly spirit. They walked in regular rows, which the Government called military formation', and chanted hymns of praise and thanks giving. No course, not even a bitter word was uttered at the insensate cruelty of the priests. In a truly prayerful mood the loss was taken as a pure sacrifice.[36]

Hence, it was the first test of the Akalis to remain non-violent in the cause of the Gurdwara Reform in which two Sikhs sacrificed their lives and became the first martyrs of the Gurdwara Reform Movement.[37] The non-violent means adopted by the Akalis in resisting the might of the Imperialists as well as the use of force by the priests was not in accordance with the Gandhian principle of non-violence as most of the historians of Gurdwara Reform Movement assert. Here the inspiration came from the Sikh Gurus : Guru Arjan Dev and Guru Teg Bahadur and the great Sikh martyrs of eighteenth century. All of them had shown marvellous endurance against State repression. However, by refusing to sue the priests in the courts, the Akalis were following the idea of non-co-operation in the true spirit of the Movement.

REFERENCES

1. Teja Singh, *The Gurdwara Reform Movement and The Sikh Awakening, Sikh Itihas Research Board (SGPC)*, Amritsar, 2002. (First 1922), p. 132; Bhai Thakar Singh Giani, *Sri Gurdware Darshan*, Bhai Labh Singh & Sons, Amritsar, 1923, p. 121; Jagjit Singh, *Itihas Sri Tarn Taran Sahib*, Tarn Taran, 1931, p. 14; *Phulwari. Lahore, Gurdwara Sri Tarn Taran Number*, April-May, 1933, p. 488; Tarn Taran Ik Sarvekhan, Kanwal Parkashan, Tarn Taran, 1981, p. 12.

2. Bhai Thakar Singh, *ibid.*, 123; *The Phulwari*; 491; *Tarn Taran Ik Sarvekhan*, 13.

3. The *amavas* of *Bhadon* used to be celebrated in commemoration of the foundation of the *Sarovar* and the city while the *amavas* of *Chetra* was celebrated to commemorate the event when in 1596 Guru Arjan Dev started making sacred tank *Pacca*; Thakar Singh, *ibid.*, pp. 121-123; The *Phulwari*, pp. 488-89; Jagjit Singth, *ibid.*, pp. 14,15, 17; *Tarn Taran Ik Sarvekhan*, 12-13.
4. *Phulwari*, pp. 493-94; Jagjit Singh, *ibid.*, p. 17; *Tarn Taran Ik Sarvekhan*, 14.
5. Principal Santokh Singh, *Central Khalsa Maja Diwan*, Bhai Chattar Singh Jiwan Singh, Amritsar, 2006, p. 43.
6. *Phulwari*, 50708; *Tarn Taran Ik Sarvekhan*, pp. 17-18; Santokh Singh, *ibid.*, pp. 43-44.
7. Bhai Mohan Singh Vaid, *Aduti Saka*, Panth Sevak Press, Amritsar nd., p. 9; *Tarn Taran Ik Sarvekhan*, pp. 17-18; *Panth Sewak*, 2 Feb., 1921, p.41.
8. Teja Singh, *ibid.*, p. 132; Mohan Singh Vaid, *ibid.*, pp. 8-9.
9. *Phulwari*, 509, 527-28, Teja Singh, *ibid.*, 133; *Tarn Taran Ik Sarvekhan*. p. 18; Mohan Singh Vaid, *ibid.*, p. 8; *Panth Sewak*, *ibid.*, p. 1.
10. Teja Singh, *ibid.*, p. 132; Mohan Singh Vaid, *Loc cit*; *The Phulwari*, p. 508.
11. Apart from the Singh Sabha Tarn Taran, *Khalsa Diwan Majha*, *Chief Khalsa Diwan*, *Khalsa Parcharak Vidiyala*, *Central Khalsa Diwan Majha*, Mata Bathanwale and Mata Ram Karu Chajjalwadi etc. used to send their preachers at Tarn Taran on the day of every *amavas* to peach Sikhism, *Phulwari*, pp. 507, 509-10.
12. *Ibid.*, p. 508.
13. *Ibid.*, pp. 508-9; Teja Singh, *ibid.*, pp. 132-33.
14. Teja Singh, *ibid.*, p. 133; *Phulwari*, p. 528; Mohan Singh Vaid, *ibid.*, p. 8.
15. Punjab Darpan, Weekly from Amritsar, 20 Jan., 1921, p. 4; Teja Singh, *ibid.*, p. 133; *Phulwari*, p. 527.
16. Teja Singh, *Loc cit.*, *Phulwari*, *Loc. cit.*;
17. *Punjab Darpan*, 27th Jan., 1921, p. 5; *Phulwari*, p. 528; Teja Singh, *ibid.*, p. 134.

18. Teja Singh, *ibid.*, p. 133; *Phulwari*, pp. 527-28.
19. 15-16 men belonged to *Khalsa Diwan Dhuri* and equal number belonged to the jatha of S. Lahora Singh Thether Ke, while the rest of them belonged to *Akali Dal Khara Sauda and Central Khalsa Diwan Majha.*
20. Teja Singh, *loc cit*; *Phulwari*, p. 529.
21. Teja Singh, *loc cit*; Phulwari, pp. 529, 530-31; Mohan Singh Vaid, *ibid.*, pp. 5-6, 12.
22. Teja Singh, *loc cit*; Mohan Singh Vaid, *ibid.*, pp. 6-7.
23. Mohan Singh Vaid, *ibid.*, p. 7; *Phulwari,* p. 530.
24. Teja Singh, *loc cit*; Phulwari, *loc cit*; Mohan Singh Vaid, *ibid.*, p. 6.
25. Mohan Singh Vaid, *ibid.*, p. 7; The *Phulwari; loc cit.*
26. Mohan Singh Vaid, *ibid.*, pp. 12-13; *Phulwari,* p. 531-32.
27. Teja Singh, *loc cit*; Mohan Singh Vaid, *ibid.*, pp. 13-15, *Phulwari*, p. 532.
28. Mohan Singh Vaid, *ibid.*, pp. 15-17; Teja Singh, *ibid.*, p. 135; *Phulwari,* pp. 532-33.
29. *Phulwari*, pp. 533-34; Mohan Singh Vaid, *ibid.*, p. 17; Teja Singh, *ibid.*, pp. 35-36,
30. Mohan Singh Vaid, *ibid.*, p. 17-18; *Phulwari*, pp. 533-34; Teja Singh, *ibid.*, pp. 135-36.
31. Teja Singh, *ibid.*, p. 136; *Phulwari,* 533-35; Mohan Singh Vaid, *Ibid.*, p. 19.
32. Mohan Singh Vaid, *ibid.*, pp. 20-21; *Phulwari*, pp. 535-36; Teja Singh, *op. cit*; *Panjab Darpan*, 27 Jan., 1921, pp. 4-5.
33. Teja Singh, *ibid.*, p. 137; Mohan Singh Vaid, *ibid.*, pp. 20-21; *Punjab Darpan,* 27 Jan. 1921, p. 5.
34. The following were the members of the Local Committee :
    1. S. Balwant Singh Ries of Kulla, President.
    2. S. Dharam Singh Ries of Usma, Vice-President.
    3. Bhai Mohan Singh Vaid, Tarn Taran, Secretary.
    4. S. Mehtab Singh (Head Master), Joint Secretary.
    5. S. Bishan Singh, Nambardar.
    6. S. Sunder Singh, Karkhanewale.

7. S. Sant Singh Ashtam Farosh.
8. S. Amar Singh Ries of Jabhal.
9. S. Teja Singh Bhuchar.
10. S. Kishan Singh Bhuchar.
11. S. Hazara Singh Jama Rai.
12. S. Hamam Singh Naushehra.
13. S. Teja Singh Pandori.
14. Baba Kehar Singh Patti.
15. S. Teja Singh Samundri.

Phulwari, pp. 536,39-40; Mohan Singh Vaid, *ibid.*, pp. 22 & 27; Teja Singh, *ibid.*, p. 139.

35. *Phulwari*, pp. 537-38; Mohan Singh Vaid, *ibid.*, pp. 23-24; Teja Singh, *ibid.*, p. 138.
36. Teja Singh, *ibid.*, p. 138; Mohan Singh Vaid, *ibid.*, pp. 25,28; *Phulwari*, pp. 538-39; *Panth Sewak*, *ibid.*, p. 2.
37. Bhai Hukam Singh Vasankot Succumbed to his injuries on 4th February, 1921, Teja Singh, *ibid.*, p. 137; *Phulwari*, p. 539.

15

The First Martyr of Gurdwara Reform Movement

Born in 1888, Bhai Hazara Singh belonged to village Aldinpur, situated about three Kilometers South of the city of Tarn Taran His parents: Mother Gulab Kaur and Father Sardar Deva Singh were pious and well off. Sardar Deva Singh was a descendant of Sardar Bhagel Singh of Karorsinghia Misal. However, Sardar Deva Singh died when Bhai Hazara was only nine year old. Later on, Bahi Hazara Singh's Younger brother Tara Singh too died at the age of ten. Thus, he was left alone to inherent his father's property which was one hundred and sixty bighas of cultivable land.[1]

At the age of 18, he was married at village Bhagrain. He had two sons. Though his wife died at young age, he never thought of second marriage. Like an ideal Sikh, his daily routine invariably started with prayer to the Almighty. Whenever he learnt about the demise of his near relative, instead of mourning, he used to meditate and always accepted it as the will of God.[2]

He was lean, lame, middle-sized man. His beard was straight. His words had have a magical effect on the audience. By nature, he was straight forward, brave, generous and always cheerful. His generosity was a model of its kind. He has given his entire land to the tenants but was never present at the time of harvest. The tenants paid his share of crops at their will. Even then, if any one of them expressed inability to pay his dues, he was exempted.[3]

He appears to be fairly educated, according to the standard of the times. For instance, in his early youth he learnt Gurmukhi alphabet from Bhai Sant Singh and Bhagat Singh and started reciting Guru Granth Sahib. When he grew to manhood, he learnt Hindi along with some treatise on ayurvedic. He evinced more interest in reading religious and historical literature rather than in worldly affairs. In fact, he had an extremely religious bent of mind. Besides giving *dasvand* (one tenth of the income) to the village Gurudwara from his annual income, he used to run Langar (free kitchen) and perform *Akhand Path* (non-stop-recitation of the bani of Guru Granth) several times in a year from the remaining amount.[4]

He was an ardent preacher of Sikhism. Himself a good player of *Taus* (a type of string instrument), he used to perform *kirtan* (devotional singing in praise of Almighty). He was a good expositor of Guru Granth Sahib. In the evening, he used to give religious discourses to his villagers at his own house, particularly, the exposition of *Panth Parkash*.[5] The villagers of Aldinpur did not like the lifestyle of the village *Granthi* (reciter of scripture). Consequently, they stopped inviting him to perform *Akhandpath*. Bhai Hazara Singh viewed it as a lack of preaching of *Gurbani* and took this responsibility to himself. What ever he received for the performance of Akhandpath and with his own funds, he donated several copies of Guru Granth Sahib, a large wooden bench, several costly canopies and rum alas etc., to the village Gurdwara. Above all, he created a permanent fund for the Gurdwara.[6]

He also started celebrating all the *Gurparbs* (anniversaries of Sikh Gurus) at his village. On all these occasions, he used to lead religious processions. Musicians and preachers were called to preach Sikhism. Thus the impact of his activities was such that many people even at the age of sixty took the Pahul of the dubble edge sword and came into the fold of Sikhism. His objective was that no child in the village of Aldinpur above the age of twelve should remain without taking the pahul.[7]

Much before the formation of Shromani Gurdwara Parbandhak Committee and the Akali Dal, he was an active reformist. For example, Bhagat Singh, the Mahant of the Gurdwara of Aldinpar, had appropriated the entire land of the Gurdwara. Through Bhai Hazara Singh persuasion, the Mahant agreed to give Rs. 250 annually to the sangat of the village to be spent for religious activities. However, when the Akalis took possession of Sri Harimandir Sahib Amritsar and Sri Akal Takht, since then Bhai Hazara Singh was in touch with the Jathedar of Sri Akal Takht and was ever ready to obey the order of the Jathedar and of the Akali Dal.[8]

On 26th January 1921, a *Jatha* of reformists Akalis under the leadership of Teja Singh Bhuchar reached Tarn Taran to pursuade the pujaris of the shrine of Tarn Taran to alleviate the grievances of the Sikh Masses. They entered the precint of the shrine around 8 a.m. After paying respects to the Holy Guru Granth Sahib, they sat to listen to the sacred music. Seeing some excitement among the priests, the leader of the Jatha tried to allay their fears by telling them, that the Jatha had come not to disturb their possession but to induce them amicably to remove the public grievances. But youthful among the priests, tried to provoke a fight by abusing and attacking the Akalis, while the latter kept quiet. However, the older priests spoke calmly, welcoming the objective of the Akalis' visit and promised to do their best to bring about peaceful settlement. Eventually, it was mutually agreed to meet in a small conference at 4 p.m.[9]

Bhai Hazara Singh was taking meal when he learnt that Akali Dal had come to liberate the Shrine of Tarn Taran. He quickly got up from the cot, threw away his food to a dog and hurriedly left his house. When his sister asked him to take some milk if he was in too hurry to take meal, he answered, 'If I could not achieve martyrdom, then I'll-definitely take.' The villagers never saw him in such a high spirit ever before. They asked him 'Jathedar ji, why are you so happy to day and where are you going so hastily? He answered, ' To day bounty of martyrdom is going to be showered. Those who wished to have their share, come along with me.' However, a good number of Sikh Sangat of his village followed him.[10]

Around 2 p.m., they joined the Diwan being held by the Akali Dal near Jhanda Bungha the parkarma of the shrine. On the other hand representative of both the parties continued to discuss the terms and conditions to be agreed, and by late evening, the representative of the *pujaris* had agreed that the priest who performed the work of *granthi* was by character unfit for the post and until a batter man was appointed in his place, Bhai Saran Singh of the Jatha should be allowed to perform the service. Accordingly, Bhai Saran Singh, accompained by Sardar Balwant Singh of Kulla, Bhai Hazara Singh, Bhai Hukam Singh and many more went into the shrine which was full of pujaris and their hired men. They were all drunk. However, when Bhai Saran Singh wished to perform service, the Granthi in charge refused. At the same time a hacket struck Sardar Balwant Singh who was bowing his head before Guru Granth Sahib. Bhai Hazara Singh who bowed next received a mortal wound and fell prostrate on the ground. As he was receiving blow after blow he was heard to say : "Brothers, you may kill me; I will not attack brother". However, the whole attack lasted only few minutes, and in all about 17 members of the Jama were wounded[11]. They were admitted to the hospital where they were attended by Dr. Sunder Singh and Dr. Harnam Singh[12].

Although, Bhai Hazara Singh got 10 inches long and 9 inches deep cut yet he was in high spirit. Bhai Asa Singh and Chanan Ram stayed to look after him while rest of the sangat of his village returned around midnight. When his son Bhai Kishan Singh came and saw him in serious condition tears flew from his eyes. Bhai Hazara Singh while patting him said, "Keep up the spirit, Singh's Children never act like this. Pray for me that I should soon achieve grace of Guru's feet". These were his last words and he succumbed to his injuries in the afternoon on 27th January, 1921[13].

His funeral took place at 2 P.M. on 28th. It was attended by thousands from far and near including several journalists from Amritsar and Tarn Taran.[14] Almost all the villagers of Aldinpur came along with the Martyr's mother, who felt proud of her son and said, 'To day I am the most blessed and the most successful woman of the world whose son has sacrificed his life for the Sikh cause.' The people too, who formed a long procession, showed remarkable calm and orderly spirit. They walked in regular rows, which the Government calls "Military formation", and chanted hymns of praise and thanks giving. There was not a course, not a bitter word uttered at the insensate cruelty of the priest. In a truly prayful mood the loss was taken as a pure sacrifice.[15] However, a Diwan was organized at the cremation ground. Prominent leaders paid homage to the martyr, illuminating his dedication for the Sikh cause. According to them his life was full of zeal, virtue, kindness, service, religious devotion, meditation, generosity, modesty etc. they also proposed to build a suitable memorial, which of course has yet not been built.[16]

REFERENCES

1. Visakha Singh, *Malwa Itihas*, Gurmat Parcharak Sabha, Ferozpur, 3 vols., n.d., vol. II, p. 525; *The Phulwari: Gurdwara Tarn Taran Number*, April-May, Lahore, 1933 p. 617.
2. *The Phulwari*, 617, 618, 619, Visakha Singh, *ibid.*, 525-26.
3. *The Phulwari*, 619.
4. Visakha Singh, *ibid.*, 525; *The Phulwari,* 617-18.
5. Visakha Singh, *op cit.*, 525; *The Phulwari,* 618.
6. *The Phulwari*, *op. cit.*
7. Visakha Singh, *ibid.*, 525-26; *The Phulwari; op.cit.*
8. *The Phulwari*, 619.
9. Teja Singh, *Gurdwara Reform Movement and the Sikh Awakening*, Sikh Itihas Research Board (SGPC), Amritsar,

2002, (first 1922). P. 134; K.S. Bajwa (ed.) *Akali Dal Scha Sauda Bar*. Sikh Itihas Research Board, Amritsar, 2002, p. 66; Bhai Mohan Singh Vaid, *Aduti Saka,* Panth Sevak Press, Amritsar n.d. 5-6, 12; *The Phulwari*, 528-29.

10. *The Phulwari, op. cit.,* Visakha Singh, *ibid.*, 526.
11. Teja Singh, *ibid.*, 136; *The Phulwari* 533-36; Mohan Singh Vaid, *ibid*, 19,20-21; K.S. Bawja, *op. cit., Punjab Darpan, Weekly* Amritsar, 27 Jan. 1921, 4-5.
12. Teja Singh, *ibid.*, 137; Mohan Singh Vaid, *ibid.*, 20-21, *Punjab Darpan*, 27 Jan. 1921, 5.
13. The Phulwari, 538 & 620; Teja Singh, *ibid.,* 138; Visakha Singh, *ibid.*, 527.
14. According to one estimate nearly 20,000 people attended this funeral; *The Panth Sewak*, Amritsar, 2 Feb., 1921, p.2.
15. *The Phulwari,* 538-39; Mohan Singh Vaid, *ibid.,* 25,28; Teja Singh, *ibid.*, 138.
16. *The Phulwari*, 539,620; Visakha Singh, *op. cit.*

16

Gurdwara Shahidganj Lahore (1764–1936)

History of the Sikhs is replete with references to Shahidganj which literally mean 'heap or store house of martyrs'[1]. Actually these places symbolize the seat of repression let loose on the Sikhs by the Mughal officials during the eighteenth century and the legendary gallantry with which the Sikhs resisted the state tyranny. The present paper aims at tracing the origin, development and dispute over the site of the Shahidganj Lahore, between the Muslims and the Sikhs with reference to the role played by the British Indian Government.

All known sources confirm that around fifties of the eighteenth century Muyun-ul-Mulk (Mir Mannu), the Governor of Lahore (1748-1753), got constructed a mosque shape building at Lahore in the Landa Bazar at *Chauk Nakhas* (Horse Market) outside the Delhi Gate. This a site became an abattior where hundred thousands Sikhs; men, women and children were mercilessly executed with the orders of the Mughal officials. Such a horrible persecution and wholesale massacre continued, unceasingly, nearly four decades at this very site.[2] Minars and pyramids of heads of those beheaded here were raised and their headless bodies were at first piled up in large heaps and then burried in this place. Subsequently, a mosque like building was built up by the power-flushed and ever zealous Mohammedan rulers who considered it a meritorius act to raise a mosque over the dead bodies of the *Kafirs* as the Muslim rulers considered the Sikhs to be. However, for the Sikhs, structure raised on the bones of the Sikh martyrs came to be known as Shahidganj (treasure-troves of martyrdom.[3]

When the Bhangi chiefs, Lehna Singh, Gujar Singh and Sobha Singh, occupied Lahore in 1764, they converted this structure into a *dharamsala* and named it *Shahidganj*. It was divided into three portions. The central chamber was used as gurdwara proper, where Guru Granth Sahib, the holy scripture of the Sikhs, was installed and recited. The southern portion was set apart for *guru ka langar* (free kitchen) and northern portion served as a storehouse. A portion of the *hamam* was used as *sukhe-di-deg* and *shabeel* from where *bang* and water were freely distributed to all devotees and travellers alike.[4] Two more memorials; *Shahidganj Singhanian* and Bhai Taru Singh, were raised by the Bhangi Sardars in the compound of Shahidganj area.[5] All the three shrines were placed in the charge of Bhai Jagga Singh. For the upkeeps and maintenance of these shrines, a gift of fifteen *bighas* of land of the *Nakhas*, with five wells, was made by the Sardars. When Maharaja Ranjit Singh occupied Lahore in 1799, he not only confirmed the gift of land made by the Bhangi Sardars but also made additional grants of land in the districts of Lahore and Amritsar. It was not withdrawn by his sons and successors.[6] The British Government too confirmed the *jagir* of Rs. 1800 per annum in the name of Bhai Jiwan Singh, son and successor of Bhai Jagga Singh, for the expenses of *Shahidganj* during his life time, to be reduced after his death to Rs., 150 per annum as 'perpetually *Muaf*' on paying one-fourth of its *Nazrana* into the Government treasury.[7]

However, encouraged by the change of the rulers, one Nur Ahmed, son of Allah Jawaya, resident of Lahore filed a criminal case on 17th April 1850 A.D. against Bhai Jiwan Singh and Ganda Singh, in the court of Major George

M'Gregor, Deputy Commissioner of Lahore. He claimed the so-called *Shahidganj* mosque and the land attached to it. Not convinced with the genuineness of the claim, the Deputy Commissioner on 1st May, 1850 A.D. ordered that 'the mosque could not be released'. An appeal was filed by the plaintiff against this judgement in the court of Commissioner Lahore Division. In this judgement on 29th June, 1850 A.D., the Commissioner up held the order of the District Court. However, the plaintiff on 18th January 1853 A.D. filed a regular civil suit which, in the wake of previous orders, was dismissed with costs on 2nd Feb, 1853 A.D.[8]

Not dismayed by these decisions, Nur Ahmed, on 26th September 1853 A.D., filed another case against Bhai Jiwan Singh, claiming 'three *canals* and fifteen *marlas* of site under Mosque', in the court of Mirza Kalab Abid Khan, Extra Assistant Commissioner, Lahore. Not only this, hoping that his correligionist officer might grant the decree in his favour, he, on 14th January, 1854 A.D. submitted an other application in the same court claiming 'thirteen bighas of cultivated land of *Muafi* estate, with a well, Mosque etc. However, Mirza Kalab Abid Khan in his order of 11th Dec. 1854 A.D. expressed his inability to award him the said property 'merely on the strength of the documents which are in his possession'.[9] An appeal in the court of Sir Henery Davis, the then settlement officer, was made on 25th February, 1854 A.D. It was dismissed. On 23rd June, 1855 A.D. then Nur Ahmed again filed a fresh case in the court of new Deputy Commissioner Mr. Robert Simon against Ganda Singh and his father Jiwan Singh with a new story.[10] Mr. Robert Simon heard the case in several sittings from June to November 1855 A.D. After examining the records and withnesses of both the parties, he dismissed the petition on 14th November 1855 A.D.[11]

This was the last- case of Nur Ahmed. Next three decades passed comparatively uneventful, except one suit filed by one Mehar Shah, Imam of a Mosque at Texali Gate Lahore, in April 1883 A.D. He submitted to the Lt. Governor Punjab that the Mosque of *Shahidganj* should be made over to the Mohammedans.[12] The Lt. Governor forwarded the petition to the Commissioner, Lahore Division, who in turn, sent it to the Deputy Commissioner, Lahore. Consequently, Sayyad Alam Shah, Extra Assistant Commissioner, Lahore was appointed to report the circumstances of the building. He examined the building on 10th July 1883 A.D. and on the 11th submitted a very lengthy report, explaining the history and current position of the building in regard to its possession. On the basis of this report, the Deputy Commissioner of Lahore, acknowledged the right of the Sikhs and dismissed the claim of Imam Mehar Shah.[13]

With the passage of the Sikh Gurdwara Act (1923) the *Shahidganj* Lahore was declared a scheduled Sikh Gurdwara as per Government notification No. 892 of 28th April, 1926 A.D. Accordingly its management was restored to the Local Gurdwara Parbandhak Committee Lahore. A consolidated list of properties belonging to the Gurdwara was published with the Punjab Government notification No. 275-G of 22nd December, 1927 A.D.[14] However, the then Mahant of *Sahidganj*, Bhai Harnam Singh was not willing to transfer the property attached to it. Consequently, a protracted litigation ensued, in the court of the Sikh Gurdwara Tribunal, between four parties, the Mahant, the Local Gurdwara Parbandhak Committee the *Anjuman-i-Islamia*, a Muslim Association of Lahore and Nazam Din and Feroze Din. The former three put forward their claims regarding the ownership of the properties attached to the *Shahidganj* whereas the latter two individuals claimed only a small area of the grave together with a right of passage from the southern road to the grave.[15] Mr. Justice Hilton, the President of the Sikh Gurdwara Tribunal, after examining the documents and evidences of all the parties, dismissed the petitions of Bhai Harnam Singh and Anjuman-i-Islamia. He wrote in his judgement that, 'the learned, council for the petitioners based his argument before us on the claim that the mosque having been built as a mosque by Mir Mannu in about 1750 A.D. must always remain a mosque and that property once dedicated to *wakf* can never be lost by adverse possessions. He did not, however, cite before us any authority to support his proposition, and in my judgement there is not sufficient ground upon which we can depart from the view which was taken in the suits of 1852 and 1855 and 1883, which are relevant under section 42 of the Act. It is clear from the documents 0/23 and 0/19, to which reference has been frequently made in the judgement, that Ganda Singh and Asa Singh were in possession of this mosque and were receiving the rent which accrued from it and that they regarded it as a part of the *Gurdwara* property. In my judgement claim of the *Anjuman-i-Islamia* has no valid foundations and the mere fact that the building is shaped as a mosque does not justify as in granting them a decree. I would therefore dismiss petition No. 1282".[16] This decision was endorsed by Rai Bahadur Muna Lal, the Second Judge of the Tribunal. While dismissing Harnam Singh's and Giani Hari Singh's petition, on 20th Jan, 1930 A.D. Mr. Hilton wrote, 'on the basis of these documents, I therefore, hold on the first issue that all the properties in dispute in all these petitions belonged originally to the notified Gurdwara and that Hari Singh and Harnam Singh do not own them, nor have ever owned them, in their private capacity. It follows from this finding that the petition of Harnam Singh and Hari Singh should fail on this main point. I would hold, therefore, that their petition is liable to dismiss in toto."[17] Petition of Nizam Din and Feroze Din too was dismissed.[18] However, Bhai Harnam Singh and Hari Singh made an appeal in the High Court. It too was dismissed with costs on 19th October, 1934 A.D. and the decision of the Gurdwara Tribunal was maintained."[19]

Thus, in March 1935 A.D., the entire property attached to the Shahidganj, including mosque shaped structure was handed over to the Local Gurdwara Parbandhak Committee (L.G.P.C.), Lahore. As the building had worn down with age, being nearly one hundred eighty five years old, the (L.G.P.K.) Shahidganj Lahore, decided to demolish all the dilapidated buildings in the precincts of the Shahidganj and to build new instead. The work of general clearance of the Shahidganj compound started on 30th May, 1935 A.D. By the evening of 7th, June 1935 A.D., most of the work of general clearance had been completed. Demolishing of the dilapidated buildings in the precincts, including the Shahidganj *Dharmsala* the so called mosque, began on 8th June, 1935 A.D. The work continued for twenty days without occuring any untoward incident. However, on 29th, June, 1935 A.D., a large crowd of local Muslims, armed with sticks and hatchets, raising, cries of *Allahu-Akbar* and other communal slogans, attempted to enter into the precincts of the shrine. It was successfully defended by a few Sikhs present inside the shrine.[20] Fearing the spread of communal violence, the Deputy Commissioner of Lahore, Mr. S. Partap, ordered the Sikhs to suspend the work of demolition until the 'examination of the relevant papers concerning the gurdwara and the mosque', was made.[21] The Sikhs, in compliance with the order, desisted from the demolition of the so called mosque. But the Muslim agitators continued with their violent activities.[22] Consequently, the number of outsider Sikhs too increased as the Muslim demonstrations increased in size and violence.[23] By 5th July, 1935 A.D., the Muslim-Sikh tension took a serious turn, when a crowd of Muslims, nearly 3000 in number, armed with lathis and bricks, marched toward the *Shahidganj* from the *Badshahi Mosque*, after '*Juma*' prayers. To control the lawless and violent crowd, the police resorted to lathi charge. However, the unruly mob retaliated; stones were thrown at the police and even lathis were used against them. As a result of this collision, several of them including the city Inspector, Sub-Inspector and Head-Constable etc. were injured.[24]

Apprehending the seriousness of the situation, Sir Herbert Emerson, the then Governor of the Punjab arrived at Lahore on 6th July, 1935 A.D. Deputations of both the communities were received by His Excellency.[25] However, His efforts to arrive at an amicable settlement met with a failure. For, the Muslims would not abide by the decision of the courts of justice and the Sikhs could not reliquish their legal rights, as recognised by the Law Courts, over the building which they claimed to be sacred to the memory of their martyrs.[26]

Eventually, on 7th July, 1935 A.D., the Sikhs decided to resume the work of demolition. It began on the early hours of 8th July, 1935 A.D.[27] A Muslim crowed assembled at near by place. On hearing it the authorities decided to prevent the Muslim crowd marching towards the Sikh shrine and creating an unpleasant situation. Consequently, cordons of British troops and the police were placed on the roads leading to *Shahidganj* and traffic along these roads completely stopped'. Not only this, the Sikhs too were forbidden to visit their shrine.[28] Excitement of the Muslims manifested itself in stray assaults on both Sikhs and Hindus. The Deputy Commissioner invoked section 144 of the Criminal Procedure Code. Any one seen committing a murderous assult or arson was proclaimed to be shot dead. Furthermore, a warning was given to the editors of the *Siyasat* and the *Zamindar* against 'any attempt to instigate the Muslims against the Sikhs'.[29] As a result of these measures, by 11th, July, 1935 A.D., the situation showed signs of improvement. To facilitate Government's efforts to bring normalcy, the Shiromani Akali Dal issued telephonic instructions to various places to stop Akali *Jathas* approaching Lahore. Even, the Akali *Jathas* present in Lahore were sent out.[30] To dissuade the Muslims from their lawless behaviour, the Government decided 'to hand the Shah chirag mosque to the Muslim community, through the *Anjuman-i-Islamia*, with as little delay as possible'.[31] However, the generosity shown by the Sikhs and the Government was misunderstood by the Muslim leaders as their weakness. A meeting was called by the Muslim leaders on 13th July, 1935 A.D. It was attended by about 10,000 with 1,000 blue shirts. Besides, thanking the Government for its generosity shown to the Muslim community, 'intemperate speeches' were made and a general call was given for the 'recruitment of volunteers for carrying on the agitation.[32]

Fearing the disturbance of peace of the province, several measures were devised by the government. These included : ban on the processions and discussions about *Shahidganj* affairs at public meeting in Lahore, censorship on the press, and to deport Muslim leaders from the town.[33] However, nearly 12,000 Muslims rallied on 14th July, 1935 A.D. and plans were announced for carrying on the agitation. Reacting to it, the Government externed, Maulana Zafar Ali, Sayyed Muhammad Habib, Mr, Ferozeddiri Ahmed and Malik Lal Khan, from Lahore and confined to certain places. Furthermore, District Magistrate strictly warned and enjoined the public not to take part in any procession within the limits of Lahore district, for a period of one month. Besides, His Excellency, Sir Herbert Emerson, made a passionate appeal for a settlement, honourable to all, of this deplorable affairs'.[34]

But these measures did not deter the Muslims to carry out their plans. On 17th July, 1935 A.D., nearly 1,000 Muslims gathered at the *Badshahi Mosque*. After the meeting, small bands of 100-200 started roaming in the bazzars and throwing stones on the police. To control them, the police resorted to lathi charge at two places; Bazar Hatta and out side Delhi gate. By 19th July, the situation become alarming when after Friday prayer at the *Badshahi* Mosque, inflamatory speeches were made and a procession was carried on to the *Shahidganj* Gurdwara. Two attempts of the processionists to reach the Gurdwara, were foiled by the police who resorted to lathi charge and made some arrest.[35] The situation turned so grim that the District Magistrate had to renew curfew order till further order. However, on 20th July, 1935 A.D., the number of agitators swelled as a violent crowed of Muslims gathered in front of the *Kotwali* with the intention of going to the Shahidganj Gurdwara. The processionists repeatedly tried to break through the police cordon, 'throwing bricks and missile at the police'. To disperse them mounted police made several charge for two hours. In the scuffle, a considerable number, from both the sides, got minor injuries while 8 were admitted in the hospital. Yet the Muslims were determined to march toward the Gurdwara. Consequently, the police resorted to firing.

Then the crowd dispersed only to reassemble on the next day.[36] On the 21st the same gory drama was repeated. During two days struggle between the police and the processionists, the number of police and troops wounded and under treatment in the Government hospitals swelled to 124.[37] By now, it appears as the strength and zeal of the organizers of the agitation had dwindled. Therefore, instead of continuing demonstrations, they decided in a meeting held on 23rd July, 1935 A.D., at *Wazir Khan's* Mosque, to launch Civil-Disobedience Movement by sending *Jathas* of five Muslims daily to the Gurdwara *Shahidganj*. However, this device practically came to an end by 25th July 1935 A.D., when some of the Muslim Government officials came to the rescue of their community saying that 'the Muslims cannot afford to forfeit the goodwill of Government'[38] Consequently, from this day onward situation in Lahore started improving and by the end of the month, Lahore settled down to normal conditions. On the 30th July 1935 A.D., the *Shahidganj* Gurdwara was opened for the devotees. By 10th August, 1935 A.D., the troops too were withdrawn from the city.[39]

However, after a gap of nearly one month, the Muslim leader appointed Pir Jamait Ali Shah as the first *Amir-i-Shariat* (Director of the community), to revive the *Shahidganj* agitation in the form of Civil-Disobedience Movement, at a conference held at Rawalpindi on 31st August and 1st September 1935 A.D.. But, Pir Sahib realizing that 'no-Government worth its salt can be cowed down by Civil-Disobedience', directed his energies to the economic boycott of the Sikhs.[40]

To maintain peace and harmony in the city, the Shiromani Gurdwara Parbandhak Committee, on 16th September, 1935 A.D. appealed to the Sikh community 'to do nothing of the coming *Shahidganj* Day', the 20th September. On the contrary, the Muslim observed '*Shahidganj* Day' which excited the feelings of the overzealous fanatics, whose blood thirstiness occasionally manifested in murderous assault on the lives of law abiding and peaceful Sikhs in several villages. For instance, Prem

Singh and Bhagwan Singh of village Meki Dhok were attacked and seriously injured by Muslims.[41] Meanwhile, Maulana Shaukat Ali expressed his desire to have on open negotiation with Master Tara Singh regarding the *Shahidganj* affairs. Consequently, on 3rd October, 1935 A.D., a meeting of the leaders of both the communities was held at Amritsar, in the Shahid Sikh Missionary College.[42] After the discussion of nearly five hours, the Muslim leaders agreed to the following press statement to be released by the Sikh leaders. 'It has given us genuine pleasure to meet Maulana Shaukat Ali, Sayyed Murtaza Sahib, Mr. K.L. Gauba and other Muslim friends in connection with the *Shahidganj* affair. Maulana Shaukat Ali has provided an occasion for us to understand and appreciate each other's point of view and for that we are grateful to him. Though the Sikh community is not prepared to part with the site, this does not preclude the possibility of further negotiations. This can only be possible if our Muslim brethren create a calm atmosphere. The prospect at present are discouraging but representatives of Sikh community would welcome a talk with representatives of Muslim community in changed circumstances".[43]

Unfortunately, the Muslims did not stop their anti-Sikh activities. For instance, on 23rd October 1935 A.D., one Hassan Muhammad of *Haveli Pathranwali* (Lahore), armed with an axe and accompanied by five other Muslims, attacked and killed Sant Singh and seriously injured Raghbir Singh, Bishan Singh and Baldev Raj. On 8th November, 1935 A.D., the crime was repeated when a Sikh named Mangal Singh of Gageki was stabbed.[44] Not only this, the *Amir-i-Shariat*, Pir Jaimat Ali Shah called a joint conference of Muslim leaders and Ulema's on 9th November, 1935 A.D., at the Barkat Ali Mohammedan Hall (Lahore). They decided to enrole ten lakhs of volunteers in the course of November and December 1935 A.D., besides establishing a communal fund to revive and strengthen the agitation.[45]

Under such circumstances, Master Tara Singh, on 4th November, 1935 A.D., closed every possibility of further negotiation with the Muslim leaders by declaring that, 'Under the circumstances it is cowardly to have any talk with the Muslims. I, therefore, wish to declare that I, at least, shall not participate in any such talk. . . No Sikh leader, no Sikh organization and not even all the Sikh organizations combined, have the power to agree to this (the Muslim) demand. Owing to Muslim threats and bullying, the Sikhs consider it an insult to the *Panth* and the Martyrs to yield an inch even."[46]

On the other hand Civil-Disobedience launched under the dictatorship of Pir Jamait Ali proved a futile exercise. In January 1936 A.D., *Ithad-i-Milat* (a committee to organise agitation) organized a conference at Amritsar to discuss action plan for the agitation. But contrary to the wishes of the organizers, Pir Jamait Ali delegated his powers to the central committee and decided to go for *Haj*. Maula Bakash, the new dictator, was unable to recruit volunteers.[47] The Muslim leaders were in a fix and in search of an excuse to terminate this agitation. Just at this juncture, Muhammad Ali Jinah, who like the Government, did not like the continuation of this agitation, offered himself to be a mediator. To meet the leaders of this agitaion, he declared to visit Lahore on 21st Feb. 1936 A.D. The leaders of the *Ithad-i-Milat* organised a Muslim conference on that day, at Lahore. They also decided not to send any *Jatha* for courting arrest on that day, as a token of honour to Mr. Muhammad Ali Jinha's visit to Lahore. The agitation thus suspended was never revived. On behalf of the Muslims, Mr. Jinah, assured the Government that, in future, they would not create any inconvenience. As a gesture of goodwill, the Government on 27th Feb. 1936 A.D. decided to release all detainees of the agitation and restore foreited sureties of seven Muslim Newpapers.[48] However, the issue was finally settled by the court on 25th May, 1936 A.D. when Session Judge Mr. S.L. Sale in his 86 pages judgement, evaluating history and earlier judgements of civil courts, recognized the claims of the Sikh community over the site of *Shahidganj* and the property attached to it. Also, he set free eleven Sikhs accused for the demolition of Kaku Shah's Mazar in the compound of *Shahidganj*.[49] To thank Almighty (*Akalpurkh*) for their success, the Sikhs pitched a tent on the plantform which they had earlier raised over the very site of Gurdwara *Shahidganj* and started a series of 101 *Akhandpaths* continual recitation of the Adi Granth).[50]

Right from the inception of the agitation, the role of the British Indian Government remained dubious. Through out the course of the agitation which lasted for nearly eight months, the Government was over anxious to placate the Muslim community. For instance, when the Sikh started demolishing the so-called *Shahidganj* mosque, the Government decided to take action against them under criminal law by invoking section 295 I.P.C. But it was found inapplicable by the law experts in this regard. Then it thought of preventing the Sikhs from its demolition by bringing it under the provisions of the Ancient Monuments Preservation Act. But this expedient too was found impracticable in the circumstances then prevailing. Thus, when it was not possible for the Government to prevent the Sikhs to exercise their legal rights and the law of the land did not provide any clue to appease the Muslim community, only then it decided to prevent the Muslims from approaching the scene of demolition. In fact, the Government allowed the Muslims to intimidate the Sikhs too long. But when their activities actually challenged the law of the land and defied the authority of the executive Government only then it decided to use force to suppress them. However, the force too was used to the minimum possible extent. For instance, the lathi charges were very mild considering the activities of the violent mob. The firing on 20th & 21st July 1935 A.D. was fully controlled. Although, it had to be resorted on ten occasions not more than 23 rounds were fired. Never, in the history of quelling disturbances of this magnitude, such a restraint had been exercised.[51]

REFERENCES

1. Shaheedganj Bhai Taru Singh (Lahore), 2. Shaheedganj Bhai Mani Singh (Lahore), 3. Shaheedganj Singhanian (Lahore), 4. Shaheed of the forty Sikhs who embtraced martyrdom on Dec. 29th 1705) at Muktsar, 5. Shaheedganj of the Sikh soldiers near Shah Bauli (Sirhind), 6. Shaheedganj Baba Dip Singh (Amaritsar), 7. Shaheedganj Baba Gurbakhsh Singh and the other Sikhs, near Akal Takhat (Amritsar), 8. Shaheedganj of the thousands of the Sikhs near Amritsar Sarovar, Darbar Sahib (Amritsar), 9. Shaheedganj Taragarh (Anandpur Sahib), built in the memory of the martyrs of the battle fought on August 29, 1700, 10. Shaheedganj Fatehgarh (Anandpur Sahib), built in the memory of the martyrs of the battle fought on August 30, 1700, 11. Shaheedganj Bhai Tiloka and 12. Sikhs near Gali Khoslian (Amritsar), 12. Shaheedganj of several Sikhs, near Katra Ramgarhian (Amritsar), 13. Shaheedganj of Baba Hira Singh and Baba Basant Singh, near Guru Ka Bagh (Amritsar), 14. Shaheedganj of several Sikhs on the South of Darbar Sahib (Amritsar), 15. Shaheedganj Bhai Jiwan Singh (Bhai Jaita) at Chamkaur Sahib (he embraced martyrdom on the bank of Sarsa rivulet), 16. Shaheedganj of the Sikhs who embraced martyrdom at Chamkaur, on Dec. 7-8, 1705, also known as Catal Garh, 17. Shaheedganj Sirhind (after the battle of Sirhind (May 1710), about six thousands Sikhs were cremated here, 18. Shaheedganj Jathedar Sukha Singh at Sirhind (martyr of the battle of Sirhind (January 1764, 19. Shaheedganj Malla Singh (Martyr of the battle of Sirhind January 1764) etc. : Bhai Kahan Singh Nabha, Mahan Kosh, LDPP (1990), 139; Harjinder Singh Dilgeer, *Sikh Reference Book*, The Sikh Educational Trust, Canada 1997, pp. 223-24.
2. The indiscriminate meassacre of the Sikhs which aimed at to extripate the community as a whole started in 1716, when an edict was issued by Farrukhsiyar directing that any Sikh falling into the hands of his officers should on refusal to embrace the Mohammadan faith, be put to the sword. To give effect to this mandate a reward was offered for the head of every Sikh. Thus, the Muslim Governors of Lahore from Abdul Samad Khan Diler-i-Jang (1713-1726) to Mir Mannu (1748-53), took all measures which an active resentment could suggest for the extirpation of the Sikhs. Consequently, movable columns of troops were despatched all over the country for hunting down the Sikh wherever they might be traced. The unfortunate

victims who were caught alive and brought to Lahore were executed in Chauk nakhas at Lahore : J.D. Cunningham, *A History of the Sikhs*, LPP, Delhi, 1990 (reprint) pp. 75-89; Teja Singh & Ganda Singh, *A Short History of the Sikhs*, Punjabi University, Patiala 1989 (reprint) pp. 91-140; Ganda Singh, *History of Gurdwara Shahidganj; Lahore*, Lahore, 1935, pp. 1-32; Khazan Singh, *History Shahidganj Lahore*, Lahore 1937, pp. 9-47; *The Daily Akali Patrika*, Lahore, 3rd July, 1935.

3. Teja Singh & Ganda Singh, *ibid.*, 111-12, 169; Ganda Singh, *ibid.*, 3-5, 8 9, 21-22, 27, 29-30, 32, 39; Baba Prem Singh Hoti, *Sher-i-Panjab Maharaja Ranjit Singh*, Lahore Book Shop, Ludhiana, 1918, p. 206; Khazan Singh, *ibid.*, pp. 12-15, 19-47.
4. Cunningham, *ibid.*, pp. 92-93; Teja Singh & Ganda Singh, p. 176; Ganda Singh, pp. 27-28, 37-39; Khazan Singh, pp. 16-17, 47-48.
5. The dungeons where Sikh Women and childrens were imprisoned and tortured during the governorship of Mir Mannu were preserved as *Shahidganj Singhanian and Shahidganj Bhai Taru Singh*, in memory of Bhai Taru Singh whose scalp was scraped off alive in June, 1745 A.D., with the order of Khan Bahadur Zaknaria Khan (governor of Lahore), on refusal to abjure the Sikh faith and to accept Islam; Teja Singh, *ibid*, pp. 37-39; Khazan Singh, *ibid.*, 41 -42; *The Akalis*, Lahore, 3rd July 1935.
6. The *muafis* and *jagirs* granted and confirmed by Maharaja Ranjit Singh were as Rs. 5 daily for *Sukhe-di-deg*; Rs. 25 daily for *Langar*, Rs. 1,100 *Jagir* in the ilaqa of Taran Taran, *Muafl* land in the villages of Chuchakwal, Bral, Wasti Ram, *muafi* land with five wells in the ilaka of Nakhas and octroi duty of the grain markets of Lahore as one *chhatak* for every donkey-load; two *chhataks* for every bullock-load and *Half a seer* for every camel-load; Ganda Singh, *ibid.*, 41-42; Prem Singh, Hoti, *ibid.*, pp. 204-6; Khazan Singh, *ibid.*, pp. 48-49.
7. Ganda Singh, *ibid.*, p. 42.
8. Ganda Singh *ibid.*, pp. 43-44; Khazan Singh, *ibid.*, p. 67.
9. Ganda Singh, *ibid.*, pp. 44-45; Khazan Singh, *ibid.*, pp. 67-69.
10. This new story was as : 'During the reign of Emperor Alamgir, Mirza Qurban Beg built the afore said mosque, shops, well and *Hammam*, in suit, and gifted the same to our grandfather. A *Khangah* was constructed by Muhammad Bakhsh and Fateh

Muhammad, our *murrids*, eight or nine years age. We have since been in continuous possession of the said property. Kahan Singh Akali had been in possession of the aforesaid mosque for the last ten years. He died sonless a year ago. The defendents, having fraudulently represented themselves to be the disciple of Kahan Singh, have taken possession of the property': Ganda Singh, *ibid.*, pp.47.

11. Ganda Singh, *ibid.*, pp. 47-48.

12. [illegible] 1935.

13. Ganda Singh, *ibid.*, pp. 50-53; Khazan Singh, *ibid.*, pp. 60-70.

14. Ganda Singh *ibid.*, pp. 50-59.

15. *Khalsa Samachar*, 18th July, 1935.

16. Ganda Singh, *ibid.*, pp. 61-62; *Khalsa Samachar*, 18th July, 1935.

17. Ganda Singh, *ibid.*, pp. 62-63; *Khalsa Samachar*, *op.cit.*; According to Khazan Singh, the litigation in the Sikh Gurdwara Tribunal started on March 18th 1928 and it was decided in favour of the Sikhs in Feb. 1930, *ibid.*, 13.

18. Khalsa Samachar, *op. cit.*, Ganda Singh.

19. Ganda Singh, *ibid.*, pp. 63-64; Khazan Singh, *ibid.*, p. 51.

20. Muslim mob came to the Gurdwara around 12.00 at night, broke the corden, and threw stones on the Sikhs inside the Gurdwara : *Khalsa Samachar*, 18th July 1935.

21. Ganda Singh, *ibid.*, p. 68.

22. For instance, on 2nd July, some 200 Muslims carrying spades, marching in a military fashion and accompanied by a crowd of nearly 3000 Muslims gathered near the Gurdwara. In another incident, S. Avtar Singh, B.A., LL.B. son of the late B. Ram Rakha Singh, his companion and the Sikh driver of the lorry in which they were travelling, had been assaulted by a Muslim crowed near Gujranwala lorry stand. S. Avtar Singh, was wounded in the right hand : Ganda Singh, *ibid.*, pp. 68-70; Khazan Singh, *ibid.*, pp. 56-58.

23. S. Kharak Singh left Sialkot for Lahore to defend the Sikh claims against a show of force. S. Mehtab Singh appealed to the Sikhs for help by saying that the *Morcha* had started. The Akali *Jathas* started coming in Lahore from different areas, the first to reach was from Amritsar. By 3rd July nearly 3000 Akalis has arrived at *Shahidganj*. Gurdwara Committee of Sri Nankana Sahib, in a meeting decided to send Rs. 1,00,000, 1,000 volunteers and 1,000 bags of flour for the *Morcha* etc: *Khalsa Samachar*, 18th July 1935; Ganda Singh, *ibid.*, p. 70; Khazan Singh, *ibid.*, p. 54.
24. *Khalsa Samachar*, 18th July 1935; Ganda Singh, *ibid.*, pp. 71 -72; Khazan Singh, *ibid.*, p. 57.
25. The Sikh deputation was led by S. Harnam Singh Advocate, S. Ishar Singh Mazail, S.B. Dr. Kartar Singh, S. Gurmukh Singh Mussafir; Giani Khazan Singh, S. Ujjal Singh etc. In three hours discussion they discussed history of the Gurdwara *Shahidgaj*, law points and the decisions of the civil courts. The Muslim deputation in its two and a half hours meeting discussed history of the so-called *Shahidganj* mosque, law of the waqaf and urged the Governor to maintain status quo and to grant assurance that the site would not be used by the Sikhs in such a manner which could hurt the feelings of the Muslim community : *Khalsa Samachar*, 18th July, 1935; Ganda Singh, *ibid.*, pp. 73-74; Khazan Singh, p. 54.
26. Ganda Singh, *ibid.*, p. 74; Khazan Singh, *op.cit.*, Khalsa Samachar, *op. cit.*, 21.
27. *Khalsa Samachar*, *op. cit.*, Ganda Singh, *ibid.*, pp. 74-75.
28. *Khalsa Samachar*, *op. cit.*, Ganda Singh, *ibid.*, pp. 75-76; Khazan Singh, *ibid.*, p. 55.
29. Ganda Singh, pp. 77-78; Khazan Singh, *ibid.*, p. 57.
30. *Khalsa Samachar, op. cit.*, Ganda Singh, *ibid.*, p. 79.
31. Ganda Singh, *op. cit.*
32. Khazan Singh, *ibid.*, pp. 58-59; Ganda Singh, *ibid.*, p. 80.
33. Ganda Singh, *ibid.*, pp. 80-81; *Khalsa Samachar*, 18th July 1935.
34. *Khalsa Samachar*, 18th July, 1935; Ganda Singh, *ibid.*, pp. 81 - 83; Khazan Singh, *ibid.*, p. 59.
35. Muslim were arrested and thrice the police resorted to Lathi charge, *Khalsa Samachar*, *op. cit.*, Ganda Singh, *ibid.*, pp 84-86.

36. Twice the police resorted to firing on 20th. But eight rounds were fired only which caused three casualities besides wounding serveral: Ganda Singh, *ibid.*, p. 87.

37. The detail of the wounded admitted in the hospitals is as :

1.	Military officers	3
2.	Police officers	7
3.	Other Ranks of British troops	12
4.	Other Ranks of Indian troops	22
5.	Other Ranks of Indian Police	80
	Total	124

: Ganda Singh, p. 88, Khazan Singh, *ibid.*, p. 60.

38. Ganda Singh, *ibid.*, p. 89; Khazan Singh, *ibid.*, p 61.

39. Ganda Singh, *op. cit*; Khazan Singh, *ibid.* pp. 61-64.

40. Ganda Singh, IInd, pp. 89-91; Khazan Singh, *ibid.*, p. 64.

41. Ganda Singh, *ibid.*, pp. 92-93; Khazan Singh, *ibid.*, pp. 64-65.

42. On the part of the Muslims, Maulana Shaukat Ali, Sayyed Murtaza Sahib, Mr. K.L. Gauba, Mir Maqbul Mahmud, Khawaza Ahmed Sadiq and Shaikh Muhammad Sadiq attended the meeting while on the part the Sikhs, Master Tara Singh, S. Dalip Singh Doabia, Giani Gurmukh Singh Mussafir, S. Kartar Singh; S. Harnam Singh; S. Partap Singh etc. joined the discussion : Ganda Singh, *ibid.*, pp. 93-95.

43. Ganda Singh, *ibid.*, pp. 95-96.

44. After inflicting two axe-blows on Sant Singh who was enjoing a musical treat between the *Shahalmi* and Mochi gates, Hassan Muhammad shouted that he was out to kill Hindus and Sikhs : Ganda Singh, *ibid.*, p. 97.

45. The conference was attended by prominent and responsible Muslims like Maulana Shaukat Ali, Nawab Muhammad Shah Nawaz Khan of Mamdot, M.L.C. Khan Bahadur, Hazi Rahim Bakhash, Sayyed Ghulam Bhaik Nairang, M.L.A., Mian Abdul Aziz, Barister of Lahore, Allama Inayat Ali Mashraqi, the founder of the '*Khaksar*' Movement, Sayyed Hamid Riza of Bareilly, Makhdum Sadar-ud-Din Gilani, Dr. Khalifa Shuja-ud-Din, Barrister, Prof. Abdul Qadir of the Islamia, College Lahore etc.: Ganda Singh, *ibid.*, 98-101.

46. Ganda Singh, *ibid.*, p. 102.

47. *Khalsa Samachar*, 23rd January 6th, 13th & 20th Feb. 1936.

48. *Khalsa Samachar*, 20th & 27th Feb. and 5th March, 1936.

49. *Ibid.*, 28th May, 1936; Khazan Singh, *ibid.*, pp. 74-89.

50. Khazan Singh, *ibid.*, p. 86.

51. Ganda Singh, *ibid.*, pp. 68-91, 104-115.

Index

A

H

I

J

M